COVET

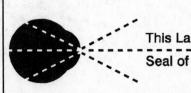

Covet

Tracey Garvis Graves

THORNDIKE PRESS
A part of Gale, Cengage Learning

GALE
CENGAGE Learning

Detroit • New York • San Francisco • New Haven, Conn • Waterville, Maine • London

GALE
CENGAGE Learning®

Thorndike Press® Large Print Basic.
The text of this Large Print edition is unabridged.
Other aspects of the book may vary from the original edition.
Set in 16 pt. Plantin.

LIBRARY OF CONGRESS CATALOGING-IN-PUBLICATION DATA

Garvis Graves, Tracey.
Covet / By Tracey Garvis Graves. — Large Print edition.
pages cm. — (Thorndike Press Large Print Basic)
ISBN-13: 978-1-4104-6260-2 (hardcover)
ISBN-10: 1-4104-6260-9 (hardcover)
1. Large type books. I. Title.
PS3607.A78296C68 2013
813'.6—dc23 2013021453

Published in 2013 by arrangement with Dutton, a member of Penguin Group (USA) LLC, a Penguin Random House Company

Printed in the United States of America
1 2 3 4 5 6 7 17 16 15 14 13

To the girls of FP: Thank you for your light, your love, and your laughter. I couldn't have done it without you.

1

CLAIRE

I'm on my way home from dropping off the kids at school when he pulls me over. I see the lights in my rearview mirror seconds before he hits the siren, giving it two short bursts. I'm not speeding, or in violation of any traffic laws that I know of, but I pull to the shoulder and the police car slows to a stop behind my bumper. When the officer walks up to the driver's-side window, I hit the button to lower it.

"Did you know you have a taillight out, ma'am?" he asks.

"Really?" I crane my neck to look behind me — as if I could possibly see it from inside the car — and immediately feel foolish.

"Yes," he says. "Passenger side. Can I see your license and registration and proof of insurance?"

I nod. "Sure."

He doesn't look like any cop I've ever seen. He looks like a model pretending to be a police officer for a photo shoot. Or maybe one of those cops who shows up at a bachelorette party and then strips down to his underwear.

Suddenly, I can't remember where anything is.

He waits patiently while I locate the necessary documents in the console and pry my license out of my wallet. I hand everything to him and he takes it to his car, and when he returns he leans down by my window and hands it all back.

Up close, I notice that his eyes are green, the exact shade of a piece of sea glass I found on the shoreline of the Gulf of Mexico two years ago when Chris and I took the kids to South Padre Island. He must be six two or three, and he's lean but broad shouldered. He doesn't look older than mid to late thirties, but there are a few flecks of gray in his dark hair, which only enhance his good looks. So unfair. He rips a piece of paper off the pad he's holding, glances down at the name he's written on it, and looks back up. "Claire?"

"Yes."

He hands me the ticket. "It's just a warning," he says, reading my expression and smiling to dispel my worry that I'm about to get slapped with a fine. His teeth are white and perfectly straight. "Have it taken care of as soon as possible, okay? It isn't safe."

"I will," I say, looking down at the ticket. It's been signed by Officer Daniel Rush. "Thank you."

He nods. "Have a nice day."

When I return home, my husband, Chris, is standing in the kitchen, a cup of coffee in his hand. He's wearing jeans and a polo shirt in accordance with casual Friday, and he smells like the cologne I gave him for his birthday.

"Have you seen my watch?" he asks, in lieu of a proper greeting. I unearth it under a stack of mail on the counter, and he straps it on. "Did you drive the kids to school?"

"Yes," I say, setting down my purse on the island. "Last day," I add, because even though I mentioned it, there's a fairly good chance Chris forgot; he's got other things, important things, to focus on right now. "I wanted to hand deliver the gifts for their teachers. I wasn't sure they'd arrive in one piece if they took them on the bus."

The kids are a safe topic, and politely exchanging information regarding their whereabouts and well-being has become our fallback method of communication. Neither of us raises our voice. I once read an article in a women's magazine that said it's a really bad sign when you and your spouse stop arguing. It means that you've given up and no longer care about saving your marriage. I hope that's not true, but I worry that it probably is. I walk to the dishwasher and start unloading it, not bothering to tell Chris about the taillight; I'll take care of it myself.

He opens the cupboard, grabs the pill bottle, and shakes a capsule into his hand, swallowing it with water. He's probably wondering if I'll say something about the pills, but I won't. I never do. He's whistling and seems eager to head out the door this morning; I should just be grateful he has a job to go to, because the twelve months we spent at home together when he was out of work were almost our undoing. Still might be. He grabs his laptop and car keys, says good-bye, and walks out the door without kissing me.

I finish unloading the dishwasher. Tucker scratches and whines at the sliding glass door, and I open it. "Go, Tuck," I say, watching as he takes off in hot pursuit of a squirrel. He never catches one because the squirrel will scamper to safety on top of our fence long before he reaches it, but that seldom stops him from trying.

It's quiet now. I pour a cup of coffee and gaze out the window as summer beckons.

I open the door to seven-year-old Jordan's room, my arms full of clean laundry. She's made her bed without being asked, and her stuffed animals are lined up neatly on her pillow. There's nothing on the floor, not a stray sock, not her pajamas, not one of the hundreds of crayons and markers she's always drawing with. Nothing. It used to bother me until my mom pointed out that I did the same thing when I was her age. "Don't go looking for trouble where there is none, Claire. She relishes order the same way you do." I never did grow out of it either, this need to have everything organized, my life segmented neatly into tidy little boxes. How karma must have had a field day with me last year.

I open nine-year-old Josh's door next and immediately trip over a pile of Matchbox cars; it appears there's been a pileup. Josh likes to crash things. He does not, however, share his sister's fondness for neatness and order. I step around the cars and navigate my way across the room, dodging piles of clothes, sports equipment, shoes, and his guitar. His navy blue comforter hangs halfway off the bed, but the sheets are pulled up and both pillows are in the right spot. I'll give him an A for effort. After I put away the clean clothes I pick up the dirty ones and reverse my steps.

In our bedroom only one side of the bed has been slept in. When he's home, which from now on will be rare, Chris often sleeps on the couch in the family room, a habit he started when his insomnia was at its worst and he didn't want to disturb me with his tossing and turning. In hindsight, I should have insisted that he stay because now I doubt he'll ever return.

I scoop up his boxer shorts and damp towel from the bathroom floor and add them to the pile in my arms, wondering if there will ever be more to life than laundry and sleeping alone in a king-size bed.

My neighbor Elisa walks into my kitchen later that morning, her yoga mat in one hand and a giant bottle of water in the other. Her light brown hair is in a perfect ballerina bun, not a messy one like mine, and her gray yoga pants coordinate nicely with her pink tank top. "I almost got run over crossing the street," she says. "What the *hell* is wrong with people? Do they not realize how many kids are in this neighborhood?" Elisa is a born and bred Texas girl whose husband, Skip, brought her back to his home state of Kansas after college, and when she's riled up you can really hear the twang in her speech.

Elisa and I live in Rockland Hills, an exclusive neighborhood in a suburb of Kansas City. We're on the Kansas side, and the single-family homes are large and stately, with a median price of three hundred and fifty thousand dollars. The architecture is a mix of styles, designed to lend a unique feel and keep the houses from looking too similar. Chris and I purchased our Tuscany-inspired four-bedroom home five years ago after we fell in love with the warm, earthy hues, expansive terra-cotta tile floors, and wrought-iron sconces. Our furniture is soft and oversize, chosen solely for comfort. We've been happy with this neighborhood except for the fact that the winding, tree-lined streets aren't heavily patrolled and not everyone watches their speed the way they should; the most frequent offenders are the newly licensed offspring of the affluent residents.

I grab my own bottle of water from the fridge. "Maybe we can check into getting one of those speed limit signs. You know, the ones that blink?" I ask.

"We need something. I can't believe how fast that car was going."

I drive us to yoga. When we walk in the front door I feel instantly calmer, the way I always do when I hear the New Age music and smell the lingering scent of incense. A potted aloe vera plant sits on a low table and paintings from local artists adorn the sage-green walls. It's all very soothing.

After we stow our gear in the locker room we stake out a spot in the back row of the studio, sitting cross-legged on our mats while we wait for the class to start. "I've got a taillight out. Can you pick me up after I drop off my car?" I ask.

"Sure," she says, stretching her arms over her head. "When?"

I take a sip from my water bottle. "I don't know. I'll call and make an appointment when I get home. I need to take care of it as soon as possible."

"Did you get pulled over?" she asks.

"Yes, this morning. By the most ridiculously good-looking cop I've ever seen."

She raises an eyebrow and grins. "Do tell."

"There's not much to it," I say, chuckling. "I was so flustered I couldn't remember where I kept my registration. It was like my brain left the building. He was nice, though." I don't tell Elisa that my mind keeps flashing back to this morning. I don't tell her that I keep thinking about the officer's smile. Maybe it's some kind of latent cop fantasy I didn't know I had. Maybe it's because it's been so long since my husband paid any attention to me at all. Maybe it's because I'm so damn lonely. It's not like it matters, anyway. There are approximately twenty-two thousand residents in this town, and the odds of running into him again are not that great.

They're not horrible, though.

I realize that these are not the thoughts of a happily married woman, but at the moment I am not very happily married.

After we return from yoga I take a shower and work on my laptop for a few hours, then cross the street to take a plate of cookies and a bowl of fruit salad over to Elisa's. Her and Skip's contemporary two-story is the polar opposite of mine: It boasts sleek, modern furniture and clean lines, and the color palette features icy blues and soft grays.

Elisa's the consummate entertainer, and her end-of-the-school-year party has become a tradition on our street with the adults looking forward to it almost as much as the kids do. I help her set up a long table on her covered patio, and we stack paper plates and sort plastic utensils. Elisa fans out a pile of brightly colored napkins.

It's barely June, but a fluke heat wave has stalled over the Midwest, and the record-breaking temperature hovers near eighty-seven. The heat and humidity make it feel as if my neighborhood has been relocated to a tropical island.

"What time are you coming over?" Elisa asks.

"Five thirty. Chris said he'd be home on time."

My guess is that Chris will still be the last one to leave the office today. If past behavior is any indication, it won't take long for Chris's workaholic tendencies to kick in, weekends and holidays be damned.

We stand back and survey our work. "I think I'm all set," Elisa says. "Thanks for helping."

"Sure. See you in a little while."

She waves. "Bye, Claire."

I'm waiting on the sidewalk an hour later when the school bus pulls up. Jordan is the first child off, and she flies down the steps and into my arms, her backpack bulging with all the treasures that used to live in her desk. She cradles a figurine in her hands; it looks like a turtle. Or maybe it's a swan. I don't dare ask. "I made you a peacock,

Mommy," she says, proudly handing it over. Her expression turns somber. "Please don't break this one."

I examine the peacock and kiss her on the forehead. "It's beautiful, honey. I'll be more careful. I promise."

Jordan looks like me, except her hair is a mass of short, sunshiny-blonde ringlets. My hair is longer, the curls stretching into waves that reach my shoulder blades, and at thirty-four I need a boost from quarterly highlights to help brighten the shade. My daughter and I share the same small nose and full lips, but she has dimples and a smattering of freckles across her cheeks. She takes my breath away.

Josh, who follows sedately behind his sister, takes after Chris. He has the same golden-boy good looks that attracted me to his father twelve years ago when we were twenty-two and fresh out of college, the ink barely dry on our degrees, Chris's in business and marketing and mine in graphic design. They're the kind of features — distinct, symmetrical, strong — that make people listen to what you have to say, buy what you're selling. When Mindy, my best friend from college, received our Christmas card and family photo a few years ago, she jokingly asked, "Has anyone ever mentioned you all look a little Stepfordish?"

I suppose we do. I'm the anomaly, though. We all have blond hair, but only Chris and the kids have blue eyes. Mine are brown.

"How was the last day of school?" I ask, taking Jordan's hand and reaching over to ruffle Josh's hair.

"Awesome!" they answer in unison. We sing a few lines of Alice Cooper's "School's Out" at the top of our lungs and walk into the house. "Who wants a snack?" I ask.

While they're eating peanut butter crackers and sipping juice I go through their backpacks, sorting the contents into piles. "Find a place in your rooms for everything you want to keep, okay?" I put Jordan's peacock on the counter.

Chris walks in the door at 5:29 and sets down his laptop and cell phone. "Daddy!" The kids barrel toward him, and he gathers them in his arms. "Do I have time to change?" he asks.

"Sure," I say. "We can wait."

He runs upstairs and returns two minutes later wearing a faded T-shirt and cargo shorts. "All right," he says, scooping up Jordan and placing her on his shoulders. She beams, liking this happy Daddy. "Let's go."

We cross the street and walk around to the back of the house. "Greetings, Canton family," Skip says as we enter his yard and approach the patio. He scoops me up in a bear hug and kisses me on the cheek. Josh and Jordan scatter, off to join the kids jumping on the trampoline.

Elisa's husband is one of my favorite people. He played football at Baylor, and he's a big strapping guy with broad shoulders and a belly that's just beginning to show the effects of too much beer and barbecue, but he's a teddy bear. I once watched him dodge traffic to rescue a turtle so it wouldn't get run over, and I saw him wipe away tears when ten-year-old Travis — his and Elisa's only child — accepted an award for collecting donations for a family who lost all their possessions in a house fire. And boy does he love his wife.

Skip sets me down and then shakes Chris's hand, clapping him on the back. "How's the job going, man?"

I tense up, forgetting for a moment that this question is preferable to "Have you found a job yet?" which is what everyone wanted to know for the twelve months Chris didn't have one. Chris answers that it's only been a month but so far things are going well, then ambles off in search of a beer, oblivious to the blip on my emotional radar. Oblivious of me entirely.

I survey the group on the patio. Julia and Justin, who live behind me and Chris, are sitting next to each other holding drinks. Justin has a beer while Julia clenches her customary glass of chardonnay; I won't know until I talk to her how many she's already had at home. Bridget and Sam and their brood, who live next door to us, our houses so close I can sometimes smell what Bridget's cooking for dinner if the windows are open, have yet to arrive. They're perpetually late; the wrangling of four boys, each born eighteen months after the last, is such a daunting task that they've mostly given up. "We'll be there when we get there," Bridget likes to say.

Justin has registered our arrival, and his eyes linger on me a bit too long. He rises from his chair and walks toward me, handing me the can of Diet 7Up he plucked from the cooler on the way. "Hey, Claire," he says, kissing me on the cheek, eyes scanning leisurely from head to toe. "You look great."

I doubt my shorts and tank top will win any fashion contests, but I smile and open the can of pop. "Thanks." This one-sided flirtation, which first developed at Elisa and Skip's Christmas party when Justin complimented my dress and then, after having way too much to drink, gave me a kiss under the mistletoe that was definitely outside the parameters of acceptable neighbor behavior, has chugged along harmlessly since December. His confidence in his own appearance borders on arrogance, and I doubt he's ever been turned down in his life. But there are many reasons I'd never open that can of worms, not the least of which is my friendship with Julia. It's nice to be noticed, though.

Justin gives me a knowing grin and then drifts off to join the men clustered near the grill. Skip takes the platter Elisa hands him and begins slapping burgers and hot dogs down on the grate. The smell of charcoal and sizzling beef fills the air. The husbands stand around watching the meat cook, drinking their beer, while the wives congregate on the patio. Even after all this time, our teen years far behind us, the boys are still across the room from the girls.

I sit down next to Julia and do a quick scan of the yard. Josh and Jordan have moved on from the trampoline and are playing freeze tag with Travis while Julia's daughters are sipping juice boxes and playing with their Polly Pockets. Elisa drops into a chair next to me and opens a beer. "Do you need help with anything?" I ask.

She tucks a tendril of hair behind her ear

and exhales. "Nope. Skip's handling the meat and everything else is ready. I just want to sit for a minute."

Julia swivels toward us. "I have big news," she says. Her eyes are glassy and her words are clipped, but she's not slurring. Two glasses at home, I'd say. Generous pours. Julia weighs all of one hundred and five pounds and can't hold her wine at all, though not for lack of trying. Her brown hair is cut in a sleek, chin-length bob that frames her pretty face, and her blue baby-doll dress brings out the color of her eyes. But her skin is starting to show the effects of daily alcohol consumption, flushed or sallow depending on whether she's drunk or hungover, and she always looks tired.

Julia pauses for dramatic effect and then says, "Justin and I are putting in a pool. It's a bit late in the season — we really should have gotten the ball rolling in the spring — but Justin's big commission finally came through, so we decided to go for it." Justin is some kind of commercial real estate whiz, and I can't help but be impressed that he's still able to do so well in this economy. We listen as Julia shares the pool's dimensions and the fact that there will be not one but two waterfalls. Construction will begin immediately, and if everything goes according to schedule, they'll be jumping off the diving board by the end of July.

Elisa, the eternal hostess, asks all the right follow-up questions and Julia prattles on, enjoying the spotlight, but then she stops suddenly and pulls a bottle — no, actually it's a jug — of cheap chardonnay out of the cooler and tops off her glass, concentrating on not spilling a drop. The fact that her next drink has so quickly replaced her enthusiasm about the pool worries me more than a little.

Bridget, looking harried, finally arrives with her four boys, but Sam does not accompany them and I wonder if we'll be graced with his presence at all; I can't remember the last time I saw him.

Skip calls out that the meat is done and everyone lines up. I make sure Josh and Jordan eat something other than potato chips and add some fruit and baby carrots to their plates. Justin brings me another Diet 7Up, smiling and popping the top before handing it to me.

After dinner I coat my children in a heavy cloud of bug spray, which they protest against. Loudly. "You'll thank me tomorrow when you're not covered in mosquito bites," I tell them. "We'll make s'mores and light sparklers in a little while, okay?" I send them off to play with the rest of the kids.

Fourteen-year-old Sebastian, Bridget's oldest, has become our de facto DJ, and the iPod blasts a variety of tunes, everything from Skip's classic country to Elisa's adult contemporary and Travis's hip-hop.

Chris stands in the yard next to Skip and Justin. The smell of cigar smoke permeates the air, and their laughter mingles with the music. It's nice to see Chris with a smile on his face, even if it isn't for me. He's gained back a little of the weight he lost and his shorts don't look so baggy anymore. His body language — shoulders back, head held a bit higher than before — tells me he's feeling a little better about himself. Watching Chris interact with the other men is bittersweet. Six months ago he might have stayed home, but now that he's here I can't help but wonder how he can effortlessly return to the way things were with his friends yet find it so difficult to get into some kind of groove with me.

The sun sets, and Justin finds me on the patio. He sits down in the chair Julia vacated when she went in to use the restroom. He says something, but I can't hear him over the music. Leaning over, he brushes my hair out of the way and says, "Julia won't mind if I take her chair." His lips graze my ear, and his fingers trail down my neck, unnoticed in the darkness.

I've known Justin for two years, ever since he and Julia moved into the neighborhood, and he's never paid this much attention to me before. Can men sense when a woman is sexually frustrated? Maybe it's like those high-pitched whistles only dogs can hear.

Justin looks up when Julia comes back outside, but he doesn't move away. I fidget and check to make sure my body language isn't giving either of them the wrong idea; I don't want Julia to think I'm remotely interested in her husband. Then again, she doesn't appear to be all that observant right now. She trips and I'm embarrassed for her, so I don't say anything. She sits down next to me. "What's going on?" She's slurring a bit and has the hiccups. I don't say anything about that, either. Justin pretends not to notice any of this, though how he can ignore it I'm not sure. "Do you want some water?" I ask, as the hiccupping sends her into a fit of giggles.

"Nope," she says, with the cheerful disposition of someone who has bypassed buzzed and is heading full speed toward blissfully wasted.

Julia never used to act this way, but in the last year her drinking has increased dramatically. I'm certain there's a reason, something it can be attributed to. None of us are doing her any favors by pretending not to notice, and someone really needs to say something. I vote for Justin. Maybe he's already tried.

Elisa brings out marshmallows, chocolate bars, and graham crackers, and Skip threads the marshmallows onto skewers and toasts them over the grill. The music is way too loud, and Bridget tells Sebastian to turn it down, threatening him with his life if he so much as glances at the volume dial on the iPod. "Where did you say Sam is?" Elisa asks when Bridget plunks herself down in the nearest chair.

"At the track." She shrugs. "Or the casino. I don't know. Does it matter?" Bridget glances over to where Chris is helping the kids with their sparklers, making sure they put the burned out ones in a metal bucket so no one will step on them. She watches as Skip hands Chris a skewer and he slides off the toasted marshmallow and sandwiches it between a chocolate bar and a graham cracker, handing it to whoever is next in line.

"I wish Sam was more like Chris," she says.

No, you don't.

But Bridget can't see the forest for the trees and doesn't realize there's a big difference between a good father and a good husband, and she probably doesn't care. Greener grass and all that. She doesn't know the mess Chris and I have made of our marriage. Neither does Julia. Elisa is the only one I share my secrets with. I've worked hard to keep the façade of this marriage, this life, intact, but only to avoid becoming fodder for the neighborhood gossip mill.

Frankly, I'm exhausted.

It's late. We gather up our children, who are tired and sticky with marshmallows and chocolate, and say our good-byes.

We're the Cantons. Sun-kissed, all-American, picture-perfect. By all appearances, we're the ideal suburban family.

As long as you don't look too closely.

2

CHRIS

On Monday morning, I stop for coffee on the way to the airport. The line for the drive-through at Starbucks reaches clear around the building and tapping impatiently on the steering wheel does nothing to make it move faster. I take a deep breath and remind myself that I've allowed plenty of time to get to the airport, and I'm in no danger of missing my flight.

Stopping at this Starbucks has become part of my new routine, and worrying about my rapidly increasing caffeine consumption accomplishes nothing, so I don't. I don't let myself worry about all this travel, either. I didn't have any choice. Claire understands; she gave me her blessing. Reluctantly, but still. The kids, though. That's another story. I try my best not to think about it.

I'm grateful to be able to spend one day at company headquarters, but my cube's chest-high walls provide zero privacy. I loathe open-plan offices, but a lot of the big software companies have embraced it like it's the next big thing. Whoever said it was better for company morale and collaboration has never tried to get anything done. The constant interruptions are a productivity killer, at least for me, which is why I don't arrive at the office earlier than 8:00 A.M. on Fridays; I get more done at home.

I miss my old company, which had one thousand fewer employees than this one. I miss my old office, with its four real walls and a door that closed.

I miss my kids and my house, and even though she probably wouldn't believe me if I told her so, I miss Claire.

I miss a lot of things.

3

DANIEL

Traffic is light on the parkway a little after 10:00 A.M. on Monday morning. Drivers who aren't speeding slow down anyway, and the ones who are going too fast slam on their brakes when they notice my police car in their rearview mirrors. I pull them over and listen to the same worn-out excuses before I write them a ticket. A man wearing a three-piece suit and driving a BMW rolls his eyes and mutters under his breath when I hand over the citation for speeding. I stand there until he looks at me. "Slow down," I say, and I don't smile when I say it.

The next car I pull over has a woman behind the wheel. She gets pissy almost immediately, exhaling loudly and glancing at her watch like I've ruined her morning on purpose. "Do you have any idea how fast you were going, ma'am?" My guess is no, because using her rearview mirror to apply her makeup and talking on the phone probably used up all her awareness. "The speed limit on this stretch is fifty-five. I clocked you going seventy."

She opens her mouth, ready to protest, but then hands me the documents I asked for and sighs loudly. "I'm going to be late," she says. She pulls a lipstick out of her purse and goes to town on her mouth as I walk back to my car.

I patrol the parkway until lunchtime and then pull into Subway to grab a sandwich and a Coke to take back to the station. Later I'll head toward the suburbs, hoping that it's quiet and that there are no unpleasant surprises waiting for me, like a missing child or a domestic dispute.

I think back to the woman I pulled over the other day. The pretty blonde in the SUV with a burned-out taillight. I remember her smile and how nice she was.

And how for the rest of my shift I kept picturing her face because she reminded me so much of Jessie.

4

CLAIRE

I'm dusting the built-in bookcases in the family room when the rumble of construction machinery, so loud and foreign in my neighborhood, startles me. I look out the window, in the direction of Justin and Julia's backyard, which abuts mine, and spot a bright yellow excavator fifty yards away. The man operating the controls lowers the bucket and metal slams into dirt. They're digging the hole for the swimming pool today.

I run my cloth over a picture of Josh and Jordan, set it down, and then smile when I pick up a hand-carved wooden sculpture Chris and I bought on the beach in Hawaii a month after he lost his job. The trip had been his idea. He bookmarked the websites for several resorts and asked me to pick one. "I may never have time off like this again, Claire," he said. "When I start a new job I might not be able to get away for a while." That was back when he thought it would be only a matter of weeks before he found another job. Before either of us knew just how bad things would get.

I'd been begging him for years to take a vacation, and it would be only the second time we'd gone away by ourselves since Josh and Jordan were born. My mom and dad took the kids for a week while we drank margaritas and swam in the ocean. We walked on the beach holding hands, and spent hours having vacation-caliber sex in the giant king-size bed in our room. If unemployment bothered Chris, he didn't let on, at least not then and not to me.

The expense of a vacation didn't worry him at all. If he found a job right away, he'd be pulling in a double income due to the eight months of severance pay his employer had agreed to pay him. We had no debt other than the house, a healthy balance in savings, retirement accounts that we told ourselves not to worry about because they'd certainly recover when the economy turned around, and college funds for the kids. On paper, we looked pretty good. I was also employed. Granted, my freelance graphic design projects didn't bring in a tenth as much as Chris's lucrative commissions had, but it supplemented our income nicely and I was able to work from home. More importantly, I enjoyed it.

We were also able to extend our health insurance benefits for eighteen months, albeit it at a very steep price. That was the only thing that really worried me back then. I'm a type 1 diabetic — I was diagnosed at age twelve — and without health insurance my disease could severely derail our careful financial planning. I wear an insulin pump, which greatly improves my quality of life, but it doesn't come cheap. There are frequent doctor visits to my endocrinologist and medical supplies that must be purchased each month. We had eighteen months before those benefits would run out.

Plenty of time.

It wasn't like the downsizing had come as a complete shock, either. It was May 2009 and we'd spent the better part of the previous year listening to the nightly news reports of the plunging stock market and the housing bubble bursting in front of everyone's eyes. The experts claimed the recession was coming to an end, but the lingering effects of high unemployment could plague the nation for months — maybe years — to come. We knew lots of people who had already lost their jobs and it seemed that everywhere we went someone was networking, leaving no stone unturned when it came to ferreting out a job lead.

The privately owned software company Chris worked for held on as long as they could, but they'd expanded quickly and relied too heavily on external funding and product revenue. Drowning in debt, they laid off their employees in waves, first the support staff and then the highest-paid executives. Chris had time to mentally prepare for what was coming. He didn't know exactly when it would happen, but he knew the sales department would be next.

"Then who will sell their product?" I asked.

"Doesn't matter," Chris said. "No one's buying it right now and they won't stay afloat long enough to ride this out. I'll be surprised if the company is still in business in six months." In the end, it took only three before they shut their doors for good.

I was sitting at the kitchen table assembling the treat bags for Jordan's upcoming birthday party — pink cellophane filled to the top with assorted candy — when I heard the garage door go up that day. My first thought was that Chris decided to knock off early, but that was wishful thinking. Chris loves to work and it isn't in his nature to stop unless he has to. He had held the position of sales manager for eight years, but when he walked into the kitchen holding a cardboard box containing the contents of his office, and a folder outlining the details of his severance package, it didn't matter that his team — under his relentless guidance — had shattered every prior sales record in the company.

Times were hard.

I walked over to him. "I am so sorry."

He set the box down on the island, pulled me into his arms, and gave me a kiss. "I know. But we both knew it was coming."

"Why didn't you call me on your way home?"

He shook his head. "I had to turn in my cell phone."

A woman in my yoga class, who often placed her mat next to mine, had recently confided that her husband lost his job and hadn't stopped crying for three days. "He just couldn't stop," she said. "He parked himself in our home office and every time I walked by he was sitting behind the desk staring at the computer screen with tears running down his face." I nodded in sympathy although I had no idea why she'd chosen to divulge this information to me because all we'd ever said to each other up until then was "Hello" and "Hard class today, huh?"

"I'm sure he'll find something soon," I said, patting her awkwardly on the shoulder.

She looked at me hopefully. "Do you really think so?"

"Sure."

She doesn't come to yoga anymore.

But Chris didn't cry. In all the years we'd been together I'd never seen him shed a single tear. In fact, he didn't even seem that upset. Everything he'd ever undertaken in his life had turned out perfectly. He'd grown up in a household where love was abundant but money was tight. The youngest of four siblings, he was accustomed to working for the things he wanted and he put himself through college, zooming through the University of Kansas with a 4.0. After graduation he landed a series of increasingly lucrative jobs, each one paying more than the one before.

Headhunters pursued him relentlessly, trying unsuccessfully to lure him away by promising to double his six-figure base salary and provide an uncapped commission structure. They dangled stock options and company cars in front of him to sweeten the deal, but he refused to budge. Loyal to a fault, he'd built the sales department from the ground up and felt personally responsible for his employees. He would never have left on his own.

None of this prepared him for the possibility that, someday, he might not land on his feet. Chris never once considered, even with the unemployment numbers looking bleaker every day, that he could be one of those left floundering, fighting for a position in a job pool that was shrinking and would end up smaller, figuratively speaking, than the inflatable one his children splashed around in on a hot day. Every man for himself.

Instead, Chris loosened his tie, smiled at me, and said, "It's been a long time since we were home alone in the afternoon." The sun's rays flooded the kitchen via the skylight above Chris's head, casting an ethereal glow on his striking features.

I smiled back. "It has." Jordan was in kindergarten and both kids were gone all day, but we'd never once taken advantage of it, because Chris was always at work. When I saw that look in his eye, the one I knew well after so many years together, I thought we'd be fine. If you still want to make love to your wife an hour after losing your job, you probably aren't that affected by the news.

Chris closed the distance between us, held my face in his hands, and kissed me tenderly, as if I was the most precious thing in the world to him. "What do you say, Claire?"

He groaned when I answered by putting my arms around him and pulling him closer so that our bodies touched. I took off his tie and unbuttoned his shirt, feeling the weight of his stare as he watched my fingers moving. Inhaling the musky, woodsy scent of his cologne, I went right for that spot on his neck, the one just below his jaw that drove him wild every time. Tracing it with my tongue, I sucked and then scraped his skin gently with my teeth. "That's it," he whispered. "Right there." He grabbed my face again and kissed me hard, then peeled off my tank top and pushed my shorts down until they landed in a puddle at my feet.

We didn't even make it upstairs.

Once we dispensed with the rest of our clothes, Chris laid me down right on our kitchen table, the one he'd always joked about being sturdy and large enough to encourage just such an act. And when his orgasm arrived, nipping right at the heels of mine, the force of it slid me just far enough across the smooth, polished surface that I collided with the treat bags, and I can still remember the sound, the rapid pitter-patter of all that candy hitting the terra-cotta tile floor, one piece after another.

I'm jerked out of my reverie by the rumble of the excavator, even louder and more jarring than before. I look longingly at the sculpture I'm holding, finish dusting it, and carefully place it back on the shelf.

5

Chris

The first thing I notice when I walk out of the Albuquerque airport is how hot and dry it is. I locate my rental car, place my suitcase in the trunk, and lay my jacket on the passenger seat. When I start the engine I adjust the vents so that the stale air doesn't blast me in the face.

Using the GPS, I drive to the potential client's office, where I spend the day pitching my company's software solutions and overcoming the objections of a conference room full of people. The more they resist, the more I persevere, and the momentum builds until I know just when to pull back and let them convince *me* that my product is exactly what they need. At the end of the day, I'm the last one to leave and I pack up my materials and laptop and drive back to my hotel, ordering a sandwich from room service so I can eat with one hand while I enter the data for my daily sales report. Adrenaline courses through me and I ride the high from the events of the day. This has happened three times now, and Jim is already showering me with accolades, which is like a balm for my badly shredded ego.

And I want more.

Around midnight, I check my phone and notice that I missed the text Claire sent at nine o'clock this morning, asking if I made it here safely. I also missed the one she sent at noon and the one that came in at 4:00 P.M. It's way too late to call her now, so I text her that everything is fine, reach for the other half of my sandwich, and turn back to my spreadsheet.

6

CLAIRE

At 6:00 A.M. the coffee finishes brewing and the sizzle of the last drop reverberates through the quiet kitchen when I remove the carafe and grab my favorite mug from the cupboard. I let Tucker out and then boot up my laptop and sit down at the island to check my e-mails, sipping slowly so I don't burn my tongue and wishing there was a way to get the caffeine into my bloodstream faster. The first one, from Chris, was sent at 3:13 A.M., so either he stayed up late working or woke up extra early to get a jump on the day. Both options are equally possible.

To: Claire Canton
From: Chris Canton
Subject: Schedule

Leaving Albuquerque by 3 p.m. then heading to Santa Fe. When is the sign-up for fall soccer? Josh told me he definitely wants to play. Repairman coming to look at irrigation system Thursday morning at nine.

To: Chris Canton
From: Claire Canton
Subject: Re: Schedule

I already signed Josh up for soccer. Will make sure to be home on Thursday morning.

I pour a second cup of coffee, check the rest of my e-mails, and work on my computer until Bridget knocks softly on my front door at 7:00 A.M. We decided a couple of weeks ago that we'd walk four miles every morning this summer, before Sam leaves for work and while Josh and Jordan are still sleeping.

Sebastian stands beside her. His hair sticks up in crazy spikes and he's wearing a Rolling Stones T-shirt and pajama pants. At fourteen, he'd rather sleep in during his summer break, but Bridget strong-armed him into babysitting because she knows Chris's travel schedule makes it impossible for me to leave the house without someone here to watch the kids. Despite my protests, she won't let Sebastian accept any money either, because it's an easy gig and we're gone only an hour. I keep an endless supply of Pop-Tarts in the cupboard for him and he's usually sitting on the couch watching TV, covered in crumbs when we return, but I don't care. He's a good kid.

Bridget's full of energy this morning, fueled by a caffeine addiction that would give me heart palpitations if I drank even half as much. Cheerful and upbeat, she wears a constant smile and reminds me of a sprinter, poised, waiting for the crack of the starter pistol. Throughout the day her children wear her down until she drops into bed only to rise and do it all again. Before she started her family, Bridget worked as a nurse in a pediatric oncology unit. She told me once that she missed it terribly, and sometimes wondered if giving it up to stay home with the boys was the right decision. "You can go back someday," I assured her, and I meant it.

Bridget's short blonde hair peeks out from under her baseball cap and she's wearing a sweatshirt and capri-length workout pants. Cooler weather has finally blown in from the west and the gray sky threatens rain. We'll be lucky if we don't get poured on before we make it back home. I grab a sweatshirt of my own and we head out, power walking our way to the corner and turning left toward the bike trail that winds for miles through our tree-lined neighborhood.

"How are you getting along with Chris traveling all the time?" she asks.

"I'm doing okay," I say. Bridget is my closest friend next to Elisa, and I could certainly admit that so far, despite my concerns, Chris's travel schedule has had little impact on any of us. He spent most of the previous year holed up in our home office with the door closed while he networked over the phone or searched employment sites on his laptop. Half the time the kids didn't even realize he was home, and when they did, they didn't care, which broke my heart. His, too.

It isn't that I don't trust Bridget; I do. And God knows she's got her own problems to deal with. Sam's prowess — or luck, depending on who you ask — at the casino and the racetrack is legendary, and Bridget knows what it's like to be alone because Sam spends all his time at work and the rest of his waking hours betting on the horses or playing poker. She admitted to me once, somewhat sheepishly, that Sam didn't really connect with the kids until they were old enough to do the things he liked to do.

"Like gamble?" I asked. I was only half kidding.

She grimaced. "Yes. He takes them to Chiefs games. They know all about point spreads."

I wouldn't have a problem telling Bridget everything, but the truth is, I'm tired of talking about it — the recession, the horrible job market, Chris's depression, and the resulting emotional upheaval that ripped through my household. I'm just done.

After a mile we pick up the pace. I strip off my sweatshirt and tie the sleeves around my waist, glancing up at the darkening sky.

"Ready for bunco tonight?" Bridget asks.

"Almost. I still need to make a Costco run."

We discussed starting a neighborhood book club, but Elisa and I are the only ones who like to read, so we decided bunco might be more our speed. A simple dice game, a drink or two, and an excuse to leave the kids at home suited everyone just fine. Tonight the teenage girl who lives at the end of our street and occasionally babysits for me is taking Josh and Jordan to the park and then back to her house to swim in her family's pool and eat hot fudge sundaes. The kids consider this the ultimate trifecta of summer fun and wish I'd host bunco more often.

We're less than a quarter mile from home when the sky opens up and pours. We sprint, laughing, not really caring that we're getting drenched. I shout good-bye as Bridget dashes into her house, and I burst through the front door of mine, wiping the water from my cheeks. Josh and Jordan are still asleep and Sebastian is watching an episode of *Family Guy* that's been on our DVR for more than a year. He rises from the couch looking so tired, I tell him to go home and go back to bed. At the front door I press a five-dollar bill into his hand. "Don't tell your mom," I say, ruffling his spiky hair.

He grins. "Thanks, Claire."

Later that day the kids and I jump in the car and drive to Costco. Josh and Jordan gorge on the best samples while I load up my cart. At home I put everything away and give the house a quick once-over to make sure it's still clean. The kids play in the backyard with Bridget's youngest son, Griffin, stopping occasionally for Popsicles or to use the restroom. I sit at the kitchen island, sipping iced tea and working on some graphics for a local car dealership advertisement until Griffin goes home and the babysitter comes to collect Josh and Jordan. “Be good and behave,” I say, bending down to kiss each of them good-bye. I caution the babysitter to keep a close eye on the kids when they’re in the pool. “Make sure you’re in the water with them, okay?”

“I will, Mrs. Canton,” she says. “My parents will be there, too.” I shut the door and turn off my laptop, then pull the fruit and cheese I picked up at Costco out of the fridge. After arranging the wedges of Brie and cheddar on a platter, and surrounding them with grapes and chunks of melon, I set a small bowl of crackers next to the platter. I have exactly five more minutes of quiet before the girls show up.

Julia arrives first, holding a bottle of chardonnay, and — I’ll be honest — she looks rough. She’s only thirty-two, but already there are deep grooves in her face, as though her skin is never fully hydrated. Her eyes look tired and her hair isn’t as shiny as it usually is.

“Hi,” I say, and I reach out and give her a spontaneous hug. She feels tiny and brittle in my arms, like she’s not eating enough.

“Well hello to you, too, Claire,” she says, surprised by my greeting. She’s not an overly affectionate person unless it’s the end of the evening. When she’s really drunk, she tells me how much she loves me, accompanied by hugs and sloppy kisses.

I shut the door and follow her into the kitchen. I hand her a corkscrew, feeling like a giant hypocrite but knowing she will drink tonight no matter what I say or how gently I suggest that she abstain. She pours a large glass and takes a drink.

The doorbell rings and I yell for whoever it is to come in. Elisa and Bridget walk into the kitchen together. Bridget holds a giant bowl of tortilla chips and has a jar of her homemade salsa tucked under her arm. Elisa balances a cheesecake in one hand and holds a six-pack of Amstel Light in the other.

"We'll never be able to eat all that," I say. I clear some space on the counter and take the bowl of chips from Bridget. Standing on my tiptoes, I open the cupboard and reach for a small bowl on the shelf and then pour the salsa into it. I love Bridget's salsa. She uses the freshest ingredients and it's spicy enough to make my lips tingle. I dunk a chip into it and groan when I pop it in my mouth. "This batch is excellent," I tell her. Elisa sets down the cheesecake on the island next to the wine bucket. I'm definitely going to have a bite or two of that.

When I first met the girls and they found

out about my diabetes, they went overboard trying to accommodate my disease. They'd show up with sugar-free cookies and platters of carrots, celery, and broccoli until I explained that my pump does most of the work for me and there's nothing I can't have in moderation as long as I pay attention to my readings and adjust my insulin accordingly. I sensed their relief when I assured them they could bring whatever they wanted, especially since no one ever touched the horrible cookies, and the veggies went right into the trash.

"Where's Chris this week?" Julia asks, topping off her glass and settling herself onto a stool next to the island.

"Santa Fe and Albuquerque."

"It must be so hard with him on the road all the time," she says. "Aren't you lonely?"

I was lonely long before Chris went out on the road, but she doesn't know that. "Yes," I say, answering honestly. "But he really needed that job, so the kids and I will just have to make do."

She snaps her fingers, like she's just come up with the best idea ever. "You should go to one of those Pure Romance parties."

"What's Pure Romance?" Bridget asks.

"You know," Julia says. "Like Pampered Chef but for vibrators. Instead of bunco, one of us could host a party next month."

Bridget laughs. "Why am I not surprised that you know this?" Julia loves to talk about her sex life, and we're used to her oversharing.

"Don't knock it, Bridge," Julia says. "They've got a fantastic product line."

Bridget opens a bottle of beer and sits down beside Julia. "I've got four kids and a husband who wants to have sex every night. How, exactly, am I supposed to make time for a vibrator?"

"I'm just saying it doesn't hurt to have a backup," Julia says. She turns toward me. "Are you even paying attention, Claire?"

"Not really," I say, taking a sip of my iced tea.

"But you're the whole reason I brought it up," she says.

"Thanks, but I'm pretty sure I can get the job done without a sex toy."

"How very boring, Claire," Julia says.

I shrug. "I'm not that fancy." I'm ready to change the subject. We usually save this kind of talk for later in the evening, after the girls have had a few drinks, but apparently we're starting early tonight. Maybe because Julia is already a few drinks ahead of everyone. The subject matter doesn't embarrass me, but it does remind me that, technically, I am in need of a replacement for Chris.

The temperature has climbed significantly since this morning and the rain has moved on, so we're going to sit on the deck to play our game. I turn on the stereo and try to remember which button activates the outdoor speakers. "Can someone pop their head outside and tell me if they hear music?"

We play several rounds of bunco and Bridget wins the pot every time. "Sam will be so proud," she says with just a hint of sarcasm. "Maybe he'll win big tonight, too."

Bridget will have to give her babysitter most of the money because her two oldest boys are at a sleepover and she had to hire someone to watch the two youngest. Sam is no more likely to stay home on bunco night than Chris is to share his feelings with me.

When we come inside, Julia tries to convince us to go back to her house. Justin and Skip are hanging out with the kids and are probably knocking back a few drinks of their own.

I beg off even though it's only nine o'clock. The babysitter has brought the kids home and they're upstairs taking showers. I'd have no one to watch them, and I'm tired and looking forward to relaxing with a DVD after I get them in bed.

Julia stands and sways slightly as she pours the last of the chardonnay into her glass. She makes her way through my kitchen, sipping the wine, and heads toward the front door. "I'll bring your glass back tomorrow, Claire," she says over her shoulder. But she won't. I always have to retrieve them.

Elisa pecks me on the cheek and gathers her things. "Thanks, Claire. I'll see you later. Bye, Bridget." She hurries out and I know it's because she wants to follow Julia and make sure she gets home okay.

Bridget yawns. This morning's caffeine boost has been eclipsed by the sedating effects of a few beers and the cumulative fatigue brought about by a day's worth of parenting.

"See you tomorrow at seven?" I ask as I walk her out.

She leans over and gives me a quick hug. "Sure. Thanks for hosting."

"You're welcome."

It takes me fifteen minutes to clean up the kitchen and the deck after I tuck the kids into bed. Before I head upstairs to slip between my own sheets, I check my e-mail.

To: Claire Canton
From: Chris Canton
Subject: Kids

I got your message. Tell the kids I'm sorry I missed them — I was on a conference call, but it was nice to hear their voices on the recording. Busy day tomorrow. I'll try to check in when I get back to the hotel. Closed the deal in Albuquerque. Hope I can do the same in Santa Fe.

7

CLAIRE

When we returned home from Hawaii last year, the first month of Chris's unemployment was almost behind us. Our lives didn't seem that different, because even though he was home all the time, he never stopped working. Idleness was a foreign concept to Chris, and he spent his days fixing things around the house and offering to drive the kids to their playdates and after-school practices. He worked tirelessly in the yard, planting trees and building a large retaining wall, which he landscaped with shrubs and rosebushes.

He was confident that the headhunters who fawned all over him would soon call to tell him they'd located the next lucrative position, complete with a sign-on bonus and six weeks of vacation time. This mind-set didn't come from a place of entitlement, and Chris certainly didn't take the recession lightly, but there were sectors of the economy that were still performing well and he thought it was only a matter of time before the headhunters found a company that needed a proven sales leader, pairing them like the matching cards in a giant game of employment concentration. Patience isn't one of Chris's stronger virtues, but he waited, and though he got a bit quieter, pensive, and slightly brooding, I don't think anyone noticed but me.

School let out and in the months that followed, Chris volunteered to coach Josh's summer baseball league and shuttle Jordan back and forth to her swimming lessons while I spent the days appeasing my clients. For the first time ever I had the freedom to take on additional work and more challenging projects. I didn't have to drop everything in time to meet the school bus or run someone to practice or facilitate a playdate.

Frequent monitoring of our bank account showed more money going out than we'd planned for. The premiums for our health insurance were so high it barely seemed legal, Chris's car needed four new tires, and our dentist referred us to an orthodontist who informed us of the costly treatment Jordan would need to correct a problem that was invisible to the untrained eye. "We can postpone it," I suggested.

Chris wouldn't even consider it. "No," he said. "If she needs it, we'll do it now."

He came home one day and found me mopping the kitchen floor. "Why don't you let Kathy do that?" he said, referring to our bimonthly cleaning lady.

I dunked the mop in the bucket and then squeezed out the excess water. "I let her go," I said. I felt horrible about it because she was a single parent and really needed the money. "I told her I'd call her back when our budget eases up a little."

Chris wouldn't look at me, or maybe I was the one who avoided his eyes, afraid to see any kind of hurt in them. "Our budget is fine," Chris said softly. He skipped dinner that night and spent the evening in our home office with the door closed.

I took on additional clients, and I hustled for more, following up on every lead I encountered. Sometimes I worked until midnight but even then Chris would stay up later, and it was around this time that he stopped coming to bed altogether, preferring the couch so he wouldn't disrupt my sleep with his restlessness. I slept worse without him next to me, but I refrained from complaining so I wouldn't add to his stress.

One night in August, after I tucked the kids into bed, I found Chris in the office with a calculator and the checkbook on the desktop in front of him, fingers flying over the numbers, his brow furrowed.

"We'll be dipping into our savings by winter," Chris said, shaking his head. He exhaled and massaged his temples.

The money he had received in one lump sum equaled eight months of his base salary but didn't include the commissions he once earned. Though we didn't have any revolving debt we paid a small fortune to our mortgage company every month. The irony was that the home Chris and I were once so proud of had lost a significant amount of its value when property values plummeted; we probably couldn't unload it if we wanted to, and we would lose money even if we found a buyer.

"I'm taking on more work than ever," I said. "If you weren't here to help me with the kids, I'd never have had the ability to bid for these jobs, and there's no way I would have had the time to devote to them."

"Well, that makes me feel so much better," he said, sighing, not bothering to hide the defeat in his voice.

I'd always thought we were equal partners, but my normally open-minded husband apparently harbored some fairly strong 1950s opinions about who should be bringing home the bacon and who should fry it up in the pan. Or maybe it was just his wounded ego that was feeling old-fashioned.

I left the room, trying my best not to crush the eggshells under my feet.

8

DANIEL

Dylan's in town. He sends me a text and asks me to meet him for a drink, so when my shift ends I go home and change out of my uniform. When I walk into the bar he's sitting on a stool, whiskey in hand, shooting the shit with the bartender. I can't even imagine what he's saying; the possibilities are endless.

"Hey," I say when I slide onto the stool next to him. "When did you get into town?" I signal the bartender to bring me the same thing Dylan is drinking.

"Couple hours ago," he says. He takes a drink of his whiskey. "You shoot anybody today?" It's an old, worn-out joke. One Dylan never tires of. His jab at my profession. Ironic, considering he refuses to choose one of his own.

I let it go. "Nope." The bartender sets down my drink. "How long are you sticking around?"

"Not long. I'm just passing through."

He needs a haircut and his wrinkled clothes tell me he's probably crashing on someone's couch and living out of a duffel bag. I take too big a drink and the whiskey burns a bit on its way down. "You see Mom and Dad yet?"

"I told you I just got here."

"You should have gone there first." I don't know why I think that's even a possibility. Dylan goes where he wants to. "They miss you."

"What do you hear from Jessie these days?" he asks.

"I don't." It's just like Dylan to mention the one thing he knows I don't want to talk about. The thing I've failed at. I take another drink, wondering why I even bothered to come. "Mom worries about you. She called me the other day. Said she couldn't get a hold of you."

"I'll try to get over there before I leave."

"You do that, Dylan." I stand up, throw some money on the bar, and walk out.

My empty house greets me when I return home. I turn on the lights and throw my keys and phone on the coffee table. Click on the TV and surf the channels. Around 10:00 P.M. my phone rings. I answer and

Melissa asks the same question she always does, her voice low and inviting.

"Want some company?"

My house seems emptier than it usually does, and I don't feel like being alone tonight, so I say, "Sure. Come on over."

She arrives twenty minutes later, and she smiles when I open the door. We don't speak, but I step aside and when she walks through the door I follow her down the hallway to my bedroom.

9

Claire

Chris flies out of the Kansas City International Airport every Monday morning and returns on Thursday night, spending Fridays in his office at the company's headquarters. He's now the director of sales for a large software development company, and from what little he's shared with me, the culture sounds dreadful. "It's ridiculously competitive," Chris said, shortly after starting, but the tone of his voice made me think he was more than a little excited about the challenge.

Even when he's not at work he is always working, sitting on the couch with his laptop or in the office with the door closed. He's on the phone a lot, too. Once he walked into the kitchen and I thought he was talking to me, so I answered. But when he turned his head and I saw the Bluetooth headset I realized he wasn't talking to me at all.

He gets in late bearing overpriced souvenirs — small stuffed animals for Jordan and unique gadgets or toys for Josh — purchased mostly from airport gift shops. In the two short months he's been back to work he's been elevated to the preferred parent, and I've become mean Mommy, the one that makes the kids eat their vegetables and go to bed on time.

"This is a bad habit to start," I warned Chris, but I know why he does it. I wanted to tell him that Josh and Jordan are too young to hold a grudge, and that their memories of the last year are already fading. Kids are remarkably resilient. More so than their parents, apparently.

He had to travel an extra day this week and we were asleep when he got home last night. The kids' summer vacation is in full swing and when Chris called from the airport he promised them a trip to the water park in Kansas City. The sun shines bright on this Saturday morning at the end of June, and the predicted high of eighty-five makes it a perfect day for careening down waterslides and splashing around in a wave pool.

Chris walks into the kitchen, rubbing his eyes. Josh puts a forkful of waffles and sausage into his mouth. "Are you still gonna take us to the water park, Dad?" he asks, wiping his mouth with the back of his hand and taking a large drink of his orange juice.

I hand him a napkin. "Finish chewing next time," I say.

"Yep," Chris says. He heads toward the coffee pot and pours a cup, then sits down at the table and yawns. Jordan smiles and Chris reaches over and tweaks her nose. "How's my baby girl this morning?"

"I'm good, Daddy," she says, smiling. She finishes her breakfast and climbs into Chris's lap, throwing her arms around him in a spontaneous hug.

He holds her tight and says, "Aw, thank you."

"If you're done eating, put your plates in the sink," I say.

"Can we change into our swimsuits?" Josh asks, barely able to contain his excitement.

"It's a little early yet, but go ahead." They tear out of the room, eager to get this show on the road.

"I can't go with you today," I tell Chris. "I'm putting the finishing touches on a big project and it's due by noon. I was supposed to turn it in yesterday, but I asked for an extension so I could take the kids to the zoo." Thankfully, my client understood;

she's a working mom, too.

"That's okay," he says. "We'll be fine."

Chris is more than capable of handling this outing alone, but since he started traveling we've lapsed into tag-team parenting, which means the kids spend plenty of time with each of us individually, but we spend very little time together as a family. I add this development to the long list of worries I already have.

"You don't need to work so much now, you know," Chris adds.

Oh, the irony.

"I'm not accepting that many new projects," I say. "This one is just time sensitive." I don't explain to Chris that my desire to scale back has more to do with the kids being home this summer than any desire to curtail my workload; I plan on adding as many projects as I can handle when school starts again. I like the independence and the satisfaction of earning an income, and there's a small part of me that also thinks I might like the idea of a safety net. That if I'm ever truly alone I'll be able to stand on my own two feet.

"I'm going to get my oil changed and do the grocery shopping," I say. "I'll drop off your suits at the cleaner's."

Chris nods, running his fingers through

sleep-tousled hair. "Okay," he says. "Thanks." There are shadows under his eyes and I'd tell him to get more sleep, but he won't listen. "Can you refill my prescription while you're out?" he asks.

"Sure," I say.

"I'm sorry," he says, so quietly I can hardly hear him. "I'm just not ready to stop taking the pills yet."

"Chris, it's okay. Really." Besides, what can I say? I'm the one who insisted on the antidepressant in the first place. I top off his coffee cup and give his shoulder a squeeze. He reaches up and grabs my hand, squeezes back. It's the first touch I've received from him in months.

When Chris and the kids leave for the water park I buckle down and finish my work, then head out to begin my errands. I finish the grocery shopping quickly, amazed at how much I can accomplish when I'm not dragging two squabbling kids along. After dropping off the groceries at home, I get my oil changed, deal with the dry cleaning, fill the prescription, and then pull into the Starbucks next door. I order an iced latte, sipping it at one of the shaded outdoor tables. The marquee for a nearby movie theater catches my eye. My family won't be home for hours, so I wander over and buy a ticket for *Sex and the City 2;* I've been dying to see it. My mood instantly improves when I find a seat in the half-empty theater, the air-conditioning a welcome contrast to the rising temperature and the blazing afternoon sunshine.

I love going to the movies; I always have. There's nothing quite like the anticipation of the story that's about to be played out on the big screen. I've never been to a movie by myself before, but once the lights go down and the previews start, I wonder why I waited so long.

That's where Chris and I met back in 1998, sitting next to each other in a movie theater when we were twenty-two years old. Kendra, a girlfriend I'd met during my internship and that I still kept in contact with, had called me up late that afternoon. "A bunch of us are getting together to see *There's Something About Mary* tonight. Are you interested?"

It was August. I'd moved into my own apartment after graduation, a cute studio in a quiet neighborhood that was within a few miles of my first postcollege, full-time job. I had no one to help me if my blood sugar got too low or too high, so managing my diabetes became more important than ever. It made my parents nervous and they tried to talk me out of it, but I'd looked forward to having my own place, relishing the thought of peace and quiet after the noise and chaos of the three friends I had roomed with for the past two years. I craved independence and wanted to prove to my parents — and myself — that I could live on my own. It wasn't until after I moved in and spent the first few nights alone that I realized how much I missed those girls and their constant companionship. The company I worked for was also very small, and even though I enjoyed preparing visual presentations for a handful of clients, it was quite solitary compared to the large groups I'd worked with on school projects.

So when Kendra called I said yes immediately, jumping at the chance to surround myself with people and noise and get out of the studio apartment that had once seemed so perfect and quaint and now just seemed lonely and claustrophobic. "Great. I'll pick you up in an hour," she said.

We met the rest of the group outside the theater, and I noticed him right away. He stood off to the side a bit, this perfect boy with blue eyes and blond hair, wearing khaki pants and a white polo shirt, as if he eschewed everything about the slovenly, multipierced, and tattooed student body he'd recently left behind. He looked like he didn't belong and he also looked as if he couldn't care less about things like that. I'd eventually find out that he had been way too busy holding down two part-time jobs and earning straight As to worry about what others thought of him. I realized I'd been staring and looked away quickly, but not before noticing that he seemed to be looking at me, too.

When we were standing in line to buy tickets, Kendra told me — when I inquired, casually, as if I really didn't care — that he was the former roommate of someone in the group. There were seven of us and we bought popcorn and found seats in the theater, and somehow he ended up sitting right next to me.

He introduced himself. "Hi, I'm Chris."

"Claire," I said, reaching out to shake his hand. "It's nice to meet you." Clean-shaven and clear-eyed, he lacked the run-down, bloodshot, hard-partying look my previous boyfriend had worn like a badge of honor. I had dated Logan for almost a year but we parted ways when it became clear that I had neither the stamina nor the desire to keep up with him. I had no interest in abusing my body the way so many of my peers did; I had enough to worry about without taking additional risks. I overheard Logan tell a friend one time, "Claire's hot, but she has issues." He was probably referring to the time my blood sugar dropped too low. I got shaky and started sweating and luckily I had glucose tablets within reach because he was no help whatsoever. Logan would have freaked out if he'd seen me during a severe low, because it isn't pretty. I say random things. I sweat profusely, and I cry. I can become belligerent pretty easily. Though Logan never came right out and said it, I always felt as if my diabetes — and my need to follow a strict schedule — put a damper on his spontaneous ways. My disease was manageable, but it required vigilant monitoring and making sure that insulin was readily available. Logan thought nothing of road-tripping two hundred miles to see a concert with only an hour's notice and he felt more at home in a smoky bar, tossing back shots of Jäger, than he ever did in a darkened movie theater. The stress of trying to fit into his world and the ups and downs of my blood sugar became something I started to hide around him, and I had enough sense to know that it wasn't a good sign. I ended the relationship a short time later and was more than a little heartbroken when he didn't seem to care.

After the movie everyone went out for pizza and beer and Chris lingered near me, making conversation and asking if I needed anything. He drove me home that night. "Can I have your number?" he asked.

"Sure," I said, digging a business card out of my purse and scribbling my home number on the back in case he didn't want to call me at work. I thought he might try to kiss me, but he pocketed the card and made sure I was safely inside before he walked back to his car. I would have let him. Even back then there was something solid, trustworthy, comforting about him. Or maybe I just liked the way he looked.

He called the very next day and invited me to another movie the following Saturday, a matinee this time. "I thought we could have lunch first," he said.

"That would be great," I said.

He picked me up and thus began one of the best dates I ever had. It was one of those idyllic summer days where the humidity seemed to vanish and the temperature hovered at a perfect seventy-five degrees, so we sat at a sidewalk table at a small bistro and ordered Bloody Marys with our lunch. I didn't often drink alcohol, but there were times when a drink sounded good and that day was one of them. I remember the way the vodka made me feel even more relaxed and carefree than I already did. Chris told me he hated olives and since I love them he laughed and popped his into my mouth, and all I could think about was the feel of his fingers as they touched my lips. When our food came we shared our entrees, feeding each other bites off our forks. To the casual observer, we probably looked like we'd been dating for a while. There were no awkward moments, and I felt instantly comfortable with him. We were having such a good time that we arrived at the movie — *Saving Private Ryan* — late, missing the previews and sliding into our seats just in time for the main feature.

When the house lights came up Chris asked, "Do you want to get some dinner? You're probably getting tired of me, but I'm hungry again and I thought you might be, too."

I looked at my watch. I didn't wear an insulin pump back then, and I needed to check my blood sugar and give myself a shot before I could eat anything else. "Maybe some other time," I said. He tried to hide it, but the surprise at being turned down when we were clearly having a great first date showed on his face. "It's just that I have to go home," I said. We walked silently to his car and he opened the door for me. When we reached my apartment and he walked me to the door, he made no move to leave. I unlocked it and he followed me down the short hallway and into the kitchen. I walked to the refrigerator and after I pulled out the bottle of insulin I filled a syringe, pulled up the hem of my skirt to expose my upper thigh, and plunged the needle in. Normally I hated giving myself a shot in front of anyone. People seemed to freak out about needles and it didn't help that Logan used to refer to it as "Claire shooting up." Chris watched, silently, his eyes lingering on the tan skin of my leg. I capped the syringe and threw it away, then looked up at him.

"I have diabetes."

He was leaning against the counter, arms crossed. "I see that." He looked confused, as if he couldn't figure out why I was being so secretive. "Now what?" he asked.

"Now I can go to dinner with you."

He smiled, his features instantly softening. "Then let's go."

He took my hand, lacing his fingers with mine as we walked to a nearby diner. "Wouldn't it have just been easier to tell me?" he gently chided.

"I didn't want it to matter." I told him about Logan and how I'd always felt that my diabetes bothered him. Like it was a burden. And even though it was way too early for what I was about to say, I said it anyway. "My disease has lifelong implications. Not everyone can handle that. Especially guys."

"Logan sounds like a tool. Taking care of you should have been his top priority."

I smiled at him, feeling sudden, inexplicable tears that I blinked back. "I can take care of myself," I said, because I didn't want him to think I was incapable of it. That I was some damsel in distress that needed rescuing. I just wanted him to know what he was up against.

"I have no doubt that you can," he said.

And this time, after we finished dinner and he walked me home, he waited until I unlocked the front door. Then he leaned in and cupped my face in his hands and kissed me. His lips were soft but there was something commanding about his kiss, something that told me that underneath his good manners and respectful demeanor I would find a guy who liked to be in charge. Who might not be so polite when we were alone in a way that I would very much enjoy. I could have stood in the doorway with him forever on that perfect summer night as he pressed the length of his body firmly against mine. I remember thinking as I lay in bed that night that Chris was the kind of guy you could plan a future with.

I went out with him three more times and the more time we spent together, the more I discovered I was right about that prediction. He had goals and dreams, and I'd never met anyone who had his life so mapped out. The girlfriend he'd had through most of college wasn't remotely interested in settling down. "She wanted to go backpacking in Europe. Stay in youth hostels and avoid getting a job for as long as she could. Things like that," he told me. "That wasn't what I wanted."

He was already climbing the ranks at work, selling cell phone packages for AT&T and working toward a position in management. Home ownership was next on his to-do list and he told me he hoped to buy within the next year. He spoke fondly of his parents and always treated me with respect. He didn't play games, and if he said he'd call, he'd call. He made me laugh, he made me feel like I mattered, and he made it so very easy for me to fall for him.

He took me out to dinner one night a week later and then we went back to his apartment. After he unlocked the door he didn't bother turning on the light. Silently, he pulled me by the hand and guided me past the kitchen and living room and down the hallway to his bedroom. Once inside, he kissed me and then slowly pulled my T-shirt over my head, throwing it onto the floor. I kissed him back and he nudged me gently until the backs of my knees made contact with his bed. He tumbled onto it with me and we kissed with abandon, both of us breathing hard when we finally came up for air. He removed my bra and I gasped when he cupped my breasts, bent his head down, and took one of my nipples in his mouth. Logan had seldom bothered with this step, and I'd forgotten how good it felt. Chris took his time, sucking on one nipple and rubbing his thumb back and forth lightly across the other, and I made sounds I hadn't made in a while. He brought his mouth back to mine and his kisses became urgent, unrestrained, and after a few minutes I broke away so I could take his shirt off and run my hands over his chest. The smell of his skin, a combination of soap, cologne, and his own scent, intoxicated me.

His fingers tugged on the button of my jeans, popping it open.

"Chris, wait. Do you have any condoms?" I should have thought of that earlier.

Oh God, please say you do.

Trailing kisses down my neck, sucking and almost biting the tender skin, he whispered, "Yes."

He slid my zipper down and took off my jeans. He listened to my quick and shallow breathing as I waited for him to touch me again. Slowly, tortuously, he finally reached out and slipped his fingers under the elastic waistband of my underwear and pulled them off. Grabbing both of my wrists, he extended my arms over my head and used one of his hands to hold them firmly in place. With the other he eased my knees apart and put his hand between my legs. The sun was setting but there was still enough light coming in through his bedroom window for me to see him touching me and to know that he was watching his fingers moving inside me. He added the gentle pressure of his thumb rubbing in a circle. It felt incredible, and I came embarrassingly fast, shuddering and crying out, but I didn't care, because Logan had never once taken the time to do that to me.

Chris brushed the hair back from my face and kissed me. "You are so beautiful." Then the mattress shifted as he rolled away and stood. He unzipped his jeans, and his belt buckle hit the floor with a clink. I heard the crinkle of a condom wrapper and Chris's body covered mine. He raised himself on his forearms and looked into my eyes when he entered me, his breathing as ragged as mine had been; we fit together perfectly. And after he came, when he was holding me in his arms, he whispered, "Claire Jones. I am falling in love with you."

Nine months later he got down on one knee and asked me to be his wife, and six months after that we stood up in front of our friends and family and promised to love and obey and cherish each other for as long as we both shall live.

I turn my focus back to the present when I realize the previews have ended and the main feature has started. I focus on the film and lose myself in the romantic comedy. It isn't so bad seeing a movie alone. I even manage to laugh spontaneously a few times.

When the lights go up I stand and follow the couples out of the theater and drive home, suddenly feeling very alone.

10

CHRIS

I throw my key card on the dresser of my hotel room, shrug out of my suit jacket, and sink into a chair. I have a headache because I skipped lunch, and my voice is hoarse from talking all day.

I've discovered that my boss, Jim, is a giant asshole. He has two sides: the one I saw during the endless rounds of interviews they put me through for this job, and the side he shows his sales managers when he doesn't think they're performing up to standards. The other day I watched him tear my counterpart to shreds in front of a packed conference room of his peers. He was condescending, short-tempered, and rude. It's unsettling, working for him. Like he could flick a switch and morph into that other guy on a dime if there's a hint of failure on my part. I'm grateful to be employed, so I don't even like having these thoughts; I'd never say them out loud to anyone. Not even Claire.

I've been with the company for two months, and I've closed every deal they've given me to close. I spend hours entering information into spreadsheets, to justify and quantify what I'm doing, and still it isn't enough. As soon as I meet my goal, it changes. Gets bigger. I'm expected to do the job of two people because the lingering effects of the recession require that companies operate as lean as they can. I get that, and I'd much rather be here in this hotel room in Denver, employed, than be without a job. Actually, I'd rather be employed and at home with my family, but it didn't work out that way.

I loosen my tie, turn on my laptop, and get to work.

11

CLAIRE

I walk into Elisa's house on the Fourth of July and find her in the kitchen talking on the phone. She motions toward the refrigerator. There's a pitcher of iced tea, so I grab a glass from the cupboard and help myself. I take a drink. It's icy cold with a hint of lemon, just the way I like it.

When Elisa hangs up she says, "Claire! You look so pretty." She takes in my white sleeveless top and knee-length, flowing white skirt and sandals. As soon as I'm reunited with my children I'll be wearing parade dirt and sticky handprints, but for now I'm pristine. I got my hair blown out this afternoon when I went in for a trim, and it lays shiny and straight to the middle of my back. A floppy, wide-brimmed sun hat and an armful of silver bangles complete my outfit.

"Thanks," I say. "I felt like mixing it up a

bit." What will probably happen is that I'll be back in shorts and a tank top by tomorrow, but it's been a long time since I was even remotely dressed up, so here I am.

I take another sip of tea and sit down on a bar stool. The kids are marching in our town's yearly Fourth of July parade, Josh and Travis with their Cub Scout troop, and Jordan with her dance studio. Chris is home for the holiday and he and Skip volunteered to drop off the kids and will follow the parade on foot and meet up with us when it's over. A carnival has been set up in the park directly across from the end of the parade route, and the kids are beyond excited about riding the Ferris wheel and Tilt-A-Whirl.

Elisa grabs a glass from the cupboard, pours some wine from an open bottle of sauvignon blanc that she pulls out of the fridge, and takes a drink.

"Did you take a test?" I ask when she plunks herself down on a stool next to me.

She shakes her head. "I didn't have to. I got my period a day early."

There's no medical reason Elisa can't get pregnant, so every month she holds out hope. Determined to have another child, she's tried everything from in vitro to acupuncture to meditation. Skip tries to convince her not to stress about it and has suggested more than once that maybe this is God's way of saying their family is complete. His words fall on deaf ears. If she's lucky enough to get pregnant, she says she won't care if it's a boy or a girl, only that the baby is healthy, but her desire for a daughter is almost tangible, like you could reach out and touch it if you wanted. Feel the solid weight of it in your palm.

After we finish our drinks we drive to the park, setting up our chairs in the front row at the end of the parade route so we can collect the kids when they're done marching. It's hot, but not unbearably so, and there isn't a cloud in the sky. Perfect parade weather.

Not much is happening, at least not yet. Two toddlers waving flags sit with their mothers on a blanket and a group of preteen girls walk by, their cheeks displaying temporary tattoos of red, white, and blue stars. The thumping music from the nearby carnival rides reach my ears, as does the smell of freshly popped popcorn.

Two police officers are leaning up against a squad car, talking. The tall, dark-haired one looks familiar. "Remember the police officer that pulled me over for that taillight last month?" I ask.

"The ridiculously good-looking one?" Elisa says.

"Yes," I say. "I'm pretty sure that's him over there. The one with the dark hair."

She shields her eyes from the late afternoon sun and looks in their direction. "Wow, you weren't kidding. He's easy on the eyes."

"I know. I can't even imagine how many propositions he must field during a normal workday," I say.

"I'm sure he's heard it *all.*"

Maybe I'm mistaken, but the dark-haired officer appears to be looking over at us, squinting slightly as though he's trying to place our faces.

"Who did you talk to at the police station when you called about the speed limit sign?" Elisa asks.

"I don't know. The dispatcher, maybe?"

I'd called the police department about getting a speed limit sign after Bridget and I encountered a speeding car while we were on one of our walks. We'd barely made it onto the sidewalk when a car roared down the street, startling us both.

"Jesus," Bridget yelled at the driver. "Slow down!"

The teenage boy behind the wheel flipped her off and we returned the salute, each of us jabbing the air with both of our middle fingers for emphasis.

"Well," Bridget said, chuckling, "we showed him." Rolling her eyes at the sheer absurdity and ineffectiveness of our actions, she said, "One of the kids is going to get hit crossing the street and then no one will be laughing."

It was a sobering thought. "I told Elisa that we need one of those speed limit signs," I replied. "I'll make a few calls and see what we need to do."

"They have one in my sister's neighborhood," Bridget said. "She says it helps."

When I called the police department I found out that we weren't the only ones who wanted one. Apparently there's a bigger demand than they're able to supply and we have to wait our turn. Who knows how long it will be before we get one?

"Do you think it would help if we talked to someone directly?" Elisa asks, motioning toward the officers. "Explain how bad the speeding is? Maybe they could bump us up a few spots on the list."

"Maybe," I say. "It can't hurt to ask."

I follow Elisa over to where they're standing, and they stop talking as we approach. The dark-haired one smiles; he's definitely the officer who pulled me over.

Elisa thrusts her hand out. "Hi. I'm Elisa Sager."

He shakes it. "Daniel Rush."

Elisa introduces me. "This is my neighbor Claire Canton."

I shake his hand. "Nice to meet you."

The officer standing with Daniel looks near retirement age, with nondescript features and strawberry-blond hair that's thinning all over. Freckles — or maybe they're age spots — dot his skin. "This is Officer Eric Spinner," Daniel says.

"It's a pleasure," he says, shaking our hands. The sound of shouting reaches us and both officers look toward a group of rowdy teenage boys. Two of them are trading insults and their language is enough to make me wince. Daniel pauses, listening, and takes a step forward. "I've got it," Officer Spinner says, and I watch as he walks toward them.

"You probably don't remember me, but you pulled me over for a burned-out taillight about a month ago," I say.

He nods. "I do remember you. Did you get it taken care of?"

"Yes."

Smiling at me, he says, "Good."

"We had a question we were wondering if you could answer."

"Sure," he says. "What is it?"

"We live in Rockland Hills and the speed limit on our street is virtually ignored. I called and we're on the waiting list to get a speed limit sign. Do you know how long it usually takes?"

"How long have you been waiting?" he asks.

"Not long," I admit. "Maybe two weeks? I'm just curious about how long it usually takes."

"It depends," he says. He opens the door of the police car, leans in, and emerges with a business card and a pen. "What's your address? I'll see what I can do."

"Really? That would be great. Thank you." I give him my address and after he writes it down he slips the card into his pocket.

"No problem," he says. He scans the crowd, his eyes roaming left to right, but his body language seems relaxed as he leans back against the car.

Elisa's phone rings and she pulls it out of her pocket. "It's Skip. I'll be right back," she says, walking away to take the call.

Now it's just the two of us. Feeling awkward, I start to say good-bye at the same time that he says, "Are you from around here?"

"Yes," I say. "What about you?"

"Overland Park."

"Shawnee Mission district?"

He nods. "I went to West."

"I went to East."

"When did you graduate?"

"Ninety-four," I say.

"I was ninety-one."

That makes him thirty-seven. There's another awkward lull. Neither of us say anything but when he smiles and looks at me, all the nerve endings in my body start vibrating, as if he can generate an electric current by virtue of his expression and his proximity. Strange, because until now I've never been one to swoon over a man in uniform. My feet move, seemingly of their own volition, and I take two steps toward him.

"I like your hat," he says.

"Thanks." I realize I'm staring and finally break eye contact. "Do you like working the parade?" I ask. Maybe this is a welcome change from his usual police responsibilities.

"Sure. It's fairly tame. Later is when it gets ugly," he says. "Holidays and hot weather bring out the worst in people. Lots of alcohol abuse. We'll see a spike in domestic assaults."

"That's horrible," I say, thinking of the

fights that will break out later and the fact that there will be children in many of those households. The sound of the marching band draws nearer. "I hope I'm not in your way," I say to Daniel, embarrassed that maybe I'm keeping him from doing his job.

He smiles and shakes his head. "You're not."

Elisa returns. "Skip said they'll be here in a few minutes."

"Do you have kids marching in the parade?" Daniel asks.

"Yes. Our sons are with the Cub Scouts, and my daughter is with her dance studio," I say. "They were really excited."

"How old are they?" he asks.

"Jordan is seven and Josh is nine. Elisa's son, Travis, is ten." Out of the corner of my eye I see the marchers approaching. I hear the sound of the band, including the loud crash of the cymbals and the distant roar created by a large number of cheering children. Elisa gives Daniel a quick wave and says, "Nice to meet you."

"You, too," he says.

"I better go," I say.

"It was nice to meet you, Claire."

"It was nice to meet you, too. Thanks for checking on the sign."

"Sure," he says. "Have a good day."

Elisa and I make our way back to our chairs. A few minutes later, Chris and Skip and the kids walk up to us and soon three enthusiastic voices are telling me about the parade, and I switch gears and give Josh, Jordan, and Travis my full attention. They want to go to the carnival now; it's all they can talk about. We tell them to be patient and that we'll head over in a minute. Chris gathers up my chair and the one I brought for him and we prepare to relocate. I grab the blanket and a small cooler that contains beer, water, and pop.

"Let me carry that," he says, taking the cooler from me.

"How did the kids do?" I ask.

"They got tired near the end, but they had a great time."

"Good."

He studies me for a second. "You're dressed up," he says.

I glance down at my outfit and notice that one of the kids has already slimed me with a smear of something sticky and blue. I rub at it with my finger, which only makes it worse. "A little bit," I say.

Chris loves skirts. When we were first dating I wore them all the time, especially after he told me how good he thought I looked in them. "You look nice," he says, smiling at me.

"Thanks," I say, and smile back at him. I can't remember the last time he paid me a compliment. He sets off toward the park, hurrying to catch up with the kids, who are trying to sprint ahead, and I follow him.

We buy wristbands and the kids stand in line for each ride, despite my observation that they all look a bit rickety. Sandwiched between Josh and Travis, Jordan waves frantically at me as the Ferris wheel begins to move, transporting them high in the sky. I smile at the joy on her face. When the ride ends we follow them as they rush to the next one. After they've ridden everything at least once, Jordan gets her face painted like a tiger while Josh and Travis eat corndogs and drink fresh-squeezed lemonade. When Jordan is done I buy her a cone of pink cotton candy and laugh when some of it sticks to her whiskers. "Don't wipe it off," she says, worried that I will smudge the paint. The kids jump in the biggest bounce house I've ever seen and, miraculously, no one throws up. Shortly before 9:00 P.M. we choose a grassy spot and settle into our chairs, the four adults sitting side by side and the kids on the blanket in front of us to watch the display. The crowd cheers when the first round of fireworks explodes in the night sky.

Daniel is out there somewhere, I imagine. Leaning against his patrol car, watching the fireworks.

Keeping everyone safe.

When we return home I hustle the kids off to bed. They're hot and dirty, and need showers, but they're so tired I decide the world won't stop turning if we wait until morning. Besides, there's no way Jordan will part with the tiger makeup just yet. Despite the late hour, Chris sits down on the couch and powers up his laptop. "You're going to work?" I ask.

He looks up at me. "I need to get a head start on these reports." His desire to prove himself to his new boss is all-encompassing, and I know he's eager to prove his worth, to make himself indispensable to the company. I've had years to adapt to his workaholic nature, and I should be used to it by now, but I'm not. When we were younger and newly married it didn't bother me as much. He wasn't out at the bars like the husbands of some of my friends (or, God forbid, the strip clubs), and I took pride in the fact that Chris had his head on straight and I never had to worry about where he'd been.

I didn't miss him as much back then because we still spent plenty of time together, preferring each other's company over anyone else's. I'd wait up for him and he'd come home at eight or nine, or sometimes even ten, and loosen his tie and I'd heat up whatever I'd made for dinner. He'd eat and we'd make love and if we didn't get to sleep until after midnight, it didn't matter. I had the boundless energy of a woman in her early twenties, and sleep was a commodity I hadn't yet learned to cherish the way I would after the kids came along.

We'd only been married for six months when we decided to start a family. When I got pregnant I spent some of the hours that Chris was at work turning one of the three bedrooms in our cozy little starter home into the perfect nursery. I agonized over what color to paint the walls, choosing a gender-neutral shade of light green since we didn't want to find out the sex of the baby. We picked out the furniture and Chris put the crib together one night while I hung up all the clothes that I'd prewashed, holding the outfits up to my nose and inhaling the fresh, clean smell. The dresser held tiny pairs of socks and sleepers, and the bookcase in the corner contained all my childhood favorites as well as the entire Dr. Seuss collection.

When Josh was born I took to mothering

with a vigor that surprised me, blocking everything but the baby out of my life. When my maternity leave was almost over I gave my employer my two weeks' notice and decided to go the freelance route so I could work from home. I breast-fed, so Chris didn't have much to do except make sure the car seat was installed properly and make diaper runs. For months, Josh and I cuddled in the rocking chair in the nursery, with the middle-of-the-night feedings quickly becoming my favorite. I was exhausted at first, but the glow of the night-light and the absolute stillness of the house — and Josh's contented sigh — satisfied me more than anything in my life ever had.

Chris stood in the doorway one evening when he got home from work, watching as I fed Josh. "Do you need anything?" he asked.

"No," I answered, barely taking the time to look up. "I don't need anything at all."

There was no reason for Chris not to work as many hours as he wanted. I was the kind of wife — the kind of mother — who had everything under control at home. And when Jordan came along I attended to her with the same devotion I'd given her brother, working twice as hard to make sure I had enough time and attention for both of them. If Chris ever felt left out, he didn't show it.

Once Jordan was sleeping through the night, I'd awaken periodically, listening from our quiet bedroom convinced I'd heard a cry or a sound. When I realized everyone was still sleeping I'd wake up Chris and we'd come together quickly. He was always receptive, and making love in the middle of the night was my way of compensating for my absence during those early years of parenting. It had nothing to do with obligation, though; I needed the closeness, the connection, as much as he did. Maybe more.

When I come back downstairs after making sure the kids are tucked in I find Chris rifling through a stack of paper, a pen clenched between his teeth. Even though Chris hasn't slept in our bed in a long, long time, I make a request. "Come up when you're done." I can't handle a blatant rejection, so I clarify. "I just want you to lie down with me," I say. "Please." I hate that I sound as if I'm begging.

He looks up at me and takes the pen out of his mouth. His desire to get back to his spreadsheets is almost palpable, but his expression softens and he nods and says, "Okay. Give me a half hour."

But in the morning I wake up alone, and when I walk downstairs to start the coffee I find Chris asleep on the couch, spreadsheets and laptop on the floor in front of him.

12

CHRIS

The sound of someone moving around in the kitchen wakes me. I hear the sliding glass door open and Claire speaking softly to Tucker. The water runs and I picture her filling the coffee pot and starting breakfast. I'm still in the shorts and T-shirt I wore to the parade, and I blink a few times, trying to clear the cobwebs; there's something I didn't do. My laptop pings, alerting me to an incoming e-mail, and I notice the spreadsheets covering the floor. I remember Claire's request and the look on her face last night when she asked me to come upstairs.

Shit.

She's been patient. More patient than I'd ever be if our situation were reversed. And yet I couldn't even give her the one small thing she asked for, which, quite frankly, is a poor substitute for the real thing.

It will take me a long time to make it up to Claire. Not just for last night, but for last year.

But I will if she can just hold on a little longer.

13

DANIEL

I stop by the desk of the officer who handles our public works, including speed limit signs. I don't know him that well, but he seems like a pretty nice guy.

"What can I do for you?" he asks.

"I need you to check a list for me. I know someone who's waiting for a speed limit sign. Her name is Claire Canton." I wait while his fingers tap the keys. After the parade I looked Claire up on the online white pages. There's an associated person in the household named Christopher, who's obviously her husband. I saw her talking to a tall, blond man after the parade, which is yet another reason why it makes no sense for me to keep thinking about her.

I can't stop, though.

She really does look like Jessie. And her hair. I don't remember what it looked like when I pulled her over, but at the parade it was straight, the way Jessie always wore hers. But Claire's mouth, that doesn't remind me of Jessie at all. Because Claire has really great lips. They're full, but they don't look as if she's done anything to make them that way. There's no way to not notice them when she talks.

The officer brings up the list on the computer and scrolls through the names. "It's gonna be a while. She's way down there."

"Can you bump her up?"

He looks at me and shrugs. "Sure. How far?"

"To the top."

He raises an eyebrow, and I pretend not to notice. "Friend of yours?"

I don't know what the hell I'd call her. I hardly *know* her. "Yeah."

"Done," he says. "She should have it in a couple days."

"Thanks," I say. "I owe you one."

He laughs. "I hope she's worth it."

14

Claire

By the fifth month of his unemployment, Chris wasn't quite as confident about finding a job. He spent hours networking on the phone in our home office and entire days online applying directly to company websites. He had relationships with four headhunters, but only one of them was still returning his calls on a regular basis. He started to pull away from me, his responses to my questions clipped, shorter. Sleep eluded him completely, and I'd wake up in the middle of the night and find him in the office, the glow of his laptop filling the room with a weak, eerie blue light. "Are you okay?" I'd ask.

"I'm fine," he'd say. "Go back to bed."

A feeling of unease would wash over me, and I remembered the woman from my yoga class whose husband had lost his job. I wondered if he ever found one. Without a job to go to, Chris simply didn't know what to do with himself. Our roles, once so set in stone, remained in a constant state of flux and Chris didn't quite know how to handle it.

In mid-August of last year, as the first day of the new school year drew near, Josh and Jordan needed clothes. They'd outgrown almost everything in their closets and the items that still fit looked decidedly worse for wear. Josh's penchant for playing football had ripped the knees from most of his jeans, and Jordan had a tendency to ruin her clothes with large splotches of Magic Marker ink. Mindful of our budget, I avoided the stores I normally shopped at and decided it would be in our best interest to economize. My kids' clothes might not be higher-end, but they'd be free of holes and unmarred by stains. Josh and Jordan didn't care where their wardrobes were purchased, and I was grateful that they were too young to pay much attention to the latest trends; those days would come soon enough.

We drove to T.J.Maxx instead of the mall. In the girls' department, Jordan zeroed in on a pink and black plaid skirt and a white button-down shirt with a necktie in the same plaid pattern threaded through the collar. “I want to wear this on the first day of school, Mommy,” she said.

“Sure,” I said, checking to make sure it was the right size before placing it in the cart. “It’s adorable.” The temperature would still be quite warm when school started in late August, so I didn’t need to worry about buying matching tights; Jordan could wear the ensemble with a cute pair of ballet flats. She selected several more outfits, choosing her favorite styles and colors, while her brother fidgeted. “We’ll pick out your clothes next, bud,” I said.

“Okay,” he said, clearly bored and grumpy that the store didn’t have a sporting goods department so he could try and talk me into buying him a new football or basketball. He gave me no input when we finally reached the boys’ department, so I picked out his clothes and decided to be happy that he didn’t have a strong opinion about what he wore.

On the first day of school, after a special breakfast of cinnamon rolls and bacon, I posed them in front of the fireplace and snapped pictures. “I want Daddy to watch us get on the school bus,” Jordan said.

“He will,” I assured her, though one glance toward the closed office door made me wonder if Chris would accompany us the way he always had in years past. I exhaled when the door opened five minutes later, noticing the circles under Chris's eyes. Had he slept at all? His shorts looked looser, almost baggy, and I made a mental note to make sure he was eating enough.

When it was time to leave, the kids hoisted their new backpacks — also from T.J.Maxx — onto their shoulders and followed me out the door, Chris lagging slightly behind.

Bridget and Elisa were already waiting at the bus stop, cameras in hand. Sam and Skip, looking a bit out of place, wore dress slacks and button-down shirts and looked as if they couldn't wait to leave for work; this would be their token appearance and it wouldn't be repeated until the following year. Julia and Justin joined us moments later; I noted her oversize sunglasses, which were hardly necessary because the sky was a dull gray.

"Rough night?" I asked.

"I'm just tired," she replied. "I was up late."

Bridget's four boys were outfitted in Nike athletic apparel from head to toe. I winced when I thought about the cost of the shoes alone, but I'd never heard her complain about money, or more specifically about not having enough. Sam worked at a stock brokerage firm and specialized in options trading, which sounded a lot like gambling except with other people's money. It was a risky profession in the best of times, and I often wondered how he was faring with the economy in its current state. Whenever anyone commented on the recession or lamented the balance in their bank accounts, Bridget would say, "Sam handles all that. I'm just the one who brings the clothes and shoes and groceries home."

"Where did you get Jordan's adorable outfit?" Elisa asked.

"T.J.Maxx," I said, taking a sip of my coffee.

"It's so cute," she said. "Josh looks great, too," she added.

"Yes, they both look wonderful," Bridget agreed.

After a flurry of final kisses and hugs, the kids boarded the bus when it pulled up at the curb, and we waved good-bye, watching as they rounded the corner and disappeared from view. The men scattered and I stood there with Elisa and Bridget for a few more minutes, talking about all the things we planned to get caught up on now that school was back in session.

When I walked back into the house Chris was standing in front of the living room window. He turned slowly when he heard me come into the room. "Are discount stores all we can afford now?" he asked, unable to look me in the eye.

"There's nothing wrong with T.J.Maxx. The kids' outfits are just as nice as anything I've bought at Gymboree or Gap, and I paid a heck of a lot less for them. We're still recovering from a recession. Everyone is cutting back and if they're not, they should be. We have nothing to prove to anyone." I took a few steps toward him, but he turned away. "The reality is that your severance and my earnings won't be enough to keep us afloat indefinitely. I'm just being cautious. That's all."

"Believe me, Claire. No one is more aware of our reality than I am. I'm the one who's carrying the full weight of it on my shoulders."

"It's not just your weight to bear. It's mine, too."

"It really isn't," he said. He left the room and walked slowly into the office, closing the door behind him.

In all the years we'd been together, I'd never experienced anything quite as heartbreaking as watching the lights of my golden boy fade.

15

Claire

The doorbell rings while I'm cleaning up the kitchen after dinner. I finally squeezed in a shower after I fed the kids and my hair is wet and combed back. I don't have any makeup on, I'm naked under my old, pink bathrobe, the one I can't seem to part with, and I'm not crazy about answering the door in my current state of undress. Why can't anyone drop by my house when I'm presentable? I glance out the back window. Josh and Jordan are playing with Bridget's boys and they look like they're having a good time, so I don't bother calling one of them in to help me out. The bell chimes again. It's probably a neighborhood child or someone trying to sell something, so I decide to answer it myself and send them on their way. But when I open the door what I'm not expecting is for Daniel Rush to be standing there in his police uniform.

Mortified, I pull the sash on my robe tighter and stutter out a greeting. "Hi."

"Hi," he says, smiling. "I just wanted to let you know that they've brought your speed limit sign."

"Right now?" I guess it's true what they say: It's not what you know, but whom. It's been less than a week since I spoke to him at the Fourth of July parade, and I wonder what kind of effort he had to exert to move us to the top of the list so fast.

There are two squad cars parked on the street. I look beyond Daniel and watch as an officer unhooks a trailer — on which the sign is mounted — and wheels it into position. I'm not sure of the protocol for this kind of service; it seems rude to just say thanks and shut the door, especially after he's gone to the trouble to help us. But I can't stand here in my bathrobe another minute. It feels all weird and desperate housewifey. Opening the door wider, I say, "Please, come in." He steps over the threshold. "Could you excuse me for a second?" I ask.

He nods. "Sure."

I run upstairs, flinging off the robe as soon as I reach the bedroom. I'd planned on putting on my pajamas after I cleaned up the kitchen, but I rifle through the laundry basket of clean clothes sitting just inside the door until I find a tank top and some shorts. I step into a pair of underwear and once I'm fully dressed, I walk back downstairs where Daniel is waiting patiently in the entryway. I'm suddenly conscious of the fact that I didn't take the time to put on a bra and I hunch forward a bit. Technically I'm small-breasted enough to go without, and the tank top has a built-in shelf bra that provides a little support, but it's the air-conditioning running full blast that I'm worried about; I have no idea what it's doing to my nipples, and I'm afraid to look down and find out. My concern kicks up a notch when Daniel glances at my chest. I turn around, looking for something to cover myself with, but the only item of clothing within reach is Jordan's Tinker Bell hoodie — size 6X — hanging on the knob of the coat closet near the front door. But when I turn back around I realize that it's the medical alert dog tag I wear around my neck that has caught his eye, not my nipples. It was probably tucked too far down into my shirt at the parade, but it's almost impossible to hide it when I wear a tank or swimsuit. I don't think much of it anymore, and my friends and family are used to seeing it. "I can't thank you enough for helping us with the sign," I say. "I really appreciate it, and I know my neighbors will, too."

"You're welcome."

"Would you like something to drink? Iced tea or a Coke?"

"No thanks. I'm good," he says, smiling at me. He points at my cheeks. "Looks like you got some sun today."

"Yes," I say. "A little too much." I noticed my pink cheeks when I got out of the shower, and I can already feel the sting of the sunburn. I made sure I put sunscreen on the kids but forgot to put enough on myself. I have to stop doing that or my face will look like shoe leather by the time I'm forty. "We spent the day at the community pool."

"Are you enjoying your summer?"

"Yes. I work from home but my schedule is flexible, so we've been able to do some fun things."

"What do you do?" he asks.

"I'm a graphic designer. Freelance," I add. "I usually work on a per-project basis."

"Do you like it?"

"Yes, very much. It's nice being able to choose what I work on."

"We're talking about redesigning our department logo. The chief has asked for ideas but we're not a real creative group."

Daniel pulls a business card out of his pocket and hands it to me. "This is our current logo. They want something similar, but updated. The last I heard they were going to set aside budget money to hire someone. Send me your rates; my e-mail address is on the card. I can put in a good word for you if you're interested in submitting a bid."

"That would be great," I say. I walk over to my purse and pull out one of my own business cards, then hand it to him. "I have professional references and testimonials listed on my website."

He takes the card. "Thanks."

The sliding glass door off of the kitchen opens, and Josh yells, "Mom?"

I call out to him. "In here, Josh."

He follows the sound of my voice and he and Griffin stop suddenly when they see Daniel. "We didn't mean to do it," Josh yells.

"It was Gage's idea," Griffin adds.

"Do what?" I ask.

"I don't know," Josh hedges, stammering.

"It was an accident," Griffin adds. He's gone ghostly white.

I turn to Daniel. "You have a lie detector down at the station, right, Officer Rush?"

"Yes, ma'am," Daniel says. "Let me know if you'd like me to take these boys off your hands."

I stare at Josh and Griffin pointedly, watching their expressions change, their shoulders slumping in defeat. "Is there something you'd like to tell me?"

"We were chasing Jordan around with a handful of worms. She said she was gonna have us arrested." He points at Daniel. "And look!"

Daniel presses his lips together, trying his best not to smile. I seize the opportunity to administer a lesson. "Well, I suggest you go outside and apologize before I turn you over to the authorities." They hightail it out of the room immediately and the sliding glass door slams.

"Nice work," Daniel says.

"I try," I say, laughing. "Those boys torment her constantly. She can hold her own, but they had this one coming."

Daniel's radio squawks and he turns up the volume and listens.

"Busy night?" I ask.

He turns it back down. "No. It's been slow. This is a nice diversion, actually. I should probably get going, though."

"Okay. Thanks again for the sign. I really appreciate it."

"Sure."

Daniel follows me to the front door and we step outside where the temperature is considerably warmer. He pauses on the front porch. “E-mail me,” he says. “About the logo.”

“I will.”

“Have a nice night, Claire,” he says, smiling at me.

For some reason, the smile makes me blush. I feel the heat on my cheeks, deepening the color I already have. Hoping he doesn’t notice, I say, “You, too, Daniel.”

I watch as he walks down my sidewalk, gets into his car, and drives away.

16

CLAIRE

When Chris had been out of work for eight months we spent the last of his severance on Christmas presents for our families and the kids, deciding to forgo gifts for ourselves, both of us insisting that we didn't need anything. We weren't often extravagant with each other, so it wasn't a big adjustment for us, but Chris seemed a little down about it. He'd always done a good job of finding just the right gift to give me and he wasn't the kind of husband who ever forgot my birthday or our anniversary.

With his severance depleted, our only source of income was our savings and the money Chris collected from his unemployment benefits, money he initially hadn't wanted to apply for at all. "You're entitled to it," I reminded him. He hated filling out the monthly paperwork, and even more than that, he hated filling out applications for jobs he was completely overqualified for just so he could show that he was indeed attempting to find a job. The realization that his applications were going unnoticed, that no one was even considering him for those jobs anyway, was even harder for him to take.

I walked into the office one snowy January day with a bowl of soup and a sandwich. The omelet I'd made him for breakfast was still sitting, untouched, on the plate I'd delivered four hours earlier. "Chris. You didn't eat your breakfast."

He didn't even look up from the computer screen. "I'm not hungry." He rubbed his temples, like I was a pain he could massage away.

"You can't just stop eating," I said.

He sighed and pushed his chair back from the desk. "I said I'm not hungry." I started to speak but Chris cut me off. "You know what, Claire? What I really need is for you to leave me alone," he said. "Stop asking me how I'm doing. Stop asking if I'm eating, or sleeping. Just stop."

He'd never lashed out at me like that before, but he had an expression on his face that worried me more than his tone or his words: It was the look of sheer desperation. The pupils of his eyes were dull and flat;

the blue lacked sparkle and the whites were streaked with red. I wanted to throw my arms around him, say something, anything that would make him feel better. But the realization that he didn't want those things from me, that I was only making it worse, brought tears to my eyes. "Okay," I said. "I'll leave you alone."

So I stopped hovering, stopped asking him how he felt or if there was anything I could do, and he retreated even further into himself, barely speaking to me. Before long, he wasn't the one with whom I shared the highlights of my day; Elisa or Bridget, or sometimes Julia, filled that role. I didn't seek Chris out the way I once had, as a partner, a confidante. Certainly not as a lover. Finding new ways to cope, to satisfy the needs he once met, unsettled me. I felt as if my world had been turned upside down, but in a completely different way than his had been. He had a goal, and once he found a job, his worries would disappear. But in the interim, I had no idea what to do about mine.

Our household dynamic shifted, buckled under the weight of its problems until the only option was to adapt lest the whole infrastructure crumble. Self-preserving in the short term, absolutely disastrous for the long haul.

We did it anyway.

I sought refuge at my parents' house one particularly lonely, desolate winter day. My mom was standing near the stove when the kids and I walked into the kitchen, and I inhaled the smell of pumpkin bread as I shrugged out of my coat. My spirits lifted instantly; it smelled like my childhood and to let someone else be the parent that day was exactly what I needed.

"Well, this is a nice surprise," my mom said when the kids ran toward her, almost knocking her over in their haste to smother her in kisses. "Your timing is perfect. I was just about to make the dough for chocolate chip cookies while the bread is baking."

"Can we help, Grandma?" Jordan asked, jumping up and down.

"I get to help, too," Josh said, elbowing his sister out of the way.

"Josh," I admonished. "Tell your sister you're sorry. You can both help."

"Sorry," he mumbled.

My mom got out the big white bowl, the same one she'd been mixing cookie dough in my whole life. She instructed the kids to wash their hands and began lining up the ingredients on the kitchen counter.

I looked around. "Where's Dad?"

She turned on the oven light and peered inside to check on the bread. "He's in the basement," she said. "Working on the train track." I heard the slight irritation in her tone, which meant my dad was in the dog house for something. "You kids be good for Grandma," I said. "No fighting. I'm going to go down and see what Grandpa's up to."

"Tell him we'll be down as soon as we make the cookies," Josh said. He loved the trains almost as much as my dad did.

I opened the basement door and walked down the stairs. My dad whirled around at the sound of my footsteps when I entered the room. "Claire!" He smiled at me, the way only he could, and held open his arms. I went to him and he enveloped me in his embrace. "What brings you by? Are the kids and Chris with you?"

"The kids are upstairs making cookies with Mom. Chris is at home." The office door was closed when we left, so I didn't tell my dad what Chris was up to because I had no idea. "How's the train track coming along?"

"I'm working on a playground. The kids will love it."

Three weeks after my dad retired, he decided he needed something to fill his days. "I'm going nuts," he told my mom.

"He's driving me crazy," my mom told me. "He's got to find something to do; he's underfoot all day."

My dad solved the problem by immersing himself in the world of model trains, and one end of the basement showcased his entire collection. He actually spent more time working on the track than he did with the trains. He'd mounted it on a large platform and the elaborate, winding track included trees and shrubs, small outbuildings, and houses. There was even a frozen pond with a miniature ice-skater on it. Jordan loved that the best. I walked over to check out his progress with the playground. He was right. The kids would love the tiny swing set and slide, and the picnic table. "What's happened here?" I asked, pointing to a jumbled pile of track that wasn't connected to anything.

"I'm switching the direction so that it winds back around. I'll probably switch it back," he muttered. I sat down on the old plaid couch. The bookshelves along the adjacent wall still held all the mementos of my youth, including my soccer trophies and my senior picture from high school. My mom had saved every award or certificate I'd ever earned and they were lined up on the shelves in their outdated eight-by-ten frames. I found the nostalgia comforting and also a little embarrassing. The room was one giant time capsule. Chris loved to come down here and tease me good-naturedly about the shrine my parents had erected in my honor. The bane of an only child.

"What's new, Claire-bear?" my dad asked.

"Nothing. Just waiting for spring."

His doubtful expression said he wasn't buying it, not for one minute. He walked toward the couch and sat down beside me, polishing his glasses on the hem of his flannel shirt. "You gonna tell your dad what's really wrong?"

His candor surprised me. I expected these kinds of questions from my mom, had in fact fielded several since Chris lost his job, but not from him.

"I can't reach him, Dad. We don't talk and he won't let me help him." Tears welled up in my eyes, maybe because it felt cathartic to finally say it out loud or maybe because everything was falling apart and I wanted nothing more than to let my dad handle it, the way he'd fixed my bicycle when the chain came off or changed the oil in my car when I started driving. I knew those thoughts were ridiculous because I was a grown woman, a mother of two, and I could hardly expect him to solve my adult problems.

"What Chris is going through is a hard thing, Claire." His tone was gentle, but his words stung. My own dad didn't think my emotions were justified. He noticed my expression. "Now, don't get your feelings hurt, honey. It's hard on you, and the kids, too. I know that. This hasn't been easy on any of you. But a man wants to take care of his family, and it doesn't matter whether they're capable of taking care of themselves or not. He's out of sorts. Doesn't know what to do with himself."

"He won't talk to me about it. I try, and he shoots me down."

"He hears what you're saying, Claire. He just can't answer you right now. Men aren't big on sharing their feelings, especially during the hard times. Don't give up on him. He needs you more than ever."

I nodded, wiping the tears that spilled onto my cheeks. "It will probably get worse before it gets better," he added. "You should remember that." He placed his hands on my shoulders and looked me in the eye. "I'm not saying you don't have a limit, when enough is enough. Don't be afraid to tell him, either. You're nobody's punching bag."

"Oh, Dad. Chris would never raise a hand to me."

"I know that. But words can hurt every bit as much."

He pulled me toward him and hugged me. I heard the thunder of footsteps on the stairs and Josh and Jordan burst into the room, eager to spend time with their grandpa and check out the track. They hugged him and after he showed them everything that was new, I told them I was heading back upstairs.

"Grandma said we're supposed to come back up, too, as soon as we're done looking at the track. The pumpkin bread is ready," Josh said. He and his sister left the room as abruptly as they had entered it. I started to follow. "You coming, Dad?" I asked.

He picked up a tiny swing and added it to the playground, giving it a slight push and watching as it swung back and forth. "I suppose. Been hiding out down here long enough."

"Why are you hiding?"

He cleared his throat. "Because your mother wants to talk about my overdue prostate exam, and I don't."

Despite my swirling emotions, and my despair, I couldn't help but smile and shake my head.

"You're gonna get it checked out though, right?"

He threw his hands in the air and snorted. "Yes."

"I love you, Dad."

"I love you, too, honey."

17

Claire

I'm playing catch with Josh in the backyard. He'd prefer to throw the ball to Chris or Travis, but Chris is in Miami and Travis has a raging case of strep throat. All Josh has left are his mom and his sister and when Jordan refused he came looking for me. His timing isn't the greatest because I'm right in the middle of cooking dinner, but he looks so hopeful that I can't bring myself to say no. I turn down the temperature on the stove, deciding that the beef stew can simmer for a while longer. After shutting off the oven that had been preheating for the crescent rolls, Jordan's favorite, I follow him outside.

I put on my glove and Josh winds up and throws.

"Good job, Mom," he says when I catch it.

He smiles when I throw it back. We play

for almost a half hour, but then I bend down to retrieve the ball that I missed and something pops in my back. I can barely straighten.

"Mom, what happened?" Josh asks, running over to me.

"Nothing," I assure him. Trying not to grimace, I say, "I'm okay."

It isn't nothing. It feels like white-hot arrows of pain are shooting from my lower back to the top of my spine, pain that's exacerbated by the slightest movement. "Let's go inside," I say. "It's almost time for dinner."

"Okay," he says.

I take two Motrin and walk over to stir the beef stew. After preheating the oven I have to ask Josh to open it; I can't bend down far enough to do it myself. "Thank you," I say. "Stand back." I slide the sheet pan of rolls inside, closing the door with my hip. When the timer goes off twelve minutes later I somehow manage to remove the rolls without dropping them.

Sitting hurts. Lying down hurts. The only thing that's remotely bearable is to keep moving. Once I stop, it becomes even harder to get going again.

The pain is much worse the next morning and the three Motrin I washed down with my coffee haven't put a dent in it. Julia calls to see if the kids and I want to meet her and her daughters at the park later this afternoon. "I don't know," I answer. "I did something to my back. I need a massage, but my regular guy is on vacation." I've been going to Walt for years; he's sixty-five, a retired marine, and he doesn't try to manhandle me or press on anything too hard. I trust him implicitly.

"You should go to my guy. If you call him and tell him I referred you, he'll get you right in."

"Is he good?"

"He's the best. I tip very well." She gives me his number and I scrawl it on a scrap of paper. As soon as I hang up I call; Julia must have some pull because her massage therapist says he'll shuffle things around and can fit me in at one o'clock. I call a babysitter to watch the kids while I'm gone.

The pain in my back has morphed into a dull, throbbing ache and the anticipation of relief prompts me to arrive early. It looks like a nice enough place, and the reception area is clean, though sparsely decorated. I thumb through a magazine and wait.

When he pops his head around the corner and calls my name, I'm relieved to discover that Julia's massage therapist is a tall, athletically built man who looks as if he's in his midtwenties. His handshake is firm, but not crushing, and once I'm on the table and he begins, I can tell he's not going to be too rough. He asks me about my pain and focuses extra attention on the small of my back where it hurts the most. Gradually I relax, and I think I could actually fall asleep.

After a while he asks me to turn onto my back and I manage to flip over without dislodging the towels that cover the parts of me that are off-limits. He resumes massaging me, starting with my feet and working his way up. I start to doze, but then his fingers graze the inside of my thigh, which is weird because Walt never touches me there.

His hand moves a little higher.

Or there.

He slides his hand between my legs, cupping me, fluttering his fingers gently along my crotch, and I fly off the table, pain ripping through my back as I try to remain upright and keep everything covered.

Walt would *never* do that.

"What the hell are you doing?" I yell.

He holds his hands up in front of him and takes a few steps backward. "I'm sorry. Julia referred you. I thought you knew."

What, that you give happy endings? No, I

didn't know that.

"Look," he says. "I'm really sorry, but I'm putting myself through grad school and I need this job. I would never have touched you if I thought you didn't want me to."

Seeing his panic-stricken expression calms me down; his explanation rings true, and I'm open-minded enough to chalk the experience up to a misunderstanding. A really big one.

"It's okay. I won't say anything."

Relieved, his shoulders slump and he takes a deep breath. "I'd be happy to work on your back some more. You look like you're in serious pain."

He seems sincere, but I say, "No thanks. I'm going to get dressed now." Before he leaves the room I add, "Hey. I was never here."

He nods, comprehending. "Okay."

We walk to the park later to meet Julia and her girls. She notes my slow rate of speed, and my shuffling gait. Her hands are wrapped around a plastic tumbler that contains a clear liquid I strongly suspect is white wine. "Didn't you call my guy, Claire? I told you he'd fix you right up." She smiles knowingly.

"I called a chiropractor instead. I don't think this is a problem that can be solved with a massage."

And certainly not with an orgasm.

It's not a lie. As soon as I got home I called a chiropractor and I've got an appointment first thing in the morning.

"You look like you're in agony," she says.

"I'll be fine."

The kids scamper off, eager to play, Josh on the jungle gym and the three girls on the swings.

Julia leans in close, so I can hear her. "Make sure you call him sometime, Claire," she whispers, and the fumes of chardonnay wafting from her mouth are so potent I'm surprised I don't catch a buzz. "You'll want to get on his rotation, especially now that Chris is gone all the time."

"I'll keep him in mind," I say, but I'm flat-out lying because I'm not so desperate for the human touch that I'm willing to outsource it to a man employed by a massage franchise sandwiched between a dry cleaner and a video store in some strip mall across town.

Not yet, anyway.

18

CLAIRE

Justin and Julia's swimming pool is finally done and she invites us over for an inaugural dip one day in early August. Josh and Jordan are thrilled and they run upstairs to change into their suits right after breakfast. Julia extends the invitation to Elisa and Bridget, too. When we arrive Julia turns on the waterfalls and points out the features of the hot tub.

"Everything turned out beautifully," I say. "It's heated, right?"

"Yes," Julia says. "If the weather stays halfway decent, we'll be able to swim until the end of October." The kids cheer, ecstatic about the prospect of having a pool at their disposal, and the air soon fills with the sounds of splashing and laughter.

"What can I get you to drink?" Julia asks. "I have beer, wine, vodka. I can make a batch of margaritas. Oh, I almost forgot. I can do mimosas."

"Do you have any iced tea?" I ask.

Her face falls. "Sure. I always forget you don't drink much." It's true that I'm not a big drinker, but I can have one or two if I adjust my insulin accordingly. But it's 10:03 A.M. A drink doesn't sound remotely appealing.

"I'll take a beer," Bridget says. "I accidentally walked in on Sebastian having some special alone time. There isn't enough alcohol in the world to erase that image."

"Oh, God," I say, laughing.

"A word of advice," she says, looking at Elisa and me. "*Always* knock first."

We groan. "I don't think we're at that stage yet," I say. "At least I hope not."

"I'll have some tea, too," Elisa says, and Julia walks into the house to get the drinks. When she returns she has a tray with a pitcher of iced tea, two glasses, a bottle of beer, and a full glass of wine. She sets the tray down on the table and hands out the drinks.

I take a sip of my tea and then spread out my towel on one of the four chaise lounges that Julia has arranged next to the pool. I strip off my cover up and lay down, rolling up another towel and placing it behind my head for a makeshift pillow. "This is fantastic," I announce, feeling the warm sun on my skin. I shield my eyes and do a quick head count: all children are safe and by the looks of it they're having a wonderful time.

"Are you still really busy, Claire?" Bridget asks.

"Not really. I've finished up a lot of my smaller jobs. I'll add more when the kids go back to school. And I might have an assignment with the police department."

"Doing what?" Bridget asks, slathering herself from head to toe with sunscreen.

"Designing a new logo. When the officer delivered the speed limit sign the other day we started talking and he asked me what kind of work I did. He told me they were interested in hiring a freelance graphic designer. I submitted a bid."

"I think someone is a little sweet on our Claire," Elisa teases. "She's failed to mention that the officer is ridiculously good-looking and that the speed limit sign showed up mere days after she asked to get bumped up on the list."

Julia spreads out her towel on the chair beside me and chugs half of her wine. "I want to hear more about this, Claire."

"Why, are we fourteen?" I ask. "There's nothing to tell. I'm sure he knows I'm married." I hold up my left hand. "I'm wearing a ring. He didn't do or say anything weird. He's just a nice guy."

Thankfully, they drop it. What I don't tell the girls is how much I've enjoyed talking to Daniel. How easy I find it. I don't have to worry about saying the wrong thing, the way I do with Chris.

Elisa settles in on my other side. She takes a drink of her tea and asks, "Can you watch Travis for a couple hours tonight?"

"Sure. Send him over," I say. "We don't have any plans. Do you and Skip have a hot date?"

"No. We're taking a class tonight."

"Couple's massage?" Julia asks, laughing.

"Maybe Elisa has finally convinced Skip to learn line dancing," Bridget says.

"No," Elisa says. "It's none of those." She pulls a pair of sunglasses out of her tote bag. "It's to learn more about getting certified to foster a child."

I sit up. "Elisa. That's wonderful." I lean over and give her a hug. "Are you and Skip thinking of becoming foster parents?"

"Maybe," she says. "There are so many kids who need good homes. A loving and stable environment. We're still trying to get pregnant, but I'm starting to think that it's not in the cards for us. When I mentioned it to Skip I had no idea what he'd say, but he was really supportive. I was worried about Travis, because he's used to having us all to himself, but he said he always wished he had a brother or sister. We'll see what happens. Tonight is just to learn more."

I reach out and squeeze her hand. "You and Skip would be fantastic foster parents." Bridget and Julia echo my sentiments.

"Thanks," she says. "We'd try very hard to do our best. I know it won't be easy."

"Keep us posted," I say. "I really hope it works out."

"Thanks, Claire."

"Who needs a refill?" Julia asks.

"I'm good," Bridget says. "I have half a beer left."

Elisa and I are still working on the pitcher of iced tea, so Julia takes her empty glass into the house and emerges with a refill. At noon, the kids take a break for lunch. We make them get out of the pool while we're inside Julia's kitchen making peanut butter and jelly sandwiches. Julia drops the jar of grape jelly on her ceramic tile floor and it explodes upon impact, making one hell of a mess. It doesn't seem to faze her, and Bridget grabs a dishcloth and helps her clean it up.

"Do you have any fruit?" I ask.

"There are apples in the fridge," Julia says.

When I grab the apples I notice that the jug of wine on the top shelf, the one that's equal to two normal-size bottles, is halfway gone. Maybe it was already open when we arrived. Because if it was a brand-new bottle and she polishes it off, she is going to be smashed. I shut the door, wash the apples, and slice them for the kids.

It turns out I was wrong. At a little after three thirty, Julia bypasses smashed and goes straight to passed out. Her five-year-old daughter, Hillary, tries to rouse her. "Mommy. Mommy, I'm thirsty."

I look over at Julia's chair and I'm alarmed to see that she isn't moving.

Julia's three-year-old daughter, Beth, walks toward her sister and says, "Is Mommy sleeping?"

Elisa and I jump out of our chairs, and Bridget tells the girls to come inside. "I'll get you a drink," she says.

Elisa gently shakes Julia, but she's out. My heart pounds when I think about Julia passing out when she's home alone with the girls. Maybe while they're in the pool.

"Do you think she's just normal passed out, or the kind of passed out where we should be worried?" I whisper.

"Why are you whispering?" Elisa asks.

"I have no idea," I say. "Maybe we should

call Justin. Ask him to come home."

"I agree," she says.

"Mom?" Travis says. "What's wrong?"

"Nothing. Why don't you all go inside and tell Bridget you need a snack," Elisa says.

After they go in I ask Elisa if she knows Justin's number.

"No," she says. "But Skip does. He calls him sometimes to play golf." Elisa calls Skip, explains the situation, and I program the number into my phone when Elisa repeats it out loud. I hit the button to call Justin and get his voice mail.

"Justin, it's Claire. Um, Julia's had a lot to drink. I think you better come home." I disconnect and look down at Julia, shaking my head. I'd like to think that she was just excited about the beautiful day and the pool being done and all of us being here. But who knows what's going on inside her head.

Justin arrives twenty minutes later, red-faced and clenching his teeth so hard I instinctively move out of his way. I've never seen him so angry before. "Julia," he says. He shakes her shoulder, and he isn't all that gentle about it. "Julia!" He runs his fingers through his hair and exhales loudly. She remains as still as a statue, albeit one who is in a reclining position.

"I can take the girls home with me," I say.

"That's okay," he says. "I'll take them inside and give them a bath. They can watch some TV after. They've probably had enough sun today." He glances down at Julia. "She can sleep it off out here for a while."

Elisa and I gather up our things and collect the kids' towels and pool toys.

"Did you see her eat anything today?" Justin asks before we go.

Actually, now that I think about it, she didn't. We made turkey sandwiches for ourselves but Julia said she wasn't hungry. "No," I say. "I don't think she did." She drank instead.

"I'll go inside and get the kids," Elisa says. "We'll go out the front door and take the sidewalk home."

"I'm right behind you," I say. I turn back toward Justin.

"Thanks for calling me," he says.

"Sure." I hesitate but then I say, "Have you talked to her about it? The drinking?"

"Yes. She knows how I feel."

I think Julia knowing how Justin feels and him doing something to help her are two totally different things, but maybe now is not the time to push. He looks spent, miserable. "Take care," I say.

He musters a weak smile. "I will."

The last thing I see when I look back on my way out is Justin rolling Julia onto her side so she won't choke in case she vomits.

At home, I tell the kids to take a shower. My cell phone rings, but I don't recognize the number. I punch the button to answer it. "Hello?"

"Hi, Claire? It's Daniel Rush." His voice sounds warm and friendly on the phone.

"Hi. How are you?"

"Fine, thanks. I just wanted to let you know the logo design job is yours if you want it."

"Really? That's great. I'm sure your recommendation helped."

"Actually, we didn't have very many applicants. It wasn't widely advertised and it's a pretty small job. But I still put in a good word for you," he quickly adds.

"I'll mock up a few designs. It shouldn't take me long. I'll let you know when I'm done."

"Keep track of how many hours you spend on it and I'll make sure you get paid."

"I will. Thanks."

"Talk to you soon," he says.

"Okay. Bye, Daniel." When I hang up I add his name and number to the contacts in my phone, feeling a bit guilty at how happy it makes me feel.

19

Claire

Bridget's husband, Sam, hits the literal jackpot shortly before the start of the new school year. A spontaneous decision to drop a quarter in a slot machine on his way out of the casino resulted in triple 7s and a seventy-five-thousand-dollar payout. This is the kind of thing that could happen only to Sam.

Bridget appropriates a chunk of the winnings and decides to invest in a new pair of breasts, which is very un-Bridget-like and embarrasses her boys to no end, especially Sebastian — who recently turned fifteen — and his younger-by-eighteen-months-brother, Finn. "They're the boobs I've always wanted," she jokes, but I wonder if they're really the boobs Sam's always wanted.

I cook dinner and bring the lasagna over two days after her surgery. Bridget's normally spotless Craftsman-style home looks like a level-five biohazard, and I trip on the giant mountain of shoes by the front door, including two pairs of mud-caked cleats. I dodge the soccer balls, baseball bats, and piles of dirty laundry that litter the hallway leading from the front door to the kitchen. The house positively reeks of adolescent boys.

I make my way into the kitchen, calling out to Bridget so she knows it's me. The counters are covered in empty frozen food containers and someone has left out a gallon of milk, uncapped. I set down the lasagna, throw the cardboard and plastic wrap into the recycle bin in the garage, and cap the milk and put it in the fridge.

"Don't look at my disgusting kitchen, Claire," Bridget shouts from the living room. "Those boys are pigs!"

I laugh as I enter the room and approach the couch where Bridget's been recuperating. She's propped up by several throw pillows, and I can't help but stare. The new breasts are unbelievably large, and I finally drag my eyes upward. "How do they feel?" I ask.

"Big," Bridget says. Straining against the thin fabric of her T-shirt, they look hard and unyielding, but I don't tell her that.

"Are they still swollen?" I ask.

"I hope so," she says. Bridget and I are both small boned and average height. Suddenly, my B-cup breasts don't bother me as much because her now-overflowing D cups seem so out of proportion. I don't mention this, either.

"As soon as I recover and get this disaster area cleaned up, we're going to have a party," Bridget says. "Sam's feeling very celebratory."

"I'm sure he is," I say. "He's a lucky man. In more ways than one."

I refill Bridget's water glass and find her pain pills. She swallows one and leans back against the pillows. A door slams and the sound of many footsteps and lots of excited shouting reaches us. Bridget sighs. "I think they found the lasagna."

I listen carefully but all I hear is the tearing of foil followed by grunting. "Wow," I say. "They're like a pack of wild dogs."

"You don't even know," Bridget says.

"Don't worry," I say. "I made two pans."

Bridget's true to her word, and two weeks later she and Sam invite everyone over. "You don't need to bring a thing," she says, when she calls me on the phone. "It's on us."

Bridget has the meal catered by one of

her and Sam's favorite barbecue restaurants. Smoky, falling-off-the-bone ribs, rotisserie chicken, baked beans, coleslaw, macaroni and cheese, and garlic bread are laid out buffet-style on the island in the kitchen. There's a large tub of beer on the patio and a full bar set up downstairs in the finished walk-out basement.

When the sun goes down, Bridget and Sam send their boys inside to watch a movie and Justin and Julia take their girls home to remain under the watchful eye of a babysitter. "Should we let the kids hang out inside for a while?" I ask Chris. It's past their bedtime, but summer vacation is coming to an end and they'll be back on their school schedule soon enough. Josh idolizes Bridget and Sam's older boys, and always jumps at the chance to check out their video games. Elisa and Skip are letting Travis stay. Jordan hates to be left out, and if Josh and Travis get to watch the movie, she'll want to as well.

"I'll take them home," Chris says. "Jordan looks tired."

She does look tired and it's probably for the best that they go to bed on time. It's just that it's been so long since Chris and I socialized with only the adults. "I'll come with you," I say. "We can get the kids settled and watch a movie or something."

"No, stay," he says. "I'm really behind. I have to get some work done."

I can almost handle that Chris is gone all the time. It's his job and I understand that. But what I struggle with is that even when he's home, his time is not his own. The kids take whatever he can give them — as they should — and then there's me, hoping to lay claim to whatever's left. But there is never anything left, and there's no point in protesting. "Okay, then," I say, turning and walking away.

"Claire," he says, catching up to me and reaching out to grab my arm. "Don't be mad."

"I'm not mad." I'm lonely, which is a lot harder to see than anger.

"It'll slow down soon. Things will get better."

"I really don't see how they can," I say.

"I just need a little more time," he says. "Please."

I nod, feeling as if I'm out of options. "Sure."

He calls out to the kids, tells them it's time to go. I kiss Josh and Jordan good night and promise to make pancakes for breakfast the next morning. They leave and one by one, the lights come on in my house. I duck into the bathroom in Bridget and Sam's basement and change into my swimsuit. I can be without my pump for a little while, so I disconnect it and leave it with my clothes.

Justin and Julia are back from taking their daughters home, so I join them, and Skip and Sam, in the hot tub, easing myself into the steaming water. Sam is puffing on one of the expensive cigars he's so partial toward. In such close quarters, it's hard to escape the smoke and I muffle a cough with the back of my hand.

We cheer when Bridget settles in next to Sam, her breasts filling out the top of her new swimsuit spectacularly. Justin lounges next to me, his leg pressed against the length of mine. His arm is behind me, resting on the back of the hot tub yet close enough to my shoulders that his fingers brush my skin often. He's drinking bourbon, which never ends well for anyone, but Julia isn't drinking anything at all, and hasn't all night. I can't imagine the argument that transpired after she finally emerged from her poolside alcoholic slumber. It must have been epic because I don't remember the last time I saw her without a drink in her hand. She's been awfully quiet tonight.

Justin is trying to convince Bridget to show off her new breasts and she's had enough to drink that she just might do it.

Skip joins in good-naturedly. "Maybe all the women should take their tops off," he says.

"Be quiet, Skip," Elisa says, but she's laughing. She decided not to get in the hot tub and she's drinking her Coke straight. I cross my fingers that she catches some of Sam's good luck.

Sam doesn't seem to have a problem with his wife displaying her new assets. On the contrary, he's fiddling with the tie on her swimsuit top. "Flaunt 'em if you've got 'em, honey," he shouts. Bridget swats his hand away. Not drunk enough, after all.

Sam looks over at me. "You should tell that husband of yours that all work and no play will make Chris a dull boy," he says, then laughs like it's the funniest thing ever. Have I mentioned that sometimes Sam acts like a complete jackass?

Bridget glares at him and gives me a sympathetic look. "I'm sorry," she mouths.

"It's okay," I mouth back. I look at Sam. "I'll keep that in mind," I say, smiling even though it's the last thing I need someone to point out. Suddenly, I don't want to be here. If I'm going to be lonely anyway I'd rather it be in my own home, in my own bed, instead of in this hot tub. I climb out and wrap a towel around my waist. I open the sliding glass doors to the walk-out basement and cross the room to where Bridget has set up the bar, then set my half-empty glass of Diet Coke on the counter.

The door opens and Justin comes up behind me and puts his arms on either side, pressing against my back and bracing himself on the countertop. He reaches one hand up and cups my right breast. "I like your tits better, Claire. They fit perfectly in the palm of my hand," he whispers, his thumb rubbing my nipple through my bikini top. It hardens immediately and he groans and nuzzles my neck.

Quickly, I move his hand and duck out of his reach. "It's never going to happen, Justin."

He laughs. "I'll wear you down eventually."

"No, you won't," I say. I have no interest in him and he knows it; it's just the bourbon talking. He's only halfheartedly fishing, checking to see if I'll bite. I turn around to face him, rolling my eyes to show him that I know he's kidding.

He laughs and heads toward the door, passing Elisa on his way out. She walks into the basement, giving Justin a curious look. "What was that all about?" she asks.

"Bourbon," I say.

"I'm sorry about Sam," she says. "That man has no filter."

"It's not just him," I say. "I guess I'm not feeling very social tonight after all." She hugs me good-bye and I slip away after thanking Bridget and Sam for their hospitality.

Entering the dark house through the garage, I notice the light showing through the crack at the bottom of the office door when I walk by. My husband is in there; I can hear his fingers tapping on the computer keys. I think about asking him how much longer he'll be working, but then I just keep on walking. I check on the kids and after I take a quick shower, I scoop a sleeping Tucker off the floor by the foot of the bed and slide between my sheets. I stroke his soft fur, happy that I have something warm-blooded to cuddle with, and he settles into the space behind my knees when I turn onto my side and close my eyes.

20

Chris

I hear Claire come in. I know she wanted me to stay at Bridget and Sam's, or to come home with me. I should have explained that they fired someone on Friday and now I've got to spend the weekend doing his work, and mine. I should have told her that I'll be traveling five nights a week now, instead of four.

I don't know why I'm not telling her these things.

Maybe because I keep thinking that I'll get caught up and then I can spend time with her without all this other shit getting in the way. But just when I think I'm close to getting caught up I get more work piled on top of me and then I fall behind again. It's a vicious cycle.

When I finally stop working around 3:00 A.M., I go upstairs and get ready for bed. Since the Fourth of July I've tried really hard not to fall asleep on the couch, because I know that sleeping with Claire makes her happy. Even if sleeping is all that I'm capable of.

She's lying on her side, with Tucker snoozing in the space behind her knees. The moonlight coming in through the window casts a slight glow on her face. I brush her hair back and my fingers trail along her cheekbone. She doesn't stir, not even when I pull the covers back and slide in next to her.

21

CLAIRE

Jordan's tennis shoes are too tight and since both kids need new shoes anyway, we drive to the mall and make a day of it, window-shopping at a toy store and stopping for lunch. As we're walking through the mall I spot Bridget standing near the cash register at Scheel's. I catch her eye and wave. "Come on, kids. Let's go say hi."

Bridget is frowning at the cashier as we approach. She takes a credit card out of her wallet, hands it over, and says, "Try this one."

The bored-looking teenager operating the cash register swipes it and hands it back. "It went through," he says.

"Hey, Bridge," I say. "What's up?"

"Oh, hi." She looks distracted. "Sorry. There was something wrong with my credit card." Her brow furrows as she slips both credit cards back into her wallet. "That's never happened before."

"Sometimes they won't go through if you're spending more than usual. It's a preventive measure. It's supposed to protect you from fraud."

"Well, I've spent a lot today," she says. "Back-to-school shopping."

"Us, too," I say. "Just shoes, though." I liked T.J.Maxx so much that I plan on buying the kids' clothes there again this year.

Bridget gathers up three enormous bags of clothes. "I'll see you later. Have fun shopping." She doesn't have a free hand, but she gives Josh and Jordan a quick smile. "Bye, kids."

We spend forty-five minutes at the shoe store, Josh acting bored and grumbling about how long it's taking his sister to choose between two pairs of shoes. "Better get used to it, buddy. Girls like to change their minds," I tease, but he's in no mood for such nonsense. He perks up when Jordan finally makes a selection. The shoes are sparkly and pink, and the soles light up when she jumps, which delights her. The sales clerk boxes up the tennis shoes Josh spent all of two minutes deciding on, but Jordan wants to wear her new shoes home. The saleslady puts her old shoes in the shoe box instead and hands the kids balloons, a red one for Jordan and blue for Josh. Jordan beams, as if her day couldn't get any better. As we're leaving the mall she lets go of her balloon and wails as it soars upward, and though I jump and grab for the string it's already way too high for me to reach. Her tears flow and I bend down to wipe them. "I'm sorry, honey. You have to hold tight to the things you love." I stand up and look toward the sky, but the balloon is a red speck I can barely make out.

And at that moment I can't help but wonder if Chris realizes just how untethered I've become.

When we get home I call Elisa. She and Skip are moving forward with becoming foster parents and they have their first home visit with a social worker today.

"I'm so nervous," Elisa says when I ask her how she's doing. "I've cleaned this house from top to bottom and I've threatened Travis with his life if he blurts out 'God damn it' like he did the other day when he dropped a hammer on his toe. I just keep worrying that one of us will say or do the wrong thing."

I laugh. "Travis said that?"

"It's not funny. I'm afraid he'll do it again. Or that Skip will, because that's obviously who Travis picked it up from."

"It's kind of funny," I say.

"Yeah," she agrees. "It is. I had to turn my back so he wouldn't see me laugh."

"Everything will be fine." If there were ever two people who were qualified to be foster parents, it's Skip and Elisa.

"What about you?" she asks. "Do you have big plans for the rest of the day?"

"I got the design job for the police department. If I can find something to occupy the kids, I'm going to get started on some mockups. I have a few ideas swirling around in my head and I don't want to lose them. Call me after the visit, okay? I want to hear how it goes."

"I will. Wish us luck."

"You don't need luck," I say. "You'll do great."

After we hang up and I convince the kids to play in the backyard, I turn on my laptop. I set Daniel's business card next to it so I can refer to the existing logo. He mentioned something about giving it an updated look. I open Adobe Illustrator and come up with a few mockups, which I promptly reject because they don't match the vision I have in my head. I don't force it and eventually I get into a groove and lose myself in my work as the ideas flow faster. When the kids come in an hour later, tired, hot, and thirsty, I have several designs that I'm happy with.

Satisfied, I turn off the computer, feeling a twinge of excitement when I think about e-mailing Daniel.

22

Claire

Last February, when Chris had been out of work for ten months, my worry turned to fear. I lost weight I couldn't afford to lose, and I slept horribly. Chris seemed to never eat or sleep at all. His clothes hung on him and the circles under his eyes turned a frightening shade of purple. Over the course of one week he spoke exactly eleven words to me; I counted. The effort required to shield the kids from the situation emotionally exhausted me, and I ran interference constantly because Chris simply didn't have the mental bandwidth necessary to deal with them.

One evening, after being holed up in the office all day, he finally walked into the kitchen when I was cleaning up after dinner. Against my better judgment, I tried to talk to him. I put my hand on his shoulder. "I'm so worried about you, Chris."

He recoiled from my touch and lashed out at me like a caged animal backed into a corner. "Really, Claire?" he yelled, running his hands through his hair in frustration. "Because I'm worried about a lot of things." He started ticking them off on his fingers. "Let's see. I can't find a job, we're going to run out of money, and eventually we'll lose our health benefits. Should I continue? I'm sure I can find some other shit to add to the list."

"You're scaring me. You're scaring the kids."

I saw a flicker of guilt in his expression when I mentioned the kids.

"I have a family to support and no means by which to accomplish it," he said, clenching his jaw so hard he could barely speak.

"We're better off than most. People have lost their homes. Some households don't have health insurance at all."

"Well, that might be us soon. When our benefits run out, we'll be lucky if we can afford some crap policy. And if we can't, we'll be at the mercy of the state of Kansas. I don't know that you'll be able to keep your pump. What if you have to go back to syringes, Claire? Would you be able to handle that? Injecting yourself twice a day, every day?"

"If I have to, yes." But he had me over a barrel and he knew it. When I switched to the insulin pump I was so happy. I felt truly blessed by the freedom it provided and my quality of life improved dramatically. Chris knew I loved my pump; I'd once told him I couldn't fathom going back to needles.

"I'm worried about *us,*" I said. "You and me." If someone had told me a year ago that my marriage could disintegrate so rapidly, it's doubtful that I would have believed them. Yet there we were.

He threw his hands in the air, as if our marriage was the last thing he was worried about. "There is nothing wrong with *us* that a job won't fix!" He swept his hand along the counter for emphasis, knocking a pile of the kids' artwork, yesterday's newspaper, and a stack of library books to the floor. The crash that accompanied it sounded like glass breaking and when I looked down I spotted the sculpture of a puppy that Jordan had made in art class, the one she cherished but had given to me two days earlier. "You look sad, Mommy," she said. "I want you to have my puppy so you'll smile." The sight of it, on the floor in pieces, enraged me.

I whirled around and faced Chris. "What is the worst thing that could happen?" I yelled. "We have to sell this house? One of the cars? Both of them? So what? We have each other. We have the kids. We have our health. Even me. If I have to inject again, I'll inject. I don't care what happens as long as we're still a family." I dropped to the floor and started picking up the pieces of Jordan's sculpture. "You are not the only person in this household. You can't shut me out when it hurts. You can't stomp around here while I walk on eggshells. I need you to talk to me!" Frustrated, stressed out, and emotionally fragile, I felt my tears fall fast and furious.

"I don't want to talk. I want a goddamned job!"

I wiped my eyes with the back of my hand. "I'm done, Chris. If you won't let me help you, then go see a doctor. Get some antidepressants, counseling, whatever. If you don't, the kids and I are going to stay with my parents for a while." Judging from his expression, I knew those words hurt my husband more than anything I could have said. I regretted having to utter them, but I didn't know what else to do. We couldn't continue like this. Chris needed help and resorting to drastic measures was the only [illegible] to ensure that he'd seek it out.

[illegible] came inside, followed by Jordan, the

door slamming behind them. They stopped in their tracks when they saw me on my hands and knees, crying, and Chris, hands clenched and red-faced, gearing up to start shouting again. Chris spun on his heel and left the room, to escape to the sanctuary of his office.

"Hey, guys, what's up?" I tried to pull myself together and act as if everything was fine. By the worried looks on their faces, I knew I was failing miserably.

"What happened?" Josh asked.

Jordan spied the pieces of her sculpture on the floor. "Mommy! Is that my puppy?"

"I'm sorry, honey. I knocked it off the counter when I was cleaning." I tried to put my arms around her but she pushed me away and ran toward her bedroom. I knew she was hurt and that she'd be more accepting of my apology if I gave her time to cool down.

Josh started walking toward me but I threw up my hand to stop him. "Don't walk over here. I don't want you to step on the pieces. They're sharp."

He didn't say anything, just watched in silence as I cleaned up the mess. "Are you and Dad gonna get a divorce?"

I looked up at him, my heart breaking at the anxious expression on his face.

"No," I said quickly. *At least I hope not.* I threw the broken sculpture into the trash and grabbed the broom and dustpan. After I swept up every last shard I hugged him and said, "Don't worry. Everything will be fine." He hugged me back and then I walked toward Jordan's room and knocked softly, hoping to make amends. She was lying in bed on her side, and I sat down next to her. "I'm so sorry, Jordan. I know how hard you worked on that puppy. And I'm so happy you gave it to me, and so sad that it's broken. It was my fault. Do you think you can forgive me?"

She rolled over to face me, her eyes swollen and red. "I forgive you, Mommy. I know it was an accident." I hugged her tight and left the room, feeling as if I'd failed her somehow.

That night, shortly after 1:00 A.M. when neither of us was sleeping, Chris walked into the bedroom. I put down the book I was attempting to read. "I'll do whatever it takes," he said. "I'll call the doctor tomorrow. Just please don't leave. Please don't take the kids away."

I wanted to go to him. Put my arms around him and tell him the same thing I told Josh. That everything would be okay. But he looked like my touching him was the last thing he wanted, so I stayed put. "I won't."

He turned around and walked back out.

Two days later, Chris got in his car and left and when he came back he walked into the kitchen. He withdrew the half sheet of paper from his wallet and threw it on the island. "I don't want to take pills," he said.

"Did the doctor say anything about counseling, instead?"

"He wants me to do both." He shook his head. "I'm not going to sit in some doctor's office and talk about what's wrong. I know what's wrong."

If he wasn't willing to talk to someone, then the pills were his only option. I had expected him to be resistant to the idea and were it not for the kids, and the promise he made, I doubt he would have ever considered antidepressants.

"Just try them," I said, the memory of our fight still too fresh to believe that there was any other way for him to dig his way out of the depression. "You said you would do whatever it took, Chris."

He got back in the car and drove to the pharmacy, and when he came home he twisted off the cap, shook the tiny pill into his hand, and knocked one back with a drink of water. He put the bottle in the cupboard and said, "There. Happy now?"

Well, not really. Maybe I was the one who needed pills; I couldn't remember the last time I was happy.

Watching him closely the next few days, I looked for a sign that the pills were working. I'd researched antidepressants online and I knew it would take time for the medication to build up in his system, but I still hoped to see some improvement, no matter how miniscule. I finally brought it up one morning a few weeks later after the kids got on the bus and Chris walked into the kitchen to take the pill. After he filled a glass of water from the sink and swallowed it down I asked, "Do you think they're helping?"

He looked out the window and shook his head. "No." He didn't seem mad, just resigned.

Bracing myself for the fight I was sure to start, I said, "Sometimes you have to try a few different ones before you find one that works."

"Maybe." Chris didn't yell. He didn't even raise his voice. But the look on his face scared me to death. His lifeless eyes told me he didn't care anymore. About anything. If he didn't catch a break soon, I wasn't sure what would happen. "If you call them, I bet they can prescribe something else." I fought back tears and walked over to him and took his hands in mine. "It will be okay," I said. I put my arms around him and tried not to take it personally when his remained at his side.

Chris called the doctor and was given a prescription for another drug. I picked it up at the pharmacy, swapped out his pills, and waited again.

This time, I didn't have to ask him if they were working; I could see it with my own eyes. As each day passed and Chris continued swallowing the pills, an amazing thing happened. He slowly emerged from the fog of depression. His step got lighter, his movements quicker, and you could hear it in his voice when he spoke: the sound of relief, of hope. He slept more and he slept deeply, as if making up for all the rest he'd missed out on. I made all his favorite foods and one day, when I brought a plate into the office, he smiled and said, "Thanks."

The pills weren't a magic bullet, and the stress of being unemployed still weighed heavily on his shoulders, but he emerged from the office more often, and he spent time with the kids, helping Jordan with a school project and throwing the football around with Josh. The circles under his eyes lightened and the pall that had been cast over our home lifted a bit. I began to breathe easier.

Six weeks after starting the new antidepressant, he landed an interview with a local software development firm. He'd applied for countless jobs within the company and had never received anything other than a form rejection letter. He prepared for the interview as if his life depended on it. He nailed it and when he made it through to the next round, I noticed an increase in his confidence. I could tell he didn't want to get his hopes up, but I also knew that the competitive side of Chris had been reawakened and if there was one thing he hated, it was to come in second.

He returned home from the third round of interviews, buoyant instead of despondent. The golden boy, whose appearance prompted most women to take a second glance, practically glowed with enthusiasm.

He followed me up the stairs that night instead of retreating to the couch to watch TV or spend time on his laptop. When he joined me in bed he kissed me for the first time in I don't know how long, and I wished I had suggested the antidepressants earlier. But after he took my clothes off, and his own, and I touched him the way I'd been touching him for years, nothing happened. I kept trying until he finally shook off my hand and rolled away. The silence that filled the room roared in my ears, and I wisely kept my mouth shut because what could I possibly say that would help?

This had only happened once before, when Chris attended the bachelor party for his college roommate. Not only could he not get it up when he came home, he passed out trying and didn't remember it the next morning. He laughed about it the next day when I told him, and said something about never drinking scotch again.

We attempted to have sex again a few nights later with the same results. Stopping the antidepressants wasn't an option — not when they were working so well — and the class of antidepressants with the fewest sexual side effects included the pills that hadn't worked for Chris.

I felt like we were all out of options. As if losing his job wasn't emasculating enough, Chris had to decide what mattered more: his mental health or his ability to make love to his wife. I assured him, repeatedly, that it didn't bother me. That it was more important that he take the pills. We'd come a long way since the dark days of late winter, and I had no intention of rocking the boat and undoing all the progress we'd made.

"Well, it bothers me," Chris said.

"Take the pills as long as you need to," I said. "Don't worry about anything else right now." He started to speak, but I cut him off before he could protest further. "Please, Chris."

"Okay," he said. He looked so dejected when he said it, and I wondered why fate felt the need to throw so many obstacles at my husband.

He walked into the laundry room one afternoon a week later. I was folding clothes and when I looked up Chris said, "I got the job."

My emotions soared. I knew our luck would finally change. Now everything would start to turn around. I gave him my biggest smile. "Congratulations."

"Thanks." His voice held no trace of the elation I was expecting.

I started to rush forward, to hug him, but his somber expression and serious tone confused me. He should have been smiling, too. He should have sounded happy. A prickle of unease worked its way down my spine and my feet remained rooted in place. "What's wrong?" I asked.

"I'll have to travel. I didn't want to say anything about it until I knew they were going to hire me."

"How often?" I asked. I had a feeling I wouldn't like the answer to this question.

"Four days a week."

My relief disappeared instantly, replaced by trepidation. "Do they have any other positions available? Anything that doesn't require so much travel?"

"No," he said. "I found out during the final interview, when they let down their guard a bit, that the only reason they're hiring someone at all is because the guy who used to have the job didn't work out. They were careful about what they said, but it sounded like he couldn't cut it." Chris leaned against the dryer and shook his head. "I don't like the travel, either, Claire, but there are ten men, maybe more, who'd be happy to have this job. The base pay and commission structure are comparable to my old job. The benefits are excellent. I'll be eligible for a promotion in six months and if I get it, I'll be able to come in from the field."

I wanted to protest, tell him to turn it down. Time apart was the one thing I didn't think our marriage could weather. We needed to work together, to repair and rebuild what we'd torn down. I couldn't imagine how we could possibly accomplish that goal if we weren't under the same roof. But when I saw the anxious look on his face, saw the desperation, I couldn't say the words. Chris needed that job, and to be employed more than he'd ever needed anything in his life, so I threw my drowning husband a lifeline and said, "Don't worry about the travel. We'll manage."

The relief on his face mingled with the sadness. The bittersweet triumph hardly seemed adequate considering what he'd been through.

He looked at me, nodded, and whispered, "Okay."

In the distance, a bell sounded. The possible death knell of our marriage. Judging from his expression, I'm almost certain Chris heard it, too.

But one week later he put on a suit, packed his bags, and got on a plane anyway.

23

Claire

On the first day of school the kids pout because Chris had to catch a 6:00 A.M. flight and won't be joining us at the bus stop this year.

"Daddy always comes to the bus stop," Jordan says, lip wobbling.

"If you haven't noticed, he's not here. He had to leave again," Josh says. "Quit being a baby."

I shoot Josh a look. "That's enough."

"Well, she is."

"I said, that's enough!"

He opens his mouth to protest and wisely shuts it. I know he's frustrated, but I'm not going to let Josh take it out on me or his sister.

I snap pictures of them standing in front of the fireplace in the family room, the same way I do every year, and try my best to make up for Chris's absence. "Daddy is very sad that he couldn't be here today. He wants us to call as soon as you get home so he can hear all about your day."

"He'll probably be in some meeting," Josh mutters under his breath.

Sighing, I let it go but only because Josh is right; that exact scenario has happened too many times to count. "He told me he'll be waiting. He'll call right back if for some reason we get his voice mail. Okay?"

"Okay," he says.

Jordan's backpack is overflowing with stuffed animals. "Let's leave some of these at home so they don't get lost," I say, as gently as I can. Lately she's developed a strong attachment to the toys Chris brings her when he comes home. She loves all of them, but the stuffed gray kitty is her favorite. "I'll babysit them for you," I say, when I see the panicked expression on her face. "They'll be safer here with me."

Reluctantly, she pulls them out of her backpack and lines them up on the couch, covering them with a throw blanket. "Please take care of them," she says somberly.

I bend down to her eye level and say, "I will. I promise, okay?"

"Okay," she says.

The kids perk up a little at the bus stop, caught up in the excitement of the first day of school.

"How did it go this morning?" Elisa asks.

I take a sip of my coffee. "They're disappointed. Josh is angry and Jordan is sad. I'm trying not to let them make it into a bigger deal than it is. Their feelings are justified, but there are worse things in the world."

When the school bus pulls away from the curb I say my good-byes to Elisa, Bridget, and Julia and head home. I pour another cup of coffee, light a scented candle, and turn on the adult contemporary station. I sit on the couch, laptop resting on my crossed legs as Tucker snoozes next to me. Reveling in the silence, I focus on my work and the morning passes quietly. At lunchtime, I send an e-mail to Daniel at the police station to let him know that I've finished mocking up the designs for their logo. An hour later my cell phone rings and Daniel's name lights up on the screen. "Hi, Daniel," I say when I answer.

"Hey, how are you?"

I let Tucker out and then open the fridge to grab a bottle of water. "I'm fine."

"Great. I got your e-mail. Can you meet me tomorrow?" he asks. "I'm working the afternoon shift, but I take a break to eat around seven."

"Sure." Since I don't rent office space and work out of my home, I often meet with my clients at restaurants and coffee shops. "Where?"

"Panera? On Mission Road."

"That'll be fine," I say. "See you then."

I arrange for a babysitter and the next day I arrive at Panera a few minutes early. Daniel is already there, waiting just inside the front door, and he smiles when he notices me walking toward him.

"Hi," he says.

"Hi." We order and when the cashier rings up our food Daniel insists on paying. "Thank you," I say. I follow him to a table and notice the other patrons glancing his way. "Do people always look at you when you're in uniform?" I ask, sitting down and putting my napkin in my lap.

"Yes," he says. "It's why I don't usually eat in restaurants. It's easier to take something back to the station."

"I could have met you there," I say.

He shakes his head. "No, this is fine. I thought you might be hungry, too."

"My husband travels during the week, so I let the kids take turns selecting the menu. It was my daughter's night to choose. You saved me from a dinner of chicken strips and Tater Tots. It's her favorite." Before I pick up my fork, I pull my pump out of my pocket and check the reading, then adjust my insulin.

"What is that?" Daniel asks, looking curiously at it.

"It's my insulin pump," I say. "I'm diabetic." I slip it back into my pocket and take a bite of my salad.

"I noticed your tag the other day, but I didn't know what it was for."

I pull my medical alert necklace out from under my T-shirt and show him the back, where it says DIABETES in capital red letters. "Yeah, I've been meaning to switch to a bracelet so I can wear a necklace that I actually like."

"How long have you been diabetic?" he asks.

"Since I was twelve."

"How does the pump work?"

I pull it back out of my pocket and show him. I've learned that it's best just to get the tutorial out of the way, especially with men. "See this?" I point to the numbers. "This tells me my current blood glucose level. Then I program it to give myself the right amount of insulin for what I'm about to eat." He turns it over in his hands, fascinated by the intricacies of it. They always are.

He hands it back, and I slip the pump into my pocket and go back to eating my salad. When we're almost done with our food, Daniel says, "Can I see the designs?"

I pull my portfolio out of my shoulder bag and place three designs next to Daniel's plate. He wipes his hands on his napkin and picks them up one by one. "These are really good."

"This one is my favorite," I say, pointing to the one in his hand. "I simplified your existing logo and gave it an updated look."

"I like it, too," Daniel says. He slides the designs back into the portfolio and sets them on the table. "I'll show these to everyone and we'll take a vote. I think they're really going to like them."

"I hope so," I say. "Let me know which one you decide on and I'll send over the master files. You'll need them if you want to order promotional materials. I can suggest some vendors if you want."

"That would be great," he says.

I take one last bite of my food and push the plate away. "How long have you been a police officer?" I ask.

He thinks about it for a second and then says, "About fifteen years. I started right after college."

"I thought policemen went to the academy."

Daniel takes a drink of his iced tea. "We do. But I went to school and got a criminology degree first. I always wanted to be a crime scene investigator."

"I don't know if I could handle a crime scene."

"They're not for the faint of heart," Daniel agrees. "Do you remember when Alex Green was abducted?"

"Yes," I say, as goose bumps break out on my arms and a chill runs through my body. Twenty-five years have passed, but everyone in the tristate area who is over a certain age knows that name. Alex Green was a twelve-year-old boy who had been abducted one afternoon on his way home from school. He was last seen talking to a man who had pulled his van over at the corner. There were signs with his picture up everywhere, for years. They never found him.

Daniel finishes his sandwich and crumples the paper wrapper. "He was my best friend."

"He was?" I ask. "Oh my God. You were so young. That had to be very traumatic for you." I can't even fathom the thought of someone abducting one of my children. And even though it was a long time ago, my heart still goes out to the missing boy's family.

Daniel nods, looking somber. "It was a difficult time. It actually bothers me more now because I can fill in the blanks about what probably happened to him, the way I really couldn't back then. I always think about Alex when we get an AMBER Alert."

"I'm so sorry," I say. I take a drink of my iced tea. "So how did you end up becoming a police officer instead?"

"There are lots of options for a criminal justice career path. I thought I'd try law enforcement for a year or two and then move on. I discovered I liked trying to prevent crimes as much as I thought I'd like solving them."

He glances at his watch. "Do you need to get going?" I ask. I check the time on my phone, and I'm surprised to see that almost an hour has passed. I've enjoyed myself. I can't remember the last time Chris and I shared a meal together, just the two of us.

"Yeah, sorry. I need to get back to work."

"No, it's fine. I told the sitter I'd only be gone an hour." Daniel grabs the designs and we gather up our trash and throw it away. He holds the door for me and follows me to my car. "Thanks again for dinner," I say.

"You're welcome." He gives me that smile,

the same one that gave my insides a little flip at the parade. "I'll let you know what we decide, okay?"

"Okay." I open my door and slide behind the wheel. Daniel closes it and when I'm waiting to pull out of the parking lot, I glance in my rearview mirror and watch him get into his car. Feeling happier than I have in days, I turn up the radio and sing all the way home.

24

Claire

I position my chair at the end of the driveway so I can supervise the lemonade stand the kids have set up. An old, dusty card table brought up from the storage room in the basement bears a handwritten sign taped to the front informing customers that drinks are twenty-five cents. Josh and Travis insisted on making the lemonade themselves, and I'd almost bet they didn't wash their hands first like I asked them to. Jordan desperately wants to help and the boys tell her she can be the server, thus proving that gender stereotypes among the elementary school set are alive and well in the suburbs. I whisper in her ear. "Tell them you'll only do it if you can also be their accountant."

The warm weather on this late afternoon in early September results in a steady stream of customers, and the boys do a brisk business; the quarters pile up in the empty pickle jar they're using to collect the money. Daniel calls a half hour later. He informed me a few days after our dinner at Panera that his fellow police officers had voted unanimously on the logo design, choosing the one that had been my favorite. I e-mailed the master image and they'd moved forward on their own, ordering an assortment of promotional materials. It's been two weeks since I last spoke to him or had any e-mail contact, and I smile when his name pops up on the screen.

"Hi, Claire," he says when I answer. "I've got temporary tattoos with the new logo. I thought your kids might like them."

"They'll be thrilled," I say. "Are you on duty? They're selling lemonade at the end of the driveway right now if you want to stop by."

"Sure. I'll swing by in about fifteen minutes," he says. "I'm not far from you."

"Great. See you soon." I tell the kids that Daniel is coming. "He's got something for you."

"What, Mom? What is it?" Josh asks.

"Tattoos."

"Aw, cool," he and Travis shout in unison. Temporary tattoos are the ultimate accessory in my household. "Does he have stickers, too?"

"I'm not sure," I say. "You'll have to ask him when he gets here."

When Daniel pulls up and parks his police car at the curb, Travis and Josh run over and lean in the open window, shouting in their excitement. "Officer Rush, do you have any stickers?"

Daniel leans over and reaches into the glove box and hands each of them a sticker in the shape of the new logo.

"My mom made these," Josh brags.

Daniel can barely get out of the car, but the boys finally move back and he opens the door. He hands each of them a tattoo and they run past me, into the house to retrieve damp paper towels. When they return, they each press a tattoo to their cheek while I hold the paper towels in place. When they peel off the backing, the logo I designed shows up in full color.

"Wow. Those turned out great," I say.

"Yeah, they did," Daniel says.

"Officer Rush, do you want some lemonade?"

The boys look at him expectantly and Daniel replies, "Sure."

The boys' excited smiles tell me they're too revved up about making money to possibly consider giving Daniel a glass on the house in exchange for the stickers and tattoos.

He approaches the table and the boys pour the lemonade into the glass. Daniel drops a quarter in the jar and takes a drink; the boys are watching his every move. He smiles and says, "Wow." Another car approaches and the boys forget all about their current customer. Waving their arms, they try and entice the car to stop. It works and soon they are busy with another transaction, Daniel all but forgotten.

"How is it?" I ask.

"It's very . . . potent."

Oh no. I pick up the pitcher and pour some into a glass, then take a drink. I nearly gag. "That's awful." The drink mix is sugar-free, but the boys have used way too much. Upon closer inspection, I notice that the liquid in the glass is quite murky.

"Boys," I say. "How many packets of drink mix did you use?"

"I don't know," Josh says. "Like, seven?"

"That's way too many. Didn't you read the directions?"

"Officer Rush said it was good. Police officers don't lie," Josh says accusingly, as if I've engineered some kind of smear campaign to force them out of business. "Right,

Officer Rush? You're going to finish it, aren't you?"

Daniel looks at me and I shake my head, smiling, because I know what he's going to do. He looks at the boys and drains the glass, coughing a bit and muffling it with the back of his hand.

"That was impressive," I say, laughing as I remove the empty glass from his hand. "I'm going to make a fresh batch, boys." I grab the pitcher and disappear into the house.

When I come back outside, Julia is standing in the driveway talking to Daniel. She's giggling and tossing her hair, and taking sips from a large plastic tumbler full of ice and God knows what. She won't be interested in the boys' virgin lemonade, that's for damn sure. I walk up to them and make the introductions. "Julia, this is Daniel Rush." I look at Daniel. "Julia is my neighbor."

"Nice to meet you," he says, shaking her outstretched hand. I turn to Julia. "Daniel is the one who told me about the design job for the police department's new logo."

"Oh, really," she says, raising her eyebrows as if I've been withholding a juicy secret.

"Yes. I mentioned it twice, remember?"

She ignores me and proceeds to talk Daniel's ear off. Unfortunately, she also sounds pretty tipsy, and I'm embarrassed for her.

The period of sobriety Justin enforced must have come to an end.

"Mom," Josh yells. "Can you get me some change, please?"

I go into the house and grab a handful of quarters out of my wallet. After I give them to the boys I sit back down in my chair.

Daniel finally breaks away from Julia and walks over to me. "I have to go."

"Okay," I say. "Thanks for stopping by." Travis and Josh run up and Daniel thanks them for the lemonade. They give him a high five. "Don't you have something to say to Officer Rush?" I prompt.

"Thank you for the stickers and tattoos," they say.

"You're welcome," Daniel answers. He turns back to me and says, "Thanks for everything with the logo. You did a great job."

"Thanks for giving me the opportunity," I say. I realize at that moment that I probably won't see him again. I'm done with the project and there's really no need for any additional follow-up. The boys have their stickers and tattoos. My invoice has been paid.

He pauses, and I think he's going to ask me a question, but then he says, "Well. Have a good evening."

"I will. You, too," I say. "Bye, Daniel."

He nods and gives Julia a friendly wave, then gets into his car and drives away. I grab another chair out of the garage and Julia sits down. Her glass is nearly empty. "Can you watch the girls for a minute while I run to the store?" she asks.

"Why do you need to go to the store?"

She rattles the ice cubes in her glass as if it should be obvious. "I'm out of vodka. Justin said he had to work late," she mutters. "Or something."

There's no way I want Julia on the road. And would she endanger her daughters' lives by taking them with her if I said no? "Just stay here, Julia. I've got vodka." There's nothing like giving someone with a drinking problem a loaded gun, but the alternative is much more worrisome. I take her glass, go inside the house, add fresh ice, and pull a bottle of Absolut out of the cupboard. Chris drinks only beer or whiskey, but sometimes I mix vodka with a diet mixer if I feel like having a drink. The bottle is more than half full.

I bring it outside, hand her the glass, and start filling it with lemonade from the pitcher. "That's good," she says, when I've filled it halfway. She grabs the vodka bottle and pours until the contents of the glass reach the rim. A drink that strong would make my eyes water. Does she not feel any remorse for her behavior that day at her pool? Does she even remember?

Julia sips her drink and I keep a watchful eye on all the kids, reminding them not to get too close to the street. I don't have to worry as much anymore though because the speed limit sign has made a world of difference. I should have said something to Daniel while he was here. Thanked him again. Thinking about the sign reminds me of how much I like talking to him.

I shouldn't be thinking about him.

I have no *reason* to be thinking about him.

But I am.

I'm thinking about how happy it made me, how I felt a momentary thrill, when my phone rang and I saw his name. I'm glad he stopped by. I wish he'd stayed longer. I wish I knew if I'd ever get the chance to talk to him again.

I look over at Julia, her glass already half empty. Maybe that's how it starts. You stumble upon something that helps you cope, fills a void. Makes you feel something different than what you currently feel. You know in the long run it probably won't be good for you, but you do it anyway. Tell yourself you can handle it.

And before you know it you're in so deep that you can't find your way back out.

25

DANIEL

I pull away from the curb, looking at Claire in my rearview mirror. I almost asked her if she'd ever want to get together, for lunch or something, but then I stopped myself. It's not exactly the kind of thing you can ask a married woman without it coming out all wrong. I like talking to her, though. And I don't know if she realizes it, but when we talk I get the sense that she likes having a conversation with me. It's the way she looks at me. But maybe she looks at everyone that way.

There are plenty of women in this town who are just as pretty and nice as Claire, so I should probably spend some time talking to them instead of spinning my wheels with someone who's already taken.

Maybe I want her because I know I can't really have her.

Maybe she wouldn't have minded staying

in contact.

Maybe I should have asked to see her again, because she kind of looked as if she might have said yes.

26

Chris

My meeting in Dallas runs so late on Friday afternoon that I miss my flight. I manage to get a seat on a later flight, but it's canceled, too. It's been a long, grueling week and all I want to do is get home so I can see Claire and the kids and catch up on some sleep in my own bed. I pull out my phone and when Claire answers I say, "Hi. I'm still at the airport. My meeting ran late and I missed my flight. The one after it was canceled, so I'm on standby for the next two. They're both pretty full so the chances of me getting home tonight are slim."

"What are you going to do?" she asks, and I can hear the concern in her voice. "Are you going to check back into the hotel?"

"I don't know. I booked myself on the 7:10 A.M. flight tomorrow morning, just in case. Something tells me that might be the one I'm on. I'll probably just stay here."

"You sound really tired."

I take a deep breath and exhale. "I'm okay. How are the kids?"

"They're missing you. They'll be disappointed if you don't make it home tonight, but they'll understand."

I don't think they'll understand. Claire told me a few weeks ago that they start watching the door a half hour before I'm due home. Nothing will make them happy but the sight of me actually walking through it.

"Tell them I'll take them somewhere fun tomorrow."

"They're supposed to go to the circus with my parents tomorrow night and then sleep over. Do you want me to keep them home instead?"

"No. That's not fair to them. If I get on the early flight, I should be home by nine thirty or so, depending on how long it takes me to find my luggage after I land. We'll have all day." I pause when an announcement comes over the loudspeaker. "Listen. I better go. I'll text you when I know more. Hopefully I'll be home by tomorrow morning at the latest."

"Okay. Good luck."

After I hang up I eat a crappy taco and wait to see if I'll be lucky enough to get on the next standby flight. Unfortunately, I'm not. I also discover that the taco was a very bad idea, and I pop a few antacids and thumb through the abandoned copy of *Time* magazine that someone left on the chair next to me. When I'm done with the magazine I put it back for the next person and open my laptop. I work for close to two hours and then I'm just as unlucky when the next standby flight takes off and I'm not on it. I'm not looking forward to spending the night at the airport, but it's almost midnight and I'm too tired to deal with checking back into a hotel. I find a seat in the corner next to a wall and I wedge my laptop in the small space between my body and the arm of the chair. Leaning my head against the wall, I doze fitfully, waking up half a dozen times. I'm the first one in line the next morning when they announce the boarding call for my flight.

I walk in the door at nine thirty, in desperate need of more coffee, a shower, and a shave; I'm way past a five o'clock shadow. The kids are eating breakfast and they fly out of their chairs and into my arms.

"Daddy!"

"Hey, guys," I say, pulling them closer. "I missed you."

"Mom said you're gonna take us someplace today," Josh says.

"Daddy might be too tired," Claire says. "Let him sit down and have some coffee."

"Are you too tired, Daddy?" Jordan asks. She looks at me, a worried expression on her face, lip wobbling.

Oh, I am putty in her hands, always will be. "I'm never too tired," I say, picking her up and giving her a kiss.

She smiles and throws her arms around me, nuzzling my cheek. "Your face is scratchy."

I give her a squeeze and set her down. "Go get dressed. You, too, Josh." Josh slurps up the last of his cereal, sets his bowl and spoon in the sink, and follows his sister.

I sit down at the kitchen table and Claire pours me a cup of coffee. "Do you want some breakfast? Eggs?" she asks.

I take a drink of the coffee, which tastes so much better than anything I had at the airport, and nod my head. "That would be great."

"Did you go back to the hotel?" she asks.

"No. I stayed all night in the terminal. By the time all the standby flights left it was so late that it just seemed easier to stay. I dozed a little, in a chair."

"Are you sure you don't want to go back to bed?"

"No. I'll be fine." I watch as Claire cracks two eggs into a bowl. She looks tired, too. "Did you get along okay while I was gone?"

"Yes," she says, whisking the eggs and pouring them into a pan. "No major problems. The kids were pretty good."

The oven timer goes off and I notice the cookies that are cooling on the baking racks that cover the countertops. "Why are you baking so many cookies?"

"Because Julia flaked on me. Today's the bake sale for the PTO and I found out at eleven o'clock last night that she forgot to make her share of the cookies. I have to take eight dozen of them to the school at noon so we'll have something to sell during the afternoon shift. I've been baking since 5:00 A.M." Claire opens the oven and removes a tray of cookies. "Let's get the diabetic to do it," she mutters under her breath.

"Why'd Julia flake?" I ask.

"She claims she doesn't remember being asked."

Around eleven, after I've had a chance to shower, shave, and respond to several e-mails that need my immediate attention, I take the kids to the pizza parlor near our house. It has an indoor arcade complete with bumper cars, inflatable bounce houses, slides, and a rock climbing wall. The kids would happily spend every Saturday here if Claire and I let them. When we get back home I mow the lawn and toss the football around with Josh while Jordan plays in the sandbox. I'm deliriously tired and running on fumes. Claire returns from the bake sale around four and tells the kids to come in and take showers.

"We need to leave for Grandma and Grandpa's house soon," she says.

"The circus!" Josh says. "I almost forgot." They rush inside, eager to move on to the next wave of entertainment.

I put the lawn mower away and when I walk back into the house, Claire is in the kitchen rubbing a chicken with spices and tucking lemon slices and pats of butter under the skin. Watching her slide it into the oven, I think about how nice it will be to eat a home-cooked meal and spend some quiet time with my wife, without the kids vying for our attention.

Josh and Jordan come downstairs after their showers and Claire checks their overnight bags, making sure they've packed everything they need and not just toys like last time.

"Bye, Dad," they say, each of them giving me a kiss and a hug before they hurry out to the car.

"Dinner will be ready in about an hour. We can eat in relative peace," Claire says, smiling.

I smile back. "Sounds good," I say, rubbing my eyes. And then I head upstairs to take another shower.

27

CLAIRE

"Best behavior, please," I remind the kids when I pull into my parents' driveway. I carry their bags into the house and give my mom a hug. "Don't let them talk you into buying a bunch of souvenirs at the circus," I say. "And don't give them too much candy unless you want one of them to throw up."

"I think your dad and I can handle it," she teases. She takes the kids' bags and places them at the bottom of the stairs. "Meanwhile, you get to spend some time with your husband tonight. Any plans?"

"Just dinner at home. It's in the oven, so I better go." I kiss Josh and Jordan good-bye. "They're all yours," I say. "Good luck."

The smell of baking chicken greets me when I walk into the kitchen. I throw my keys and purse on the counter and prepare the rest of the meal. It takes me a half hour to make the risotto, but it's Chris's favorite.

Rummaging around in the fridge, I locate a fresh bag of salad. Perfect. It occurs to me suddenly that the house is rather quiet. I call out to Chris. No response. He's not in the office or the family room, so I walk upstairs. He's passed out on our bed, wearing only a towel.

When he's asleep he looks so calm, like the demons that once plagued him are finally gone. I try to rouse him. "Hey," I say, giving his shoulder a gentle shake. "Chris." He doesn't even flinch. Sleep is a basic human need, and I can hardly fault him for requiring it, especially when it's been in such short supply, but the selfish part of me, the lonely part, wants him to wake up. I run my hand over his chest; it's been so long since I've touched him, or he's touched me, and the warmth of his skin brings back memories of a happier time. I shake him a little harder. "Chris. Wake up." He continues to sleep. Giving up, I walk back downstairs and set a place for myself at the kitchen table. I eat in silence, giving Tucker scraps when he begs. When I'm done I put the leftovers in the refrigerator.

Restless, I slip my phone into my pocket, and grab my purse. In the garage, I slide behind the wheel, wiping away tears, feeling frustrated and mentally chastising myself for being so emotional.

I back out and crank the stereo. Sheryl Crow wants to know if he's strong enough to be her man. I just want to know if mine will ever be awake and at home. The sun blazes in the sky, still burning brightly at 6:00 P.M., and I reach for my sunglasses, driving aimlessly, enjoying the music. After a while some of my frustration melts away. It's nice to be out of the house, with no responsibilities.

I could see a movie; I'm starting to get used to seeing them alone. But it's Saturday night and I don't feel like mingling with the couples on date night. I could go to a bookstore and browse, maybe order a latte and read for a while.

Driving sounds better, though. *Delilah* is on the radio and sometimes the stories of lost love and heartache depress me, but tonight I feel a kinship, so I listen. My hip vibrates, but I let the call go to voice mail. I'm in no mood to talk, especially if it's Chris feeling remorseful. But then I worry that the call was from my parents and there's a problem with Josh or Jordan. I dig the phone out of my pocket and punch the code for my voice mail. I smile when I hear my mom's voice assuring me that everything is fine and the kids are having a great time.

"We just finished dinner and we're on our way to the circus." She knows me too well. I delete the message but then I'm surprised when I realize I have one more to listen to. It came in the day before, around noon, but somehow I missed it.

"Hey, Claire. It's Daniel Rush. Give me a call when you get a chance."

His voice mail message has sent a frisson of excitement through me. I scroll through my contacts until I find his number, and he answers on the third ring.

"Daniel? It's Claire. Sorry I missed your call yesterday. I didn't realize you'd left a message until a few minutes ago." Suddenly I feel awkward calling his cell phone on a Saturday night. What if he's sitting around with a girlfriend or something? Or out on a date?

I hear the sound of a TV in the background, but then the volume cuts out and I don't hear anything but him. "That's okay," he says. "I just wanted to see if the speed limit sign was helping. I forgot to ask you about it when I dropped off the tattoos and stickers."

"It is. The cars are going much slower. Sometimes my neighbor and I sit in the driveway while the kids are playing and watch people slam on their brakes. It's highly entertaining."

He starts laughing. "Oh, I have no doubt."

"Elisa brings out a pad of paper and pretends to take down license plates."

"Maybe you should just start issuing tickets," he says. "Have a little fun."

"Maybe we should," I say.

The conversation lifts my mood and I'm trying to think of something to say so Daniel won't hang up, when he asks, "Where are you?"

"Nowhere. Just driving." I expect him to give me a hard time for talking on my cell phone while I'm behind the wheel, but he doesn't.

"Alone?"

"Yes."

"Any plans?"

"No."

"Do you want to go for a motorcycle ride?"

The invitation catches me off guard. But instead of wondering why Daniel is asking another man's wife to take a ride on his motorcycle, I say sure and pull over so I can program his address into my GPS.

He lives near the edge of town, beyond our subdivision where the houses are farther apart and about twenty years older. It takes fifteen minutes to get there and when I pull up he's sitting on the front steps of a small ranch-style home. The landscape has a rural feel to it, and Daniel's house is bordered on one side by vibrant yellow prairie grass. I park and turn off my SUV, wondering what the hell I'm doing as I open the door and get out of the car. He stands as I approach, and when he smiles at me his whole face lights up. It looks as if he hasn't shaved in a couple of days and the dark stubble that covers his face, and the worn jeans and long-sleeved gray T-shirt he's wearing are a radical change from the clean-shaven, uniformed police officer I'm used to; he's absolutely smoldering.

"Hi, Claire. Hold on a second." He goes into the house, screen door slamming behind him, and when he returns he hands me a sweatshirt. I'm wearing jeans but he points to my short-sleeved shirt and says, "You might be a little warm, but you should have something covering your arms." I pull the sweatshirt over my head and inhale a hint of cologne and a musky, male scent that makes me think he's worn it recently.

I follow Daniel to the garage. He pushes the bike, a Honda, out onto the driveway and shuts the door. It's a sport bike, the kind of motorcycle where the rider has to lean forward to reach the handlebars.

"Have you ever ridden on a motorcycle before?" he asks.

"No. What do I need to do?"

"Hold on tight. Keep your feet on the pegs. Stay centered over the seat."

He hands me a helmet and after I put it on he reaches out and buckles it, pulling it tight. It has a visor that comes all the way down and covers my face. I take the ponytail holder I'm wearing on my wrist and twist my hair into a low knot.

Daniel swings one leg over the seat, and I follow his lead. He puts his helmet on and looks over his shoulder. "Put your arms around me," he says, and then slides his own visor down with a snap. I place my hands on his waist, feeling a ridge of muscle under his shirt. He starts the engine and grips the handlebars; his sleeves are pushed up a little and his forearms look strong, lightly tanned and corded with veins.

When we pull out onto the road he opens up the throttle and the wind slams into me. "Put your head down," he shouts, and I do, curving my body around him, breasts pressing into his back. I hardly know him, and there's something so intimate about holding on to him this tightly.

The winding roads lend a hypnotic feel to the ride. The trees blur as we pass by; it feels like flying. The highway narrows and becomes two lanes. Very few cars share the road with us as dusk approaches, and the hum of the motorcycle's engine, like white noise, relaxes me. For the first time in a long time I don't think about Chris, or the kids, or any of my myriad worries and concerns. I exist solely in the moment. Fifteen minutes later Daniel turns around, and we head back the way we came.

The sun has almost set when we pull into his driveway. He parks in front of the garage and turns off the motorcycle. My feet touch the ground, and I put my weight on one leg and swing the other off of the bike. I unbuckle the helmet and lift it off, pulling the ponytail holder out of my hair and sliding it back onto my wrist.

Daniel puts the kickstand down, takes his helmet off, and runs a hand through his hair. "Did you like that?" he asks, grinning.

I smile back at him and say, "That was great."

He gets off the bike and I hand him my helmet. We walk toward the front steps of his house. "Do you want a beer?" he asks.

"No thanks. I don't drink alcohol very often."

"What do you normally drink?"

"Anything diet."

He laughs and shakes his head. "Wow, I am zero for two. How about a bottle of water?"

"Perfect," I say.

He sets the helmets down, goes inside, and returns with the drinks. The smell of cut grass lingers in the air and fireflies light up his yard on this sultry September evening. The stars are out and it's a perfect night for being outside. I sit down next to Daniel and take a drink of my water.

He looks over at me and smiles. "Where are the kids?"

"They're spending the night with my parents. They took them to the circus."

"What about your husband?" He doesn't look at me, just stares straight ahead, takes a drink of his beer, and waits for my reply.

"He's at home. Sleeping." I take another drink of my water. Daniel doesn't comment. He nods and sets his beer bottle down. The fact that I'm here, sitting next to him, probably says a little about the state of my marriage. I don't want to talk about my marriage though, so I change the subject. "Do you ride a lot?" I gesture toward the motorcycle.

"Yes, when the weather cooperates. Some of the other guys down at the station ride. We go out as a group sometimes."

"I'm surprised by how much I liked it. It was so relaxing."

He nods. "That's what I like about it, too."

"How long have you lived here?" I ask.

"About a year."

I wonder where he lived before this house. And who lived with him. "It's nice. Quiet."

"I like it."

"Do you have to work tomorrow?"

"Yes. I had yesterday and today off."

I put the cap back on my water bottle. "I should probably go," I say. Chris could be awake by now and I've been gone long enough that he might actually ask where I've been. I have no idea what I'll tell him.

"Okay," he says.

He watches as I pull his sweatshirt over my head and hand it back. We walk to my car and I punch in the code for the keyless entry. It's suddenly too quiet, and I turn toward Daniel, wanting to fill the awkward silence with words. "Thanks for the ride," I say.

"You're welcome," he says. "Drive safe."

I get in the car. Daniel closes my door and I pull out of his driveway and head back to my neighborhood.

The house is dark when I get home, so maybe Chris isn't that concerned about where I've been after all. When I climb into bed he's still stretched out on top of the covers, wearing only the towel.

The guilt creeps in like a slow-moving fog as I lie next to my husband, and it works its way into the tiny cracks in my conscience. It's not as if Daniel and I had some clandestine meeting set up. I didn't drive across town to join him for a secret rendezvous. But how would I feel if Chris had spent the evening with another woman, no matter how platonically? And tomorrow morning, when he apologizes for sleeping through our dinner and the first evening we've had to ourselves in a long time, I'm certainly not going to tell him what I did instead.

I roll over and try to get comfortable, but it takes me a long time before I'm able to fall asleep.

28

DANIEL

I watch Claire drive away.

I can't believe I asked her to go for a ride with me. It was easily the most impulsive thing I've done in a long time, and the words came out before I could stop them.

I'm never impulsive. Cops rarely are. We think things through, look at the situation from all angles before we proceed. We don't charge into the unknown. Doing that will get you killed.

She sounded lonely. That's the only reason I can come up with for why I asked her if she wanted to go for a ride with me.

It's also the only reason I can come up with for why she said yes.

It doesn't matter if I think she's sweet. That she's easy to talk to. That I've always thought that there's nothing prettier than a brown-eyed blonde.

The most we could ever be is friends,

because it's definitely not my style to mess with another man's wife.

Especially since he never seems to be around.

29

Claire

I'm sitting in the backyard with Bridget almost a week later, watching the kids run around after dinner. Chris flew to Atlanta on Monday, and I've had my hands full with work and the kids' after-school activities. It feels good to just sit for a while. Let my mind wander. When my phone rings and I see Daniel's name on the screen, I silence the ringer and let it go to voice mail. I'm curious about what he wants, but I don't want to have a conversation with him in front of Bridget.

I probably shouldn't be having a conversation with him at all.

"Claire. Did you hear me?" Bridget asks, giving me a poke.

"No, sorry. What did you say?"

"I was wondering if you could run Gage and Griffin to soccer practice tomorrow. Sebastian and Finn have a football game and they really want me to be there. Sam has an all-day offsite meeting in Kansas City and won't be home until late. I hate to ask you, but I haven't figured out how to clone myself yet."

"It's no problem, Bridget," I say, nodding. "I can help you."

"Thanks. I don't know what I'd do without you and Elisa sometimes."

"You've helped Elisa and me out plenty of times," I say.

"Not nearly as much as you've both helped me," she says.

I smile and say, "You've got more kids than we do. You're entitled."

Later, when Josh and Jordan are in bed, I listen to his voice mail. "Hey, Claire. It's Daniel. I'm off tomorrow and I'm taking the bike out. Let me know if you want to come with me."

It's been five days since I went to Daniel's house, and the guilt I felt about enjoying his company has faded a bit, like the colors of an old photograph. Or maybe I've just rationalized it away: Nothing happened. He was just being friendly.

He's a nice guy and I have no reason to believe that his intentions are anything less than honorable. But agreeing to see him again is going to send a mixed signal, and at thirty-four I'm way too old to be a tease. I take the easy way out and text him my response. *I'm sorry. I can't. Thank you for asking though. Best, Claire.*

He responds thirty seconds later. *No problem. Thanks, Daniel.*

His reply tells me that he got the message loud and clear.

It's too bad, because I would have really liked to go for another ride.

I get into bed, turn on the TV, and flip aimlessly through the channels, trying to find something to watch. There's a book on my nightstand, and I read a few pages, but that doesn't hold my attention either. I turn off the TV and lie there in the dark.

And remind myself that I made the right choice.

I'm sitting at a stoplight in front of the credit union at eleven thirty the next morning. A man who looks a lot like Bridget's husband, Sam, is walking up the sidewalk in front of the building. I'm just far enough away that I can't be sure. He has the same stocky build and dark hair as Sam, but he's wearing jeans and a gray sweatshirt. The driver behind me honks his horn and I look up and see that the light has turned green.

Later that day, when I'm driving Gage and

Griffin to soccer practice I decide I must have been mistaken. The man walking into the credit union couldn't have been Sam. The whole reason I'm helping Bridget out is because Sam's at an all-day meeting downtown. Instead of jeans he's probably wearing a three-piece suit and trying to one-up his peers.

It sure looked like him, though.

30

Claire

I'm weaving through the late-afternoon traffic, trying to make it home before the kids are dropped off by their respective carpools. The thumping starts as I'm mentally reviewing my to-do list and thinking about what to make for dinner. I quickly look in the rearview mirror to make sure I haven't run over something, but the pavement is clear and it takes only a few additional seconds before my brain processes that the thumping is coming from one of my tires. I pull off onto the shoulder and turn on my hazard lights, then reach for my cell phone, hoping that Elisa will answer. She picks up on the fourth ring and I exhale.

"Hi, Claire," she says. "What's up?"

"I've got a flat tire," I say. "Josh and Jordan will be home in twenty minutes. Can you meet them and take them to your house?"

"Sure, no problem. What are you going to do about the tire?"

"I don't know yet." In the past I'd called AAA, but that was one of the things I canceled when I was going through our expenses, eliminating everything I thought we could live without, no matter how little it cost. When I told Chris he was livid. "What if you and the kids get stuck on the side of the road? Jesus, Claire. I don't think AAA is going to break the bank." I give silent thanks that the kids aren't with me and mentally reprimand myself; we really didn't save that much by dropping the service, and perhaps I was a bit militant in my efforts to save us from financial ruin.

"Skip will be back in an hour," Elisa says. "I can send him."

"Thanks, but I'll try my dad first." I call my parents but the phone rings and rings. They should be sitting in the kitchen eating dinner, within arm's reach of the phone that hangs on the wall, because they are, if nothing else, creatures of habit and five thirty is dinnertime in their household. It always has been. I'd call their cell phones, but they both keep them in their glove boxes, turned off. They have no time for such gadgets, except in an emergency, and the only reason they agreed to them at all was because I insisted. My frustration and anger at myself grows.

I don't want to try to change the tire myself. My inner feminist chafes, but the truth is that dusk is fast approaching and my skills are rudimentary at best. I know how to change a tire, of course, know the basics of how to work the jack and remove the lug nuts. But my fear is that knowing how and executing the job successfully are two very different things. The cars whiz by outside my window; I'm probably not pulled over far enough for this to be remotely safe. I call the toll-free number on my insurance card, but the person I speak with informs me that I have to call my own tow truck and then submit a claim to be reimbursed for the cost. Using the Internet browser on my phone, I search for a nearby service station, but when I call, the man who answers says that their truck is already out assisting another motorist. They can send someone but they can't tell me how long it will be. I hang up and think about searching for another service station but then an idea pops into my head. It's been a little more than a week since I turned down his offer to go for a ride, and if I call him it's as good as admitting that I do want to see him again. I'll be opening a door that I told myself I'd be better off keeping closed.

I know I *should* keep it closed.

But I'm not so sure I *want* to keep it closed.

I scroll through my phone until I find his number, crossing my fingers that he's off duty.

He answers right away, sounding surprised. "Claire?" So either he recognizes my number or he's saved my contact information in his phone.

"Hi. I'm really sorry to bother you, but I've got a flat tire. Chris is out of town and I can't get a hold of my dad. The service station I called said they didn't know how long it would be before they can send someone."

"Where are you?" I give him my location.

"Stay in the car," he says. "I'll be right there."

He pulls in behind me fifteen minutes later, and I get out of the car and walk toward him. He's dressed in jeans and a sweatshirt and he's wearing a beat-up baseball cap. He looks rugged, like the kind of man who could change a flat tire with ease. He's smiling at me but his smile fades when he says, "This is not a safe situation for you to be in."

"I have my phone," I say, holding it up.

"You should have a towing service," he says, gently chastising me.

"I did," I admit. "I'll call tomorrow and renew."

The flat tire is on the driver's side and Daniel glances at the swiftly moving traffic. "Pull over a little farther, okay?"

"Okay." I get back in the car and pull over as far as I can. When I park and get out Daniel says, "Go sit in my car."

"You don't want me to help you?" I ask as he opens the back of my vehicle and starts rooting around for the jack.

"No, I've got it."

Daniel drives a sporty black two-door Toyota. Wildly impractical compared to my kid-hauling SUV or Chris's roomy Lexus sedan, but Daniel apparently doesn't need space for booster seats, sports equipment, and all the other paraphernalia children require. Unlike my vehicle, littered with empty juice boxes and smelling faintly of McDonald's French fries, his spotless interior smells like leather and citrus.

I settle into the passenger seat and text Elisa. *Police changing tire. Home soon. Thank you.*

She texts back right away. *Kids are playing with Travis. I'll feed them dinner. Take your time.*

Fifteen minutes later Daniel opens the driver's-side door and gets in, wiping his hands on his jeans. A smudge of grease remains on his thumb and I stare at it, transfixed. "Are you cold?" he asks. The daytime temperatures are still in the high seventies, but once the sun starts to go down it gets chilly fast.

"Just a little." Daniel starts the car and turns the heat on low. He reaches over and hits the button for my seat warmer. "Thanks again," I say. "I hope I wasn't interrupting anything."

"You weren't," he says, smiling at me.

I smile, too. "I seem to always be asking for your help."

"Don't worry about it, Claire," he says. "It's not like you've asked for one of my kidneys." He grins and we both laugh.

"Maybe I'll ask for one of those next," I say. It takes all the willpower I have not to reach out and touch him. I tell myself it's a physical manifestation of my gratitude, but that's utter crap. I'm drawn to him, pure and simple, and I'd have to be pretty unobservant not to notice that my presence seems to be doing something to him, too. It's the way he looks at me, the warm tone of his voice, not to mention the classic knight-in-shining-armor scenario that's just been played out. I think for a moment what it would be like to trail my fingers along his jaw and feel the stubble there, and instantly feel ashamed. I have never had so much as a thought about anyone other than Chris. It's heady stuff, but I come to my senses and pull back.

What I'm about to say next will feel awkward, but I take a deep breath and proceed anyway. "The other day, when you left a message about going for a ride? I wanted to go. I only said no because I didn't want to give you the wrong idea."

"Okay," he says, slowly, turning toward me. His tone tells me he's not one hundred percent sure where I'm going with this.

"I don't know what you're looking for." I hesitate and he looks at me as if he's trying to decipher my meaning, which is probably difficult because I'm not being very clear. "I can't read you," I finally blurt.

"I know you're married, if that's what you're worried about," he says.

"Not worried," I say. "Just curious."

"What do you want to know?" he asks.

"Why did you ask me to go on that motorcycle ride? The first time, I mean."

He shrugs slightly, looking pensive. "I thought you might say yes. You seemed lonely."

"Am I transmitting?"

"What?" he asks, clearly confused by my question.

"Nothing. Never mind."

"Why *did* you say yes?" he asks.

"Because I am lonely." It's almost fully dark, which makes this conversation slightly less uncomfortable. I can still see his face, in the weak glow of the dashboard light, but it's easier somehow with nightfall all around us. "But I'm not looking for anything other than friendship."

"You seem really nice, Claire. I thought we hit it off and that you might like getting together again sometime. But I don't want to make you feel uncomfortable."

"You aren't. I just needed to know your intentions. Make sure I hadn't given you the wrong idea." It seems like such a strange, unnecessary conversation, but it isn't, really. Deep down I know we need to draw the boundaries if there's any chance of us spending more time together.

I tell him about Chris losing his job. "Things were pretty bad for a while. He found a new job and now he's never home. He's a great dad, he gives everything he has to the kids, but he just . . ." I look away and shake my head. "He just doesn't have a lot of time for me right now."

"I'm sorry," he says.

"It's okay. It's just the way things are." I fiddle with the zipper on my jacket. "Have you ever been married?" I ask.

"Yes."

"What happened?"

He shakes his head. "It just didn't work out."

"Any kids?"

An expression I can't read clouds his features. "No."

We sit in silence for a minute, but surprisingly it doesn't feel weird. Finally I say, "I better go pick up the kids. Elisa has them."

"Okay," he says.

"I'd like to go for another ride sometime."

He smiles at me. "Sure. I'll text you," he says.

"Thanks again for changing the tire."

"You're welcome. Have a good night."

"You, too." I get out of Daniel's car and slide behind the wheel of mine. When the traffic clears I pull away from the shoulder, watching in my rearview mirror as Daniel pulls out after me and heads in the opposite direction.

31

Daniel

I watch Claire pull away from the side of the road. I'm glad she called, because I really didn't think I'd ever hear from her again. I understand why she shot me down when I called her: She's got a husband, a family. It's probably not a bad idea that she set some parameters, asked me my intentions. Now we both know what to expect.

Maybe I should have my head examined for even thinking I can spend time with her platonically, but it's not as if I'm some hormonal sixteen-year-old who can't think with his brain. I'm thirty-seven, and staying in control is seldom a problem. Then again, I don't know that I've ever been friends with a woman without wanting her, at least a little bit.

I tell myself that a friendship with Claire is the next best thing, and I tell myself that it's enough.

32

CLAIRE

In the days that follow, Daniel sends me a text to make sure I swapped out the spare tire for a new one. I respond and let him know that I did. He follows up with a voice mail a day later, letting me know that there's a big accident on the parkway and cautioning me to take a different route so I don't get stuck in the gridlock in case I'm headed that way. The e-mail he sends a few days after that, with the funny video that's gone viral, brings a smile to my face.

His last text, which came in at midnight when I was already in bed, says, *I pulled over a guy who wasn't wearing pants tonight. He told me he knew he'd forgotten something, but couldn't figure out what it was. But no worries because he had underwear on. Women's underwear, but still.*

I laugh and type out a response while I'm drinking my coffee. *You are a lucky,*

lucky man.

The guilt I once felt about Daniel has been slowly replaced with anticipation: When will he call next? When I check my phone will there be a text from him? It's subtle yet omnipresent, weaving its way through the minutiae of my ordinary life. Lifting it up. Making it more exciting. The rationalizing has already started: I'm not doing anything wrong. I speak to clients on the phone all the time, and I've become very friendly with many of them over the years. It's no big deal.

Daniel texts me a week later. *I'm off tomorrow. Do you want to go for a ride? There won't be very many nice days left.*

It's early October and the weather isn't going to hold out much longer. Soon I'll be bundling the kids into warmer coats and buying their new winter boots.

Sure. What time?

Noon?

Okay. See you then.

The sound of thunder wakes me the next morning and when I go downstairs to start the coffee, I open the blinds and watch the raindrops hit the window. I feel a wave of disappointment, but when I check my phone there's a text from Daniel and it says,

Come anyway. I text him back and say *Okay.*

After I get the kids off to school I shower and then stand in the middle of my closet, trying to decide what to wear. We're not going for a motorcycle ride, that much is clear, but I don't know what Daniel has planned for an alternative. I choose my favorite pair of jeans and a simple, white T-shirt, worn untucked to hide my pump, which is clipped to my belt. I put on my favorite burnt-orange cardigan, that one that I dig out every fall, and pull on my well-worn brown leather boots. Silver hoop earrings and my wedding ring are my only jewelry. I spritz on perfume and apply mascara and blush. The humidity wreaks havoc with my hair, so I let it air-dry and leave it alone, not daring to even finger-comb the waves in order to avoid the frizz.

When I pull into Daniel's driveway I park and grab my umbrella, then walk quickly toward the front door. It opens and Daniel stands in the doorway, waiting. I'm about to cross the threshold when a loud clap of thunder startles me and I jump. We both laugh and he pulls me inside, shutting the door behind me.

"I guess we're not going for that ride," I say.

"Not today," Daniel says. "We'll have to

take my car instead."

"Where are we going?" I ask.

He grabs his car keys off the coffee table and smiles. "I thought we could go to lunch. Is that okay?"

"Sure," I say. "Why not?"

Once we're in the car Daniel backs out of the garage, turns on the windshield wipers, and presses buttons on the radio. "What kind of music do you like?"

"I usually just listen to whatever the kids want. I know the words to every Disney soundtrack."

Daniel laughs. "Impressive." He chooses a station. "Is this okay?"

I hear the opening verse of "Mr. Jones" by Counting Crows. "I love that song. It reminds me of my senior year of high school."

"I like it, too," he says. "Someone was always blasting it in my frat house."

It seems odd, driving somewhere together. I can't help but feel that there's something covert about it, and I worry that someone will see us, which is ridiculous because we aren't doing anything wrong. And it's not as if I don't have male friends. I do. I just haven't seen most of them since college. Aware that I'm fidgeting, I try to relax, lacing my fingers together and resting my hands on my lap. He didn't ask for my input on lunch, so I'm curious about where we're going. "Do you have a destination in mind?" I ask.

"Yes," he says. "Have you ever been to Bella Cucina?"

I shake my head. "No. I've heard it's good, though."

"It's a little out of the way, but I think it's worth the trip."

The gray sky batters the car with a relentless deluge. It's the kind of weather most people would not venture out in, but Daniel seems undeterred, his hands resting easily on the wheel. When he pulls into the restaurant parking lot twenty minutes later, he tells me he'll drop me off at the door.

"I admire your chivalry, but I'm not that delicate."

"Humor me," he says, smiling and stopping in front of the restaurant entrance.

"I bet you help little old ladies across the street, don't you?"

He laughs. "Only when I'm not getting the kitty cats out of the trees."

Smiling at him, I say, "That's the fire department."

"Actually, it's animal control."

I grin, step out of the car, and open my umbrella, which isn't really necessary since

I have to take only ten steps before reaching the striped awning over the front door. Daniel parks the car and joins me.

The smell hits me when we walk in: sizzling pancetta, yeasty focaccia bread, garlic, and tomatoes. My stomach rumbles.

"I hope you like Italian," Daniel says, shaking the raindrops from his umbrella and holding out his hand for mine. "Or this was a really bad move on my part."

I hand him my umbrella and say, "I love Italian."

There are very few patrons, and Daniel requests a small table in the corner, tucked away on the other side of the bar. Once we're seated, our knees almost touching underneath the table, the waitress takes our drink order — iced tea for both of us — and we peruse our menus. "What's good here?" I ask.

"Everything. The marinara especially. It's got a bit of a kick, though."

Daniel orders pasta and I choose the chicken parmesan with a side of steamed broccoli. We help ourselves to the bread basket and I select a sourdough roll while Daniel goes for the focaccia. We dip the bread in olive oil that has been sprinkled with freshly ground black pepper. It's delicious. When our entrees come I take a bite of my chicken. It's smothered in the marinara and Daniel's right: It does have a bit of a kick.

It occurs to me suddenly that I haven't been out with my own husband in a very long time, but this is the second meal I've shared with Daniel.

"Are you working on any new projects?" he asks.

"I have a few new clients. I take yoga classes almost every morning and I've been hired to design some brochures and promotional materials for the studio. I'm looking forward to digging into that project."

"I hope I'm not keeping you from getting your work done."

"I worked for a few hours this morning. I'll work some more after the kids are in bed. I'm kind of a night owl."

"Me, too," he says. "That's why I'm glad I switched from the morning to the afternoon shift. I don't have to be there as early now."

When we're done eating the waitress clears our plates and asks if we want dessert. "Claire?" Daniel says.

"No thank you."

Daniel shakes his head. She leaves the check and I reach for my wallet, but Daniel says, "I've got it." He puts his credit card on the table and the waitress takes it away.

"Thank you," I say. "The next one's on me."

Daniel smiles and says, "Okay." He leans back in his seat and studies me. I meet his gaze, wishing I had a clue about the thoughts running through his head. Maybe he isn't thinking about anything at all. The moment ends when the waitress returns. Daniel looks down to sign the check and then we get up and head toward the door. The rain has ended and the sky lightens as we drive home. The rumble of thunder in the distance grows softer and he turns off the windshield wipers. The sun tries valiantly to break through the clouds.

He pulls into his garage and kills the engine. I'm surprised to find that it's almost three. "Thank you for lunch," I say. "I better get going."

"You're welcome."

I grip the door handle and open it. He walks me to my car and waits until I'm seated. "Enjoy the rest of your day off," I say.

"Thanks. I will." He closes the door and I head for home.

33

CLAIRE

I'm not sure how it starts, but by some unspoken agreement Daniel and I begin spending at least one day a week together. Because he works a rotating schedule the chances are good that the two days a week he has off will fall between Monday and Friday, when the rest of the world is at work. My schedule is flexible enough that I can spend my daytime hours any way I want, and I don't mind working at night after the kids go to bed, because it gives me something to do.

Sometimes we meet for lunch and sometimes we run errands together. I helped him pick out new carpeting for his living room, weighing in with an opinion on my favorites, and he picked me up from the car dealership when I took my vehicle in for an oil change. We often end up at his house afterward, depending on how much time I have before I need to be home to meet the school bus. I've gradually become comfortable at Daniel's; he goes about his business, and I make myself right at home. I think nothing of poking my head into his refrigerator or changing the channel on the TV if he's not watching it. Daniel runs five miles most mornings and one day when I showed up earlier than usual he answered the door with wet hair, wearing only a pair of jeans. It took some effort to drag my eyes away from his bare chest.

I try my best not to dwell on how comfortable we've become with each other, and how quickly it happened, pushing away the thought that maybe it's not okay. That under the guise of friendship we're starting to walk down a road I said I wouldn't travel with him.

Daniel discovered that I like to go to movies and I detected a hint of pity in his expression when I told him that I often went alone. "It doesn't bother me," I said. "I'm used to it."

"Call me next time. I'll go with you."

"Okay," I said. And I did. We had a great time, sharing popcorn in the mostly deserted theater. I don't think *Eat Pray Love* would have been Daniel's first choice, but he didn't complain once. "You can choose the next movie," I promised when it was over. "Something with a car chase or an explosion."

"Deal," he said.

"How can you even sit like that?" he asked one day.

I was sitting cross-legged on his couch with a throw blanket around my shoulders while I thumbed through a magazine. "What? It's comfortable. I twist myself into much more difficult poses in my yoga class." I continued to meet Elisa for yoga almost every morning, but so far I hadn't said anything about spending time with Daniel.

"I can't even get into that position anymore," he said, setting down a bottle of diet peach Snapple on the side table next to me.

"That's my favorite drink," I said.

"I know that, Claire," he said, looking at me as if I was a bit slow. "That's why I bought some at the store the other day."

The doorbell rings one cloudy afternoon while I'm there. Daniel ran out to grab us some lunch, and I'm not sure what to do. I walk over to the door, but there's no peephole. The doorbell rings again. Hoping it's just a delivery, I open the door and find myself at a complete loss for words because there's a woman standing there. Her surprised look and her scowl tell me that she wasn't expecting me to be here and isn't very happy about it.

She's wearing a business suit and looks a few years younger than me. Her brown hair is pulled back in a sleek ponytail and she's wearing an awful lot of makeup for noon on a Tuesday. She's striking, with cheekbones that could cut glass. "Where's Daniel?" she asks.

I'm about to tell her that he stepped out for a minute, but the crunch of tires on gravel as he pulls into the driveway saves me from having to say anything. Her head whips around when she hears the car. Daniel parks and walks toward us, paper bag in one hand, cardboard drink carrier in the other. When he reaches the front door I take the bag from him.

"Hi," he says, greeting the brunette. "Claire, this is Melissa."

She says hello to me and her tone is lukewarm at best.

I hold out my hand and she gives it a brief shake. "Nice to meet you," I say.

The whole exchange is a giant ball of awkward.

Strangely, Daniel doesn't seem flustered at all. I turn to him and quietly say, "I can go."

He grabs my wrist and says, "No."

The three of us go into the house. I put the bag on the counter in the kitchen and Daniel leans over and says, "Why don't you wait in my room."

I walk down the hallway. I know which door is his because I often pass it on my way to the bathroom. After entering the bedroom I shut the door behind me.

It's such a private space for me to be occupying, although being inside this room with Daniel would be even more intimate. His king-size bed is unmade and from the looks of it he's a restless sleeper. The sheets are twisted and the comforter is halfway off the bed. He's not much for decorating either, and the walls are bare except for a large TV mounted directly across from the bed. On the dresser there are two bottles of cologne, a pile of change, and an iPod dock. I uncap one of the bottles and inhale. I've smelled this cologne on him before. There's also a flashlight and a police radio plugged into chargers, but no gun. I'm sure Daniel keeps that someplace safe. A picture frame lying flat catches my eye. It contains a small photo of a baby boy, which seems so out of place among the other items. I pick it up and peer at the image closely, then set it back down, wondering who it is.

At a loss for what to do with myself, I make the bed, complete with hospital corners and fluffed pillows. The murmur of voices reaches me, hers louder than his, but I can't hear what they're saying. I sit cross-legged in the center of the bed, but I'm uncomfortable, so I scoot up toward the headboard and lean back against it, one of Daniel's pillows wedged behind my lower back. It feels weird to be using his bed in any fashion, but there's nowhere else to sit. The minutes crawl by but finally the door opens. Daniel pauses, a ghost of a smile on his face, looking at me in a way that makes me wonder what he thinks about seeing me stretched out on his bed like I belong here. He eases himself down beside me, close enough that our shoulders are almost touching, and leans back against the headboard. "Sorry about that," he says.

"It's okay," I say. "Was that your girlfriend?" I never asked if he was seeing someone, and I feel foolish for assuming he wasn't. And it's not as if I'm in a position to care if he is.

He looks contemplative but then says, "No. I don't have a girlfriend." He blows out a breath, as if the whole situation has exhausted him. "She's someone I used to see. I haven't called her in a while."

"I'm guessing she isn't too happy about that."

He shrugs. "It was just a casual thing."

"It doesn't always feel casual to women, especially if you were sleeping together." I regret the words the minute they come out of my mouth. We never talk about this kind of thing. Never. And initiating a conversation about Daniel's sex life when we're sharing his bed — no matter how platonically — may not have been my best move. Now the air feels charged, as if the dynamic in the room has abruptly changed. All my fault.

"I'm not sleeping with her," he says. "Well, not anymore."

"Why? Are you sleeping with somebody else instead?"

Shut up, Claire.

Daniel shakes his head. "No."

"Then why not her?" I have no idea why I'm still talking, still asking him these things. I'm even more alarmed by the fact that suddenly all I can think about is sex and how long it's been since Chris and I made love.

"I don't know. I'm just not really feeling it."

"Do you date much?" I've never given much thought to how he spends his evenings and weekends.

"Not really."

So maybe Daniel is lonely, too.

"How long have you been divorced?"

"A little over a year. My wife kept the house and I moved here."

There's more to the story, of this I'm certain, but I don't push.

Daniel runs his hands along the comforter. "You made my bed."

"I didn't know what to do with myself."

"Thanks," he says, smiling. "Come on. Let's go see how cold our lunch is."

34

Claire

In late October, Chris's boss informs him that he'll be on the road for the next two weeks, with no time to fly home on the weekend. "I'm sorry," he says when he calls me from his hotel room to break the news.

"It's okay," I say. It's not like it matters if I'm okay with it or not. It's going to happen anyway.

I should be upset, and I do feel horrible for the kids, but the more Chris travels, the more I adapt to our current household situation. When he comes home he disrupts the routine I've so carefully put in place to give the kids a sense of normalcy, and I'm the one who deals with the fallout when he leaves again. It takes at least a day for everyone to adjust. Josh gets moody and won't listen, and Jordan develops an unnatural attachment to her stuffed animals, especially the ones Chris has bought her since he's been out on the road. He's gone so often that now it feels odd sharing a bed with him on the weekends. Before he lost his job, we used to go upstairs at the same time every night, to make love, to watch TV, to talk. Sometimes all three. Now he stays up late working and when he finally slips between the sheets it wakes me up and I toss and turn for hours, trying to get back to sleep.

It's not that I'm happy about him being gone — far from it. It's just that Chris being gone is now what I'm used to.

The brilliant sunshine and the soaring temperatures of a brief, last burst of Indian summer at the end of the month offer a temporary respite from the approaching chill of fall. The kids are ecstatic and on our way to the bus stop Jordan asks if we can go to the swimming pool after school. "How about the park?" I say as we walk to the bus stop. "The pools are all closed until next summer." She sighs and reluctantly agrees that the park will have to do.

My phone rings as I'm walking back into the house. I answer it and say, "Hey."

"Let's go for a ride," Daniel says. "It might be the last one for a while."

I'm just as eager to enjoy the last few

warm days of the season so I say, "Sure. That sounds fun."

"You're not too busy today?"

"I have a few things I'm working on, but I can pick them back up tonight when the kids go to bed."

"Great. Noon?"

"Sure. See you then."

When I arrive at Daniel's he's standing in the doorway. He watches me walk toward him and my breath catches a little when he smiles. I remember when Chris's face used to brighten like that whenever I walked into the room. How the smile reached all the way to the corners of his eyes.

"Hi," he says. "How are you?"

"I'm great," I say. "It's beautiful out. Jordan wanted to know if we could go swimming when she got home from school."

Daniel laughs. "It's certainly warm enough." He appraises me quickly from head to toe, to make sure I'm dressed properly; I know better than to show up in short sleeves, no matter how high the temperature is, so I'm wearing a long-sleeved cotton T-shirt, a light jacket, jeans, and tennis shoes. No flip-flops on the motorcycle.

In the garage, I pull the helmets off the shelf while Daniel pushes the bike out onto the driveway and shuts the door. He grabs the end of my helmet strap and buckles it for me, giving it a gentle tug to make sure it's tight enough. I'm perfectly capable of doing this myself, but I don't say anything. After he puts his own helmet on he swings a leg over and I do the same, adjusting my position on the seat and settling in behind him.

The hum of the engine fills my ears and then Daniel puts the bike in gear. When we reach the highway and he opens up the throttle he doesn't have to tell me to put my head down. I've been waiting for this, for him to go faster, so I could have a legitimate excuse to curve my body around his. Something tells me he's been waiting for it, too. That maybe the main reason for asking me to go on a ride had nothing to do with the beautiful weather and everything to do with us being able to touch each other, to feel.

I hook my thumbs in his belt loops. The warmth of the sun beats down on me and I turn my head sideways and rest it on Daniel's back. It isn't ideal, because of the bulky helmet, but I feel boneless, liquid, pliant, as if I've taken on the shape of Daniel. Aching for physical contact, I want someone to hold me and I wish I was in front and Daniel was in back, but I'll take what I can get. Unable to resist, I inch forward a little more, tightening my hold on him and gripping him with my thighs. He notices, I know he does, because he turns his head back toward me for a second.

We ride for a long time and then Daniel pulls over at a gas station to refuel. I uncoil myself from him and get off the bike. We both take off our helmets. "How's your butt?" he asks.

He watches as I place the helmet on the ground, stretch my arms over my head, and arch my back, working out the kinks. "Not too bad. How about you?"

"I'm fine. I'm used to it."

I hold his helmet while he pumps the gas and when he's done we walk inside.

"Do you want something to drink?" he asks.

"Sure." We walk to the cooler. My hands are full with both helmets so Daniel grabs a regular Coke and scans the shelves for my drink. "No Snapple," he says.

"That's okay. Diet Coke is fine."

After he pays we walk outside and Daniel pushes the bike away from the pump, toward a grassy area with one lone tree. I put the helmets down beside it.

"Thanks," I say when he hands me my drink.

Daniel opens his Coke, takes a big swallow, and runs his fingers through his hair. Shrugging out of my jacket, I sit cross-legged on the grass, in the shade of the tree, and redo my ponytail so that it's high up on my head and the hair is off my neck. I instantly feel cooler. Daniel sits beside me, his legs stretched out in front of him.

"Are you hot?" he asks.

"Yes. Especially my neck. It's all this hair."

He takes another drink. "I like your hair."

I pull my phone out of my pocket to make sure I haven't missed any calls.

"Everything okay?" Daniel asks.

"Yep. Just checking." I take another drink. "How long will it take us to get back?"

"About forty-five minutes."

"We should probably head out soon."

"Okay," he says.

We finish our drinks and I tell him I need to use the restroom. On the way into the gas station I drop our empty cans in the recycle bin near the door. When I come back out, Daniel is standing beside the bike with his helmet on. I walk toward him, taking my hair out of its high ponytail and gathering it into a knot down low. Daniel holds my helmet in his hands, but instead of handing it over he puts it on me, tucking my hair into it and reaching under my chin to buckle the strap.

"I can do that myself, you know."

"I know," he says, and then he slides down my visor until it clicks into place. Once we're on the bike I put my hands on his waist and he starts the engine. He turns around and even though his voice is a bit muffled, I can understand him when he says, "Hold on tight."

When the ride is over Daniel pulls into the driveway and parks the bike next to the garage. I climb off and remove my helmet.

"What time is it?" he asks, flipping up his visor so I can hear him.

"Time for me to get going. I have to meet the bus in less than an hour, and I have a couple of errands to run on the way home." It's convenient having a cut-off time. It takes the decision out of my hands. I have no choice but to go.

He puts down the kickstand, climbs off the bike, and unbuckles his helmet, setting it on the ground next to mine. There's an expression on his face I've never seen before, and I swear his eyes look different, like the pupils are darker than usual.

Daniel follows me to my car. Pausing with my hand on the door, I turn to say good-bye, leaning up against the car, never completely sure what to say. And never sure about what he's thinking. "Thanks for the ride," I say, smiling at him. "It was a great way to spend the day."

He's not smiling. He's staring at me and it looks as if he's studying my mouth, but then he looks away for a moment. He turns back to me and says, "Come again tomorrow?"

I've already come once this week, but I meet his gaze and say, "Yes."

Elisa and I take the kids to the park after school. The temperature may be atypical, but the leaves are changing right on schedule and their red and yellow colors blaze like fiery sunsets as we make our way through the tree-lined streets, trailing slightly behind the kids. Once we arrive we settle ourselves at a picnic table and watch them scatter, eager to hit the monkey bars and play on the swings.

"This weather is absolutely gorgeous," I exclaim. We've surely surpassed the forecasted high of eighty, and I turn my face to the sun, closing my eyes and letting the rays warm my skin. I take a deep breath and exhale slowly. Jordan rushes over and hands me her stuffed kitty. "Will you hold this for me, Mommy?"

I smile and cradle the kitty on my lap. "Of course."

"How long can we stay at the park?" she asks. No matter how long we stay, Jordan always wants to stay longer. The park is her favorite place and she usually has to be coerced to leave. "We'll stay until dinnertime, if you want."

"And then we'll go to McDonald's?" she asks, smiling brightly as though this fantastic idea has just occurred to her even though it's probably been percolating in the back of her mind since she got off the school bus.

"Sure," I say. What the hell. It will make her and Josh's day.

"Yay!" She scampers off, announcing the good news to her brother, joining him and Travis near the slide.

"You're in a good mood," Elisa says. She twists the cap off a bottle of water and takes a drink. "You've been smiling for the last half hour."

I'm still feeling relaxed from the motorcycle ride with Daniel. "It's been a good day," I answer truthfully.

"It's so great to see you like this," Elisa continues. "I know it's hard with Chris out of town all the time, but you seem so much happier. I knew things would get better."

She smiles brightly, satisfied that everything has worked out okay. Elisa's eternal optimism is one of the things I love about her the most, but she's way off in her assessment.

I take a deep breath and say, "I spent the day with Daniel Rush."

Her forehead creases as she mentally filters through the names in her head and her eyes widen. "The ridiculously good-looking cop?" she asks.

"Yes. It wasn't the first time, either."

"Oh, Claire. Are you serious?" She looks so disappointed in me.

"It's not what you think," I say. "We're just friends."

Her relief upon hearing this clarification is evident in her expression. I can almost see the tension drain out of her when she realizes I'm not having an affair with Daniel. "Okay," she says, nodding as if she's analyzing the information. "How did this happen?"

I tell her about finishing the logo project and how Daniel kept in touch. I tell her about the flat tire and the phone calls and texts. "Didn't Travis tell you he stopped by when the boys had their lemonade stand?"

"He just said he got stickers and tattoos when he was at your house. I assumed you gave them to him."

"No, Daniel did."

"How long has this been going on?"

"Not long. Since mid-August."

She's silent, and I mistake it for disapproval. "I would never cheat on Chris," I say, clutching Jordan's kitty tighter and examining it so I have something to do with my hands and don't have to look at her. "I still love him. I just don't feel very connected to him right now."

"I've known you for five years, Claire." She turns to me and I finally meet her gaze. Her expression is a mixture of caring and understanding. "I know you know right from wrong. I also know that the last year has been hard on you and Chris. But he loves you, too. I truly believe that."

"Sometimes I wonder," I say. "I was thinking about it the other day, and worrying that maybe Chris and I got married too young, before we really knew each other well enough. This is the first real test of our marriage and we're failing. What if our current problems have nothing to do with him being out of work? And now being gone all the time? Maybe he's not in love with me anymore." I rest my head in my hands, massaging my temples. If this is true, I'm not sure that there's anything I can do to fix it.

"But you and Skip got married young, younger than us even. And look at you. You're so happy."

Elisa snorts. "Let me tell you a story about me and Skip. Because things weren't always so great between us."

This admission surprises me, because I've never seen two people who are more in love. I forget sometimes that I didn't know Elisa and Bridget and Julia until we became neighbors. We're friends — genuine friends — but that's due more to our physical location, our proximity to each other, than anything else. I know about their present, but I wasn't there for their pasts. I turn toward Elisa, eager to hear what she has to say.

"I started dating Skip in college, you know that part already."

"Yes." Elisa was a sophomore at Baylor when she met Skip in a bar on an otherwise boring Thursday, on her way home from studying at the library with her sorority sisters.

"He was the quintessential big man on campus: handsome, personable, and a star quarterback who also made pretty good grades. Everyone expected big things from him and he delivered every time. I fell in love with him, and I fell hard. He did, too.

But dating a football player, especially one as revered as Skip, didn't come without challenges. Girls threw themselves at him constantly, and his ego was out of control. I was only twenty, and I had a jealous side that reared its ugly head frequently, especially if I'd had too much to drink."

I have a hard time picturing Elisa — the epitome of Southern charm and grace — as a jealous, beer-swilling co-ed.

"By the time we were juniors, our relationship had deteriorated to toxic levels. Screaming, fighting, flinging accusations at each other, almost all of them unfounded. I needed him, though, and he needed me, too, no matter how much of a mess we made of the relationship. Then, toward the end of my junior year, I got pregnant."

I do the math. Not Travis.

"Surprisingly, the news that he would be a father made Skip happy. The scouts were filling his head with dreams of being drafted by the NFL and I guess he pictured me and the baby waiting at home while he lived the dream, posing for pictures and granting interviews. We got married at the courthouse when I was eight weeks along and forty-eight hours later I lost the baby." Elisa turns toward me, tears in her eyes. "That changed everything. At least it did for me. Even though I knew I was being irrational, I couldn't believe Skip would want to stay married now that there was no baby. Now it was just him and me and a tiny apartment off campus. *Sports Illustrated* is never interested in a picture of that. Then, during our senior year, he blew out his knee in the third game of the season."

I recalled Elisa saying something once about an injury ending Skip's football career.

"It turned out that he had the same insecurities I did. He thought that not being a football player anymore would influence my desire to stay with him, the same way losing the baby had made me doubt his loyalty. Ridiculous on both sides, but we were too young, and too stubborn to see how foolish we were being. Skip started partying way too hard, staying out all night and skipping class. I found out he cheated on me, so I cheated on him. More than once."

I stare at Elisa. All this seems so out of character.

"Finally, we had a major fight and I kicked him out. The days that followed were dark. I was only twenty-two and already well on my way to a divorce."

"Then what happened?" I ask.

"He came back one night. Knocked on the door even though half of his stuff was still in the apartment. I asked him what he wanted and he said, 'I can't live without you. I tried. I can't do it.' We decided, right then and there, that we would cut through all the crap and make our relationship work. My parents had retired and moved to Florida by then and there wasn't much of a reason to stay in Texas. I probably would have followed him anywhere if you want to know the truth. We moved here and we started over. Skip went to work for his dad's insurance agency and then took over when he retired. It made him happy, and trust me, no one was more surprised by that than Skip."

"And you had Travis," I say.

"Yes. But I miscarried twice before we were blessed with him." I put my hand on Elisa's arm and rub it gently. If my prayers are answered, she'll have the second baby she so desperately wants.

"What I'm trying to tell you, Claire, is that at the end of the day it's me and Skip. He's my best friend. And we have Travis and he's our world. It was hard on Skip, giving up his dream, but he's happy with his life. Chris seems happier than he was, but he's still not there. And when you're not happy with your own life, and yourself, you can't be happy with anyone else. You're not happy either, and rightly so. I imagine there are lots of couples going through the same thing you and Chris are. Give him time. But don't find refuge in another man's arms. I understand how Daniel can seem like a knight on a white horse right now, but all you're seeing is the best of each other." She pauses, and asks, "What's his story, anyway?"

"I don't know. He's divorced. No kids. I don't think he's looking for any big commitment."

"He knows you're married, right?"

"Yes. And I made it clear I wasn't looking for anything more than friendship."

"A guy that looks like him can be pretty tempting," she warns.

"I don't even notice anymore." That's not entirely true. Sometimes I still do, especially when he smiles. What I don't tell Elisa is that it isn't his appearance that keeps me coming back. It's the way I feel when I'm with him, like I matter. It's the way he looks at me, listens to me, in a way that Chris can't — or won't — right now.

"Do you think men and women can be friends?" Elisa asks. "Just friends?"

"I think it's a slippery slope."

"What's in it for him?"

"I don't know. Maybe he thinks if he's patient, if he waits long enough, I'll cross that line."

"Will you?"

"It'll only make things worse if I do," I say, which doesn't really answer her question. "Do I seem lonely? Do you get a vibe from me?"

"I've sensed your loneliness. You don't appear desperate, though. If that's what you're asking."

"Maybe it's selfish, but I need to feel Chris's love. I need to wrap myself up in it and have something solid to hold on to. I don't want to have to beg my husband to put his arms around me, especially at a time when I need it the most. We're not making enough progress, back to the way things used to be, because it takes time and togetherness and those two things are in very short supply right now." I shake my head and pause, watching the kids as they climb to the top of the jungle gym and then hurl themselves down the twisty slide they all love. "I swore I would never be one of those wives who complain about how much their husbands work. Chris has always wanted to provide for us and his career has always made him happy. It's not like he doesn't come home because he's out at the bar getting wasted."

"Or the track or casino," Elisa adds. I nod my head in agreement, knowing that we're both thinking of Bridget.

"He needed that job and I gave him my blessing. But that doesn't mean his absence has gone unnoticed or that it's without repercussion." Tears well up in my eyes and I blink them back. "I'm trying to hold on, Elisa. I am. But there is always something more important to Chris than me."

"Just don't let it go too far, Claire. Don't make the same mistakes Skip and I made."

Her words slap me in the face, like being doused with cold water. "It's nothing like that, Elisa. I'm happy when I'm with Daniel. It's uncomplicated." But even I know how ridiculous that sounds. Of course it's complicated. Daniel might be my friend, but he's still a man. It would be wise for me to remember that.

"It is now. But eventually, it might not be."

Her words echo in my ears as we collect our children and walk home, the dazzling sunshine beginning to fade as dusk approaches. The kids shuffle along excitedly, pointing at the Halloween decorations on our street. One of the neighbors has really outdone themselves with a giant blow-up witch in the yard and creepy black spiders that look as if they're climbing the house. There's a giant pile of bones near the sidewalk, a skull perched precariously on top.

And it occurs to me that Halloween is the only time that any of us willingly bring our skeletons out of the closet.

35

DANIEL

"What sounds good for lunch?" I ask. I'm standing in the doorway of my living room and Claire's sitting cross-legged on my couch, as she always does, reading a book.

She smiles and shivers, grabbing the blanket I keep folded at the end of the couch and placing it on her lap. "Something warm."

The gray November sky could just as easily bypass rain and go straight to snow if the temperature drops any lower. "You look like you're on the verge of hypothermia," I say. She runs so much colder than I do. "When do you need to eat?" When Claire's around I try to follow her schedule since she needs to eat regularly.

"Soon. Are you going to cook?" she asks, putting her book down and looking up at me.

"I don't know if there will be any cooking

involved," I admit. "But I can make you one hell of a sandwich. Do you want turkey? Ham? Roast beef? I have all three. I bought some Swiss, too." I walk over to the thermostat on the wall and kick up the heat a few degrees. Out of the corner of my eye I notice Claire studying me. When I turn to look at her she blushes, as though she didn't expect me to catch her doing it. "What are you looking at?" I ask.

Her blush deepens. "You are ridiculously good-looking," she says. She looks away quickly, flustered. Like she didn't mean to blurt it out like that. She's always so careful around me, never saying anything overly suggestive.

I grin. "You think I'm good-looking?" I like knowing that she thinks so, and there's no way I'm letting this go.

"I'm sure everyone thinks you're good-looking," she says. "Quit fishing."

"Probably not everyone," I say, crossing the room to sit next to her on the couch.

"Your false modesty is refreshing, but I'm not buying it. I can only imagine the propositions you receive when you pull women over."

I snort. "I don't get that many."

"Sure," she says.

"Okay, fine. I have, on occasion, been offered very specific acts in exchange for my leniency."

"Awkward," she says, making a face.

"Yeah." I stand up and head toward the kitchen. Over my shoulder I say, "Turkey and Swiss?"

She says, "Yes, please," just like I knew she would. They're her favorite.

My mom calls while I'm making the sandwiches. I put down the knife and listen as she tells me how worried she is about Dylan. "I haven't talked to him in ages. He's not answering his phone, either," she says.

I guarantee he's answering his phone, just not when she calls. Dylan's excellent at avoidance.

"Have you talked to him lately?" she asks.

"It's been a few weeks but he sounded fine," I say as I put the turkey and cheese away. "He's a grown man. He can take care of himself, Mom." I want to tell her to stop worrying about Dylan, but I don't because she will anyway. "I'm sure he'll make it home for Thanksgiving." I'm not sure though. I'd place the odds at about fifty percent. "I'll try to get a hold of him and if I do, I'll call you back, okay?"

She says okay and when I hang up and walk back into the living room with the sandwiches, Claire doesn't have the blanket on her lap anymore.

"Are you warmer now?" I ask.

She stares down at the floor and mumbles a response.

I can't quite understand her. "Claire?"

She looks at me but her eyes are unfocused and she seems kind of out of it. Sweat dots her upper lip and forehead. I've never seen Claire sweat. Ever. And it's not as though the room is that much warmer.

"Hey. Are you okay?"

She still won't answer and it's starting to freak me out a little. She says my name and tries to speak, but her words trail off and she slumps over on the couch as if she's beyond exhausted.

"Claire. Claire!" I reach for her and pull her up.

"Stop it," she says. "I'm fine. I don't need your help." Clearly, she does need my help.

The realization of what's happening to her suddenly hits me, and I rack my brain trying to recall what I read, what I should do when her blood sugar gets too low. I think about calling 911, but then I remember. Juice. Juice is best. Adrenaline courses through me as I hurry to the kitchen and grab the quart bottle of orange juice and a glass. I fill it to the top and when I return to the living room I have to set the glass on the coffee table so I can get my arms under Claire and help her sit up. She fights me and as she's flailing about she lands a pretty good punch near my eye. She starts crying when I raise the glass to her lips and try to get her to open her mouth. "Come on," I say. I tip the glass up and she coughs and sputters and hardly any of the juice goes down her throat. "Stop it, Claire!" I hold her jaw tight with one hand and I worry that I'm hurting her, but there's no other way to keep her still. I try again and some of the juice actually makes it into her mouth but the rest runs down her chin and neck. "You have to drink this, Claire." This time I tilt her head back a little and manage to get a decent amount into her. She finally stops struggling and starts working with me instead of against me, almost childlike in the way she follows my instructions. I help her take another drink and then I keep giving her sips until it's all gone. She's trembling and crying softly and taking these little gasping breaths. "Shhh, it's okay," I tell her. I set down the empty glass on the coffee table and rock her in my arms until she calms down.

"I'm cold, Daniel." Grabbing the blanket, I throw it over Claire and pull her toward me so that her head rests on my chest.

Eventually, when the shaking and the tears subside, she says, "I'm so embarrassed."

I brush the hair back from her sweaty temples. "Hey, don't be." I'm suddenly aware of just how close our bodies are, and how tightly I'm holding Claire. Her head is tucked under my chin and I can smell her shampoo. "What happened?" I ask.

"I just had a little too much insulin in my system." As much as I'd like to keep holding her I know I should probably feed her instead. I ease her off my chest. "Stay here. I'll be right back." I go to my room and grab a sweatshirt and when I get back to the living room I hand it to Claire. Her shirt is wet from all the juice that spilled. "Go change. There are towels in the bathroom if you want to wash the juice off." I pull her to her feet and she stands, shaking a bit. "Do you need me to help you?" I ask.

She shakes her head. "I can do it." Reaching up, her fingers graze the skin near my eye. "Did I do that?"

I smile at her, to ease her concern. "I'll live. You've got a decent right hook, though, especially when you're pissed off."

She walks back into the room a few minutes later, wearing my sweatshirt. We eat side by side on the couch. "Do you want to lie down for a while?" I ask when she finishes eating.

"Yes. I'm wiped out." She stretches out on the couch and I cover her with the blanket. "Don't let me sleep past two thirty, okay?"

"I won't." She closes her eyes and falls asleep instantly.

I click on the TV, keeping the volume low so I won't wake her up. I watch an old movie on cable but every once in a while, just for a few seconds, I watch Claire sleep.

"I can drive you home in your car," I tell her, after I wake her up. "One of the guys can meet me and bring me back here."

"No. I'm fine. I feel much better now. Really." She stretches and rubs her eyes. "I want to go home and take a shower and put on my comfiest pajamas."

"Are you sure?"

She pulls out her pump and checks her readings. "I'm positive. Everything looks good."

"You'll text me the minute you're home?" I ask.

"Of course."

Claire gathers up her things and I help her on with her coat. Outside, the air feels even colder. I open her door but before she slides behind the wheel she says, "How did you know what to do?"

"I looked it up on the Internet one day. I didn't know anything about diabetes. I wanted to know what to do if you ever needed help."

She looks surprised, and like she might start crying again. "Lucky for me you like orange juice."

"I don't."

"But you always have it in your fridge."

"I keep it there for you."

She looks into my eyes and holds my gaze as something unspoken passes between us. "Thank you."

"You're welcome. Be careful, okay?"

"I will. I'll text you as soon as I'm home."

I close her door and twenty minutes later I get a text. *I'm home.*

I write back immediately. *Good. Take it easy tonight.*

36

CLAIRE

The kids are upstairs taking showers and putting on their pajamas when Chris gets home a little after eight on a Friday night in mid-November.

"Hi," he says. He shrugs out of his suit coat and drapes it over the back of a kitchen chair.

"Hi. How was your week?" I'm amazed at how formal our communication has become. I miss how easy it used to be to talk to Chris. Now our weekly debriefing sessions — filled with snippets of our workweek and what the kids are up to — are polite, sterile exchanges that are only slightly more passionate and significant than discussing the weather. Gone are the days when we sat down and ate dinner as a family, listening as the kids shared the highlights of their day. And then after, when the kids were asleep, back when Chris worked for only an hour or so in the evening, we'd go to bed and share different things with each other.

"Busy," he says. "We're still understaffed, in the field and at headquarters." Another by-product of the recession: companies trying to make do with as few resources on the payroll as they can get by with, which means it's the employees who must pick up the slack. "But I closed every sale I was working on." Chris smiles, and vibrates with an energy I haven't seen in a while. He looks good. Tired, but good. No longer underweight, he's filling out his shirt nicely thanks to the workouts he told me he was squeezing in at the hotel fitness centers. "It makes me feel better," he said. "Relieves a little of my stress."

He reaches into the refrigerator and grabs a beer.

"Congratulations," I say, and I mean it. I finish loading the dishwasher and then fill the coffeepot with water and fresh grounds, setting the timer so it will brew automatically the next morning.

He opens the beer and takes a long drink. "Thanks."

I yell upstairs to the kids. "Hey, guys, Dad's home." Jordan comes tearing down the stairs, hair wet, wearing her Hello Kitty nightgown, and launches herself into his arms. We'll have trouble getting her to bed tonight. Her requests for one more book and for Chris to stay with her until she falls asleep will continue until I finally go in and play the heavy, which will leave me feeling drained and sad. She misses him. Why wouldn't she? Jordan fires off a stream-of-consciousness-style recap of her entire week, barely stopping to take a breath, and Chris listens attentively. They relocate to the couch and Jordan snuggles up close. I smile when he kisses the top of her head.

Josh hasn't come downstairs, so I go up to see what's taking him so long. He's sitting on his bed, halfheartedly strumming his guitar. "Hey, buddy. Dad's home. Aren't you coming downstairs?"

"Yeah," he says, without enthusiasm.

I sit down next to him on the bed. "What's wrong?"

"Nothin'," he says. I wait patiently, to see if I can coax a bit more out of him by not pushing. He strums a few more times and then puts down the guitar. "It's just that Jordan won't shut up long enough to let me talk to Dad. And he's just gonna leave again anyway."

"He'll be home all weekend," I point out.

"Yeah, working."

This isn't really fair, because Chris tries

hard to make sure he spends plenty of time with the kids, and Josh knows it. My belief is that his attitude stems more from his overall frustration at having one of his parents unavailable five nights out of seven than any real sense of injustice. I feel his pain.

"Come on down," I say. "Dad wants to see you. He misses you guys a lot."

"Okay," he says, finally acquiescing. "But tell Jordan I get a turn."

I ruffle his hair. "I will. I promise." He follows me down the stairs. When Chris looks up and opens his arms, Josh goes to him, and watching them embrace puts a smile on my face. I will never say that Chris doesn't love his children with his whole heart. He does.

After we put the kids to bed Chris goes into the office and shuts the door. I read a book on the couch with Tucker curled up next to me. An hour later I finish my book, but I don't really feel like starting a new one. I peruse the movies in our extensive DVD collection instead. I'm not in the mood for anything violent, but Chris isn't really a fan of chick flicks, so I compromise with *Up in the Air.* I've already watched it, more than once in fact, but George Clooney stars in it and I never get tired of him. I poke my head into the office.

"Do you want to watch a movie?" I ask, hoping he'll be willing to take a break.

"Sure. Go ahead and pick one."

"I already did," I say, holding up the case.

He doesn't respond.

"Chris?"

He finally stops typing and looks up. "Sure. Go ahead and start it. I'll be out in a minute."

I pop the disk into the DVD player and sit down on the couch. We used to watch movies all the time, snuggled under the same blanket. Sometimes I'd fall asleep, my head in Chris's lap.

I sit through several previews but they end and the movie starts. I'm still waiting for Chris to join me forty-five minutes later. I click off the DVD player and the TV.

"I'm tired," I say when I poke my head into the office. "I'm going to bed."

"You are?" Chris asks, without looking up from his computer. It's as if he's fallen into an alternate reality, and I'm surprised he even heard me. "I thought we were going to watch a movie?"

"Yeah, me, too. Maybe some other night."

In our bedroom, I strip off my clothes and put on my pajamas. After I brush my teeth and wash my face I slide underneath the covers. There's nothing on TV when I click through the channels, and I don't feel like walking back downstairs to find another book. Strangely, I'm both tired *and* restless. And bored. I shut off the lamp and lie there in the dark. It's almost ten thirty, but I grab my phone from the nightstand and call Daniel. I haven't heard from him since I received his last text a few hours earlier.

He answers on the third ring. "Claire?"

I can hardly hear him over the noise in the background. "Where are you?" I ask.

"Out with the guys. We're watching the game."

"Oh, I'm sorry. I'll talk to you tomorrow."

Before I can hang up he says, "No. Just give me a second." A minute later the noise disappears, save for the occasional sound of a car honking its horn.

"Are you outside?"

"Yes. Couldn't hear you in there."

"It's cold out."

"It's not that bad."

"I don't want to interrupt your evening. Go back to your friends."

"It's no big deal. What are you doing?"

"I'm lying in bed." I didn't think before I spoke and now that the words are out of my mouth, I realize they sounded more suggestive than I intended them to.

"Oh?" he says. "Tell me more."

Suddenly, I'm not so bored.

This is very different in context and tone from anything Daniel has ever said to me in person. I don't think he's drunk, but there's a slightly flirtatious lilt to his words that tells me he's had a few.

"I'm just tired. But now I can't sleep." It's very difficult not to imagine Daniel here in this bed with me. Holding me close. Touching my skin. His lips on mine. I tell myself that it's okay to imagine. These are my thoughts and they won't hurt anything. It's no different than thinking about George Clooney.

Except that I'm not on the phone with George Clooney.

"Is he home?" He rarely mentions Chris by name.

"Yes. He's downstairs, working."

"And you're lying there? In the dark?"

My body temperature rises when he says those words. I'm fairly certain that Daniel is now imagining scenarios of his own, which means that we have just skated into very unfamiliar territory. "Yes."

"You told me, the night I changed your tire, that you were lonely. Are you always lonely?"

"Not always."

"But a lot of the time?"

"Yes." I know I shouldn't be saying any of this, shouldn't be encouraging him. But I don't care. At this moment I want to be selfish. I want to think things I shouldn't and say them out loud.

He's stronger than I am, though, because he says, "I need to hang up before I say something I can't take back. Something you may not want to hear," he adds, and the sound of his voice, loaded with things unsaid, nearly sends me over the edge.

Every nerve ending in my body is on fire. "Okay. Go back to your friends."

"Good night, Claire. Sleep tight."

"Good night."

I set the phone on the nightstand and take a deep breath. There's a man downstairs who has every right to be in this bed with me, but he isn't interested. And there's a man who doesn't have any right at all, yet he sounds as though he'd give just about anything for the opportunity.

I have never felt more alone.

37

Chris

I fly home from Utah late on Wednesday night. Tomorrow is Thanksgiving. Claire and I alternate whose family we celebrate with and this year it's hers. Frankly, I'm glad. My parents try to pack my siblings, their spouses, all the grandkids, and various assorted relatives into their small two-story house and by the end of the day I usually have a raging headache. It's much quieter and calmer when we celebrate with Claire's family.

She's taking a pie out of the oven when I walk in the door a little after 11:00 P.M. My house smells a hell of a lot better than any of the hotel rooms I stay in, and now that I'm sleeping better I miss my bed when I'm away. I can't believe how many months I wasted sleeping on the couch.

I watch as Claire sets the pie on a wire rack. She's wearing her hair in a ponytail and a few strands have escaped. I suddenly have the urge to tuck them behind her ears, so I set down my laptop and suitcase and walk to where she's standing.

"Hi," she says, reaching over to turn off the oven.

"Hi," I say.

She picks up a casserole dish from the counter and steps around me, like I'm in her way.

"Can I help you with anything?" I ask.

She puts the casserole in the fridge. "No thanks." Exhaling, she says, "I'm almost done."

Sometimes I forget how busy she is, holding down the fort at home. She's got her own work, the kids, and the house. Just because she makes it look easy doesn't mean it is. She's wearing a pair of pink flannel pajama pants with white snowflakes on them. Her pink cotton long-sleeved T-shirt is just snug enough that I can see the outline of her breasts. I take off my jacket and think about how nice it will be to sleep in my own bed tonight, next to Claire. Spend the day with her and the kids tomorrow. Just knowing that most of the country will be taking the day off and that I can get away without working at all if I want to has put me in a good mood. "Do you want to watch a movie, or something?"

"No," she says. "I'm exhausted. I've been baking and cooking and trying to keep the kids from bouncing off the walls all day. I'm going to bed."

"Okay. Good night." I want to kiss her, even if it's just a quick peck before she goes to bed, but I'm not fast enough, because before I can even reach out for her, she's gone, grabbing her phone and walking toward the stairs without a backward glance.

38

Claire

I'm lying in bed waiting for Daniel's call. Chris's request to watch a movie together caught me off guard, and I feel some remorse for saying no. It's what I've been yearning for. Spending time with him would have been the right thing to do, but I'm not that eager to fulfill his request. Not out of spite. Not out of any sense of retaliation. I simply don't want to watch a movie. I'm tired and I'd rather stretch out under the covers of my warm bed and talk to Daniel. He texted earlier. *Can I call you tonight? Late?* I texted back. *Yes.* It's all I've been able to think about.

We never discussed the things he said on the phone the night I called him when he was out with the guys. I thought it might be weird the next time I saw him, but I didn't say anything and neither did he. We simply acted as if the whole thing never happened.

And I certainly didn't mention it to Elisa when she asked if I'd talked to Daniel recently. I was certain she'd warn me to be careful. Tell me I was heading toward the deep end.

I've always been careful, but I wouldn't mind being a little *less* careful.

Then, about a week later, he called me. It was late and I'd been watching a movie in bed. When my phone rang I answered it and without preamble he said, "Are you in bed?"

I knew instantly that we were back on that unfamiliar ground, and a ripple of excitement washed over me. I reveled in the anticipation, wondering what he might say. "Yes," I said.

"Were you sleeping?" he asked.

"Not yet."

"How was your day?" I pictured him settling in for a long conversation, maybe lying in bed the way I was.

"Uneventful. How was yours? Did you help your friend move?" Daniel didn't have to work that day, but he'd volunteered to help one of his fellow officers move into a new home.

"Yes. My back is killing me. He had the heaviest furniture I've ever carried. I need a massage. Know anyone who's good at them?" I could tell by his suggestive tone that he wouldn't mind if I was the one who rubbed him down.

"I've got a guy, actually," I said. "Just let me know if you want his number."

"You have a guy?" His voice had taken on a very different tone when he asked that question. Flirty to curious in less than ten seconds.

"Oh, relax. Walt doesn't give happy endings. Not like my neighbor Julia's guy."

"Julia has a guy, too? She told you he gives her happy endings?"

"No, she *didn't* tell me. And then I went to him when Walt was on vacation. That was the problem."

"Are you saying her guy got you off?" By that point Daniel just sounded pissed.

"No! I flew off the table as soon as he touched me."

"He touched you?"

"Just barely."

"Where?"

"Well, it wasn't my back."

"I will shut them down tomorrow, Claire."

"Don't, please. It was an epic miscommunication. He stopped immediately and apologized profusely. Besides, you and I both know this probably goes on all the time."

"It's illegal."

"I know that. But there are women who seek it out and there will always be someone willing to give it to them. Julia's guy is putting himself through college by giving the big O to any woman who wants one."

"Did you entertain the possibility of letting him give you one, even for a second?"

"No. Of course not."

"Why?"

I answered Daniel honestly. "Because he was just some guy I didn't know."

Daniel and I never got back on track after that and we hung up a short time later. I'm guessing he was as unsatisfied by the conversation as I was. Maybe tonight will be different.

He calls a little after eleven. I put my phone on vibrate so Chris wouldn't hear it ring if he happened to come upstairs.

"Can you still talk?" He speaks softly and I wonder if he's in bed or lying on the couch.

"I can talk," I say.

"Is he home?"

"Yeah. But it's okay." Once I declined his offer to watch a movie Chris probably opened his laptop and started working. Who knows when he'll make it upstairs?

"How was your day?" Daniel asks.

"Busy."

"Did you get everything done?"
"Yep. I finished the last pie an hour ago."
"Did you stay inside?"
"Yes. The kids wanted to go to the mall to see Santa, but it was so cold and dreary that I just couldn't do it. I paid for it, though. They had a raging case of cabin fever."
"But you're warm now," he says.
"Yes. Definitely," I murmur, certain he can hear the change in my voice, the timbre of my words as they roll slowly off my tongue. "What about you?" I ask.
He chuckles softly. "I'm nowhere near as hot as you."
"I beg to differ," I say, wondering if we're going to speak in double entendres the whole conversation and not minding a bit if we do.
"What are you wearing that's keeping you so warm? Or not wearing," he asks, laughing. "I really have no idea."
"Flannel pajama pants and a long-sleeved T-shirt. Nothing that you or any man would find remotely interesting, I'm afraid." I often wore lingerie for Chris, but the opportunity hadn't presented itself in a very long time. "The last time I checked, the Victoria's Secret models weren't covered in cotton from head to toe. Sorry to disappoint you."

"That's okay," he says. "In my head you're wearing something entirely different."

My heart rate speeds up a bit. "Sounds like you have a preference in women's lingerie." Chris has always been partial to black silk chemises.

"Not really. It's nice, don't get me wrong, but there's something I like even better. Call me a minimalist."

Now all I can think about is being naked. And I'm pretty sure that's all Daniel's thinking about, too.

Suddenly, I wouldn't *mind* being naked.

But I'm not at all comfortable with taking this much further, because I don't think Daniel and I could ignore it the next time we're together. And I like this tension we're building; I don't want to release it yet. "See? You do have a preference," I say, hoping the light, teasing tone of my voice is enough to bring us back from the edge a bit.

He just laughs and says, "I do, indeed. I also like women with blonde hair and brown eyes, who eat turkey and Swiss sandwiches and wear way too many layers of clothing because they're cold all the time."

"You can't see me, but I'm smiling."

"I wish I could see you," he says. "Will he? Later?"

I hear the longing in his voice, and I want

to tell him he has nothing to worry about. But some things are just off-limits, and the intimacy issues that Chris and I have are between us and no one else. "No," I say. "I'm tired. I'll be asleep long before he comes up."

"I don't understand that."

"I know."

"I should let you go," he says.

I suppose that's one way to ensure that I really am asleep before Chris comes upstairs.

"Sweet dreams."

"You, too. Bye, Daniel."

I don't fall asleep right away, though. Mostly because I can't stop thinking about what it would be like to make love with Daniel.

39

Claire

To: Claire Canton
From: Chris Canton
Subject: December

It looks like I'll be on the road the rest of the month. We're rolling out the new product line and the sales directors are responsible for making sure the implementation team doesn't screw it up. We'll be meeting with clients first thing Monday morning and won't be done until late on Friday night. I'd only be able to fly home for one day and the company doesn't think that's "economical" so they've asked us to stay in the field. If we finish by the twenty-third I can take a week off between Christmas and New Year's.

I'm sorry, Claire.

By now, seven months into his new job, I'm so used to Chris being gone that this news has almost no emotional impact on me. He could be telling me he'll be gone for the next three months and I doubt it would make much of a difference. We've become like the proverbial two ships that pass in the night. No time for connecting, fixing, rebuilding. Just as I'd feared. I wonder how many marriages are fractured and damaged beyond repair by complacency rather than any single traumatic event. One day you wake up and realize that the distance between you and your spouse has grown to such an enormous width that neither of you are capable of clearing the distance. No matter how much speed you build up, or how far you can jump, it's just there. Gaping and unforgiving.

Surprisingly, the kids understand, in the same way that I do. I break the news to them at dinner on Thursday night. "Dad won't be coming home for a while, guys. He's really busy at work, but he'll be back before Christmas and then he's going to take a week off."

Josh shrugs. "Okay." He's trying to act like he doesn't care, but his feigned indifference tells me that it bothers him more than he's letting on.

"Okay," Jordan says. But her voice is barely more than a whisper and she squeezes her stuffed gray kitty, the one Chris gave her that never leaves her side, a bit more tightly.

My heart breaks. Though I'm grateful for their adaptability, I wouldn't mind seeing a little more emotion, a sign that they miss Chris. I know deep down they do, but I also know that it's amazing what you can get used to if it goes on long enough. Chris being gone has become their normal.

Later that night I talk to my mom on the phone. "Chris will be on the road most of this month," I say.

"Oh, Claire," she says. "I don't like that at all." She doesn't think it's safe for me to be alone so much, because of my diabetes. Her concern and my need for independence have always mixed about as well as oil and water. And I understand, I really do. Especially after what happened at Daniel's. I'd like to think I could have handled that one on my own eventually, but I'm not so sure. "The holidays are stressful enough," she says. "How did the kids take the news?"

"They were surprisingly okay with it. Too okay," I say.

"Oh. I see. Well. Your dad and I would love to keep them overnight on one of those

weekends. You can get some Christm
shopping done. Have a manicure. Go out
lunch with one of your friends. It'll give yo
a break, Claire," she says.

"That would be great, Mom. Thanks."

To: Chris Canton
From: Claire Canton
Subject: Re: December

That's okay. I'll handle the Christmas shopping and whatever else needs to be taken care of. The kids understand.

I realize after I sign off and shut down my computer that the brevity of my response, and telling Chris that the kids understand, might have been insensitive, as if none of us really care. Though I chafe at how little time he has for me when he's here, he's out there every day, working hard, whether he wants to or not. Away from his home and his family.

And in this particular situation a little more emotion from me might have gone a long way.

40

Claire

Daniel has been running indoors since it turned cold, on a treadmill he keeps in one of his spare bedrooms.

"I'd rather run outside," he says. "But I'm not a big fan of falling on the ice and breaking my leg." He usually runs early, but he had to work late last night and had just rolled out of bed when I arrived at twelve.

"Slacker," I said, when he opened the door and I noticed his sleep-tousled hair, wrinkled T-shirt, and pajama pants.

He yawned and rubbed his eyes. "Yeah, and I'm still tired."

He's had time to eat breakfast and read the paper and now he's on the treadmill. I brought my laptop today and the whir of the machine, and the cadence of his footsteps, mixes with the sound of my computer keys clicking. When he finishes his workout he walks into the living room, chest bare,

wearing only athletic shorts. He's drying his face off with a towel and swigging from a water bottle.

I watch the rise and fall of his chest, lightly sheened with sweat as he stands a few feet away from the couch, still breathing hard. His shorts are hanging low on his hips and I can see the top of the V muscle that extends from his lower abdomen down to his hip flexors as well as the trail of hair that starts near his navel and runs downward. A scar, two inches to the left of his belly button, puckered and silvery, catches my eye. I can't tell how long it is because it disappears down the front of his shorts.

I get up and walk toward him. Looking down, I lean forward to get a better look and say, "What happened?"

"Knife," he says. "I learned the hard way not to take away a man's cocaine before making sure he's completely disarmed." He takes another drink. "Rookie mistake. Never made it again."

"Oh," I say, and without thinking, without even stopping to consider my actions, I place my hand flat against his skin and trace the scar with my finger, imagining the knife piercing him. The wound ragged and bleeding. He stands perfectly still, unflinching, as I touch him. "That must have hurt." My hands are cold and the warmth of his skin sends a wave of heat across my palm. It travels to other parts of my body and even though I know I should move my hand, should stop touching Daniel immediately, I don't seem to be able to.

Daniel looks at me, his eyes heavy, half lidded. "It was a long time ago," he murmurs. Grabbing my wrist, he moves my hand away and takes two steps back. "I'm going to take a shower," he says.

Embarrassed about what I've done, I say, "Okay." I sit back down on the couch and try to concentrate on my work while Daniel takes an incredibly long shower.

Later, when it's almost time for me to leave, I ask Daniel what his plans are for Christmas. "I'll go to my parents' house on Christmas Eve. I have to work on Christmas Day."

"I wish you didn't have to work on Christmas Day," I say.

"It's okay. I'd rather that someone who has a family gets the day off." He says it matter-of-factly, but I can't help but wonder if it bothers him. I'm sure the holidays meant something else to him when he was married.

"Will your brother be in town?" Daniel has a younger brother named Dylan. He told me once that they're not close.

"Who knows with Dylan?" Daniel says, sitting down beside me on the couch. "That's just one of the many reasons we don't get along."

"What are some of the others?" I ask. Maybe it's because I'm an only child and always fervently wished I had a brother or sister, but I don't understand discontent between siblings. Chris is always squabbling with one of his sisters. It perplexes me.

"He's really smart. Brilliant, even. Charming when he wants to be. He scored off the charts on some IQ test back in elementary school. He had a ton of behavioral problems, but it turned out that he was just bored. They gave my parents the option of letting him skip a grade, but they decided not to because they didn't think he was mature enough. Even now as an adult, he's very socially inept."

"What does he do for a living?" I expect Daniel to tell me that Dylan is a brain surgeon or an actual rocket scientist.

"He does nothing. He has three advanced degrees but no desire to actually find and hold down a job. He's so worried about making sure his boss and coworkers know how smart he is that he's a horrible employee. He has a tendency to quit before they can fire him, and believe me, eventually they all would have. The only reason he's gotten away with his lifestyle for so long is because he refuses to put down roots anywhere. He lives frugally, crashing on friends' couches, and rolls in and out of town whenever he feels like it. Most of the time we don't even know where he is. It upsets my mom. She already worries about me, because of my job, and it's not fair that she has to worry about him, too."

"That's too bad."

"Well. We're used to it by now. What about you? What are your plans for the holidays?"

I tell him that we'll split the time between my family and Chris's. "He'll be home for a week."

"Oh, that's good," Daniel says, but he doesn't look at me when he says it. "Kids will be happy about that."

"Yeah," I say.

"Do you think you can go out for dinner some night before everything gets too crazy?" he asks.

"Sure. My parents want to take the kids for the weekend soon, to give me a break. We could do it then."

"That would be great," he says. "Just let me know when."

41

CLAIRE

A week before Christmas, I drop Josh and Jordan off at my parents' house and drive to Daniel's.

The sound of music greets me when he opens the door — something by Coldplay — and he smiles when I cross the threshold. When I shrug out of my coat he looks me up and down slowly, and smiles.

"Whoa," he says, whistling appreciatively. "Where have you been?"

His compliment puts a smile on my face. I'm wearing a black pencil skirt, very high heels, and a tightly fitted, feminine version of a man's white button-down shirt. "I went to a holiday open house today. One of my bigger clients. Very swanky. Champagne in the afternoon. I had half a glass."

"You look very nice," he says softly.

"Thanks."

"How long has it been since you ate?" he asks.

I glance at my watch. It's a little after six thirty. "A while."

"Should we go now?" Daniel asks. "I know it's early, but we'll probably be able to get a table somewhere without too much trouble. I would have made a reservation, but I wasn't sure what time you'd need to eat."

I'm glad he didn't make a reservation. That would have made this feel too much like a date. And it is certainly not a date. But how would I feel if Chris went out to dinner with a female friend? It suddenly occurs to me that there's a good chance that Chris *is* going out to dinner with a female, maybe a coworker, someone on his team. He's never mentioned it, but I've never asked. This possibility simultaneously consoles and worries me.

"Bella Cucina?" I ask. I'm in no mood for a crowded, noisy chain restaurant.

"I was going to suggest that," he says, smiling at me.

Daniel is wearing a black V-neck sweater. He's paired it with jeans but they're nice jeans, dark, not the faded and worn kind that he prefers. He grabs a coat and helps me back into mine and we drive to the restaurant. The light dusting of snow that meteorologists have been excitedly predicting all day has started to fall and after Daniel parks the car he extends his arm for me to hold on to so I won't slip in my high heels. "Maybe I should have insisted that I drop you off at the door again," he teases.

"Not necessary," I say. Besides, it's nice holding on to Daniel's arm.

There are more patrons tonight than there were when Daniel and I came here for lunch. Thankfully we don't have to wait long and soon the maître d' leads us to one of the wedge-shaped booths in the corner that allow diners to sit next to each other instead of across from one another.

"Would you like me to take your coats?" she asks.

We hand them to her and then a waitress takes our drink order — a glass of wine for Daniel and sparkling water for me — and we open our menus.

"What sounds good to you?" Daniel asks.

"I'm not sure." After a few minutes I decide on the salmon and Daniel chooses the shrimp and linguini. The ambience is more romantic tonight, with dim lighting and candles burning on every table. A quick scan of the room yields no familiar faces, and I relax a bit. I won't have to introduce Daniel and have any "it's not what it looks like" conversations.

The waitress brings our drinks, and when she leaves, I lean back against the low, padded leather seat rest. Daniel takes a drink, looks at me, and smiles, resting his arm along the back of the booth, near my shoulders. There's a small jazz trio in the corner and the sound of instruments being tuned rises above the diners' conversations and the clinking of silver and glassware.

Our entrees arrive and while we are eating, a well-dressed gentleman approaches our table. The proprietor, I presume.

"How is everything?" he asks. "Is there anything I can bring you?"

Daniel and I praise the food and tell him that we don't need a thing.

He smiles and says, "Wonderful. Enjoy your evening." Before he goes he turns to Daniel and says, with a slight bow and flourish of his hand, "Your wife is very lovely."

Daniel's smile falters, but he recovers almost immediately and says, "Yes, she is. Beautiful, in fact."

I could say the proprietor was being assumptive, but I *am* wearing a wedding ring. To an outsider, Daniel and I look like a married couple, and I am, perhaps, enjoying the quintessential best of both worlds: husband, albeit absentee, and handsome, attentive companion.

I look at Daniel and whisper, "Thank you."

He nods and turns away to take a drink of his wine. The waitress returns, clears our plates, and asks us if we want dessert. We both say no and she leaves the check.

"Please let me get this one," I say.

Daniel shakes his head and smiles. "No." He pays the bill and we walk through the restaurant toward the glass doors of the entrance, Daniel's hand resting heavily on the small of my back. The weight of his touch sends a delicate shiver up my spine. We retrieve our coats and he helps me into mine, and when we step outside the cold night air almost diffuses the romantic vibe we had going in the restaurant. Almost, but not completely. Large snowflakes are still falling and once again Daniel gives me his arm to hold on to. He opens my car door, waits until I'm seated, and then closes it. He walks around to the driver's side and slides behind the wheel, then starts the car and turns the defrost on high.

"Thank you for dinner," I say.

He puts the car in gear and says, "Anytime, Claire."

When we return home Daniel lights a fire in the fireplace. It's wood burning, not gas like the one at my house.

"I love that smell," I say, inhaling deeply and listening to the tinder crackle as it ignites.

"Can you stay for a while?" Daniel asks.

"Sure." There's nowhere I have to be. No one waiting on me. I kick off my shoes, which have begun to hurt my feet, and sit down on the couch, tucking my legs up under my skirt. The logs catch and the flames grow higher.

"Do you want something to drink?" Daniel asks. "I've got some Snapple in the fridge."

"I'll get it," I say. I walk into the kitchen and take a glass out of the cupboard, then fill it with ice. Daniel opens a drawer and removes a corkscrew. There are two bottles of wine on the counter, both red, and he selects one and opens it, then pours himself a glass. I grab a diet peach Snapple from the fridge and follow him back into the living room, setting down the bottle next to his glass of wine on the coffee table. He leaves the room and when he comes back in he's holding a gift bag.

Oh, shit.

"Is that for me?" I ask. I didn't buy him anything. Why didn't I buy him something?

I should have seen this coming from a mile away.

"I saw it in the store window when I walked by. It reminded me of something you said once, so I bought it." He sits down beside me and hands me the bag.

I open it. Inside are two wrapped presents. One is wrapped in gold and the other in silver. The small boxes are roughly the same size and I don't know which one to open first. Daniel does, though, because he points to the silver one. "You shouldn't have," I say.

"Just open it," he says.

I tear off the paper and smile when I lift the lid of the box. It's a rubber bracelet, like the Livestrong ones and the hundreds of copycats that followed. It's pink and it has the medical alert symbol and says DIABETES in capital letters. "You remembered." I slip it onto my wrist.

I open the second box. It's a small round sterling silver pendant hanging from a silky black cord. It's exactly what I would have chosen if I'd been asked to pick out a gift for myself. Large chunky jewelry looks out of proportion on my small frame, but the dimensions of the delicate silver disk fit me perfectly.

"Do you like it?" he asks.

"I love it." I take it out of the box and undo the clasp, then hand it to Daniel. "Take the other one off and put this one on me, please." Turning around, I lift up my hair and Daniel leans in, removing my medical alert necklace and replacing it with his gift. The disk rests in the small dip between my breasts and when I turn back around his gaze lingers there. "It's beautiful," I say. "Thank you." I hug him, the way I always do when someone gives me a gift. It catches him off guard and he finally realizes what I'm doing and tries to hug me back at the exact same time that I pull away. Really, it's almost comical. You'd think that we don't know how hugging works.

"You're welcome," he says, gathering up the scraps of wrapping paper. He goes into the kitchen to throw it away and when he returns he says, "Music or TV?"

"Music, please."

Daniel crosses the room and hits the button on the stereo, scanning through the channels. "Holiday favorites?"

"Yes," I say. "That would be perfect." He sits back down beside me, takes a drink of his wine, and places the glass on the coffee table. I'm suddenly aware of how close we're sitting, and how completely alone we are. I'm slightly worried that my active participation in our late-night phone calls has given him the wrong impression, some kind of green light. But he's been a perfect gentleman this evening and my instincts tell me he will continue in the same manner. Daniel doesn't seem like the type of man who would lay his cards on the table without knowing exactly what the outcome would be.

I take a sip of my drink and place the bottle back down on the table next to his. A yawn escapes before I can stifle it with the back of my hand.

"Tired?" Daniel asks.

"A little. It's been a long day. And it's so nice and cozy in here. Makes me sleepy." Daniel's house reminds me of the starter home Chris and I bought when we were newly married. Ours was also a ranch and had the same arched entryways and hardwood floors. I love my current home, but sometimes I miss that first house and all that it signified: the untarnished and unchallenged beginning of my life with Chris.

I wander over to the built-in bookcase that reaches from floor to ceiling on one wall of the living room. If it were my home, I'd fill the shelves with decorative accessories, my collection of hardback books, and framed photos, but Daniel doesn't utilize the space much. There's a clock and a few pieces of mail. A magazine. His home lacks a woman's touch, but maybe he likes it just the way it is. I look up and three photo albums on the highest shelf catch my eye. I have to stand on my tiptoes to reach them and I pull down one of them, its cover dusty, and crack it open. The album must be from Daniel's college days because the first picture I see shows him wearing a sweatshirt with the letters of his fraternity house on it. He's holding a beer, surrounded by at least ten other guys doing the same. I sink to the floor, the album in my lap, and smile. "Fraternity brothers?"

He nods his head. "I did some serious partying with those guys." He sits down on the floor beside me, drinking his wine, and watches me flip through the pages. There aren't many pictures and most of them are shoved in haphazardly, as if he couldn't be bothered to slide them into the individual pockets.

"Are there any pictures where you're not drinking beer?" I ask. "Or holding a beer? Or standing beside a keg of beer?"

"Probably not," he answers.

I laugh when I notice Daniel's floppy, middle-part hairstyle, and I can't help but tease him. "Tell me, how influential were the Backstreet Boys in shaping your look back then?"

"Very funny," he says. "I'll have you know I got a lot of attention from the girls with that hair."

"I'm sure you did," I agree. The truth is, it didn't detract from his looks, not in the least. But if anything, he's more attractive now, as if each year that passes only improves his appearance.

I stand up and swap the first photo album for the next — this one even dustier. The first picture is of Daniel and a girl. She has blonde hair and she's wearing it in a shoulder-length, fully layered style just like I wore in the nineties and that neither of us would be caught dead in today. Her eyes are blue, not brown, yet the resemblance is such that we could be sisters. She's sitting on Daniel's lap with a red Solo cup in her hand. They appear to be laughing, as if the photographer snapped the photo at just the right time. Midjoke. Page after page of Daniel and the blonde girl follow: pictures of them in formal attire, in jeans and sweatshirts, and two full pages of them enjoying a tropical vacation.

When I reach the end of the album the blonde girl is still in it. In one photo they have their arms around each other and she's wearing a diamond ring on her left hand. Engagement photos. It hits me suddenly that I'm looking at Daniel's ex-wife. "Is this her?" I ask.

He nods, his eyes a bit glassy. I've never even seen him tipsy before, but he's well on his way.

"What's her name?"

"Jessica. Jessie."

I come to the end of the album and stand to retrieve the last one. The cover of this one isn't dusty at all. Daniel goes and sits on the couch, knocking back a big drink of wine. I sit down on the couch next to him and open to the first page. There's a picture of Daniel in a cap and gown at his college graduation, and several more when he completed his training at the police academy. One of him as a rookie policeman, in full uniform. The next photos are from his wedding. I look at them silently. Jessie looks beautiful, the big hair now smoothed into a low chignon with flowers surrounding it. Daniel's wineglass is empty and he heads to the kitchen for a refill. I flip past the wedding photos and think that maybe this was a bad idea. He probably doesn't want me looking at pictures of his other life, but he's too polite to tell me not to.

I flip to the next page and the pictures on

it take my breath away.

Jessie is very, very pregnant. She's smiling and Daniel is sitting beside her, his hand on her stomach, fingers splayed as if he's trying to encompass all that's inside of her in one handful, which would be impossible because she is clearly full-term. Time stands still and yet speeds up as I turn the pages, and my sense of foreboding increases. Daniel sits back down on the couch, but he's not watching me; he's staring off into space, very still.

On the next page a smiling baby, cradled in Jessie's arms, wears a blue cap and looks minutes old. Now I know whose photo is in the frame on Daniel's dresser. The images that follow — Jessie holding the baby, Daniel holding the baby, and one of Daniel kissing the baby's forehead — bring tears to my eyes because I know where this is heading. Feel it in the pit of my stomach and yet I can't look away.

There are pages and pages of pictures and then suddenly there aren't.

I close the album and set it on the coffee table, blinking back the tears. "What's your son's name?" I ask.

"Gabriel."

"That's a beautiful name." I don't ask any more questions. If I've learned one thing about men, it's that if Daniel wants to share, he'll share.

"He died of SIDS when he was three months old," Daniel says, and when he looks at me I see the mournful expression on his face.

"I'm so sorry." Tears fill my eyes and I scold myself because they won't help anything, but I can't stem their flow. I wipe my eyes and will the tears to stop, which only makes them multiply.

Daniel begins to speak. "I came home late. There was a multicar accident on the parkway and I'd been up most of the night tying up loose ends and submitting paperwork. I checked on Gabriel when I got home. He was just getting over his first cold and hadn't been sleeping well, but he seemed fine. I went to bed and the sound of Jessie screaming when she went in to get him the next morning woke me up. We called an ambulance right away, but he was already gone. She just kept screaming, and I will never forget that sound."

I look at Daniel and the sorrow I see in his eyes cuts me to the quick. "I'm so sorry," I say. The problems Chris and I have faced suddenly pale in comparison. It's one thing to lose a job, but losing a child is life altering. Incomprehensible to me.

"We buried him and we tried our best to get on with our lives. But Jessie just couldn't. We had a huge fight one night and she admitted that she blamed me. She said maybe if I'd picked him up when I came home that night he might not have died. But the doctor told us it would have been nearly impossible to pinpoint the exact minute he stopped breathing."

I nod but don't say anything. Daniel doesn't need me to tell him that it wasn't his fault. That it was a tragic accident. I'm sure he's heard every variation of those sentiments.

"We stayed together for another year. Went to counseling. Talked about having another baby. But she was just so angry, and I was the nearest thing to it. I told her I'd let her go, so she could find someone new and start over."

"Did she?"

"I don't know."

He looks so incredibly sad. Overwhelmed by my need to comfort him, I ignore the warning bells clanging in my head that *this is a very bad idea,* and I reach out and put my arms around Daniel and lay my head on his chest. He doesn't do anything at first. His heartbeat pounds under my cheek and his breathing speeds up, but his hands remain at his sides. Finally, he wraps his arms around me, and after a few minutes he seems calmer.

"Do you still love her?"

"It doesn't matter," he says.

He holds me tight and one of his hands slips under the back of my blouse. He rubs my skin in a circular pattern with his fingertips. It feels amazing. My brain is sending all kinds of fight or flight signals, but the light pressure of his touch eventually dispels my anxiety, and I tell myself that there is nothing even remotely sexual about this situation, at least not to me. After a while, I lift my head off his chest.

"Stay with me for a while," he says.

I'm suddenly exhausted, and the fatigue runs bone deep. It's as if the weight of his words is more than I can handle; I can't imagine what it's like to be the one to say them. The temperature in the room feels as if it's dropped ten degrees, and the cold surrounds me. "Okay," I whisper.

Daniel reaches over and flicks off the lamp on the table beside the couch. The firelight is the only thing that illuminates the room. Daniel shifts me, so that my head is in his lap. He strokes my hair.

"Do I remind you of her?" I ask.

"You remind me of the good parts," he

says. He notices my shivering and the soft fabric of the throw blanket settles over my body. "Better?"

"Yes."

"Does he know about me?" Daniel asks.

Right before I fall asleep I say, "No."

When I wake up the room is dark and it takes a few moments for my eyes to adjust. My head still rests on Daniel's lap and his arm is thrown across my shoulders. The guilt arrives full force. I may feel completely disconnected from Chris, but falling asleep at another man's house, no matter what the circumstances are, is a significant transgression. I sit up and glance at my watch. Almost 3:00 A.M. I'm completely wide awake and all I can think about is leaving.

Daniel stirs. "Claire?"

"It's okay. I'm going home. Don't get up."

He gets up. The last dying embers in the fireplace emit a soft glow and Daniel turns on the lamp so I can find my shoes, cell phone, and purse. He helps me into my coat and I don't know what to say, so I hug him tightly. He hugs me back until I finally pull away.

"I have to go."

He slips on his shoes and walks me to my car. The snow has stopped falling and the winter sky looks clear. The air feels crisp and cold.

"Be careful," he says. "Watch the roads. They might be slick."

I hear something in his voice, but I can't identify it. Melancholy. Longing. Regret. Or maybe he's just tired.

"Text me so that I know you made it home safely."

"I will." I drive away, feeling guilty, conflicted, and empty.

42

Claire

When Chris walks in the door on the evening of December 23, a fresh wave of remorse washes over me, especially when I notice how tired he looks. While I was asleep on Daniel's lap, Chris was probably still burning the midnight oil at a Holiday Inn Express somewhere.

He sets down his suitcase seconds before Josh and Jordan tackle him. He gathers them in his arms, holding them tight. It isn't hard to tell from the expression on his face and the way he kisses Jordan's cheek and ruffles Josh's hair that he missed them.

"Do you think you're on Santa's nice list or his naughty one?" Chris asks.

"Nice!" they yell.

"I was maybe naughty once," Jordan admits.

"Just once, huh?" Chris teases. "I wonder if your mom might tell me otherwise." Chris looks over at me and grins.

"Maybe twice," I say.

Chris's good mood fills the room. He's been looking forward to this break for a while now, and I was worried he might call to say that his boss changed his mind about letting him have the time off. The kids would have been crushed.

"Do you want something to eat?"

He shakes his head. "I ate at the airport. And frankly, I'm looking forward to not doing so for a while."

"I'll make all your favorites while you're home," I say.

He nods and smiles. "That would be great."

"Go get your pajamas on," I tell the kids. "Santa wants you to go to bed on time."

They don't want to leave Chris, but they do as I ask because they're more worried about upsetting Santa.

"I got promoted," Chris says. I can tell by the smile on his face how happy he is.

I smile, too. "That's fantastic, Chris! I knew you would."

The kids will be thrilled. My household can find its equilibrium.

"So you won't have to travel anymore, right?"

"Eventually." Chris leans up against the

counter, arms crossed. "I'm not even gonna try and spin this, Claire. The promotion is great, but I'm going to be even busier than I was, if that's possible. I'll be doing both jobs until they hire my replacement. I don't know how soon they'll bring me back to headquarters. Hopefully it won't take too long."

I don't want Chris to know how disappointed I am that his return from the field isn't imminent, so I say, "It's okay. We'll get by."

"I don't think we should say anything to the kids just yet."

"No." I don't mention that I never say anything to the kids unless I know it's set in stone. I've learned that lesson the hard way.

Jordan comes tearing back into the room. "Dad, will you watch *Frosty* with me? Please?"

"Let me get changed, okay?" Chris comes back downstairs a few minutes later, wearing gray sweatpants and an old KU T-shirt. Josh and I pop popcorn and join them on the couch.

"This is nice," Josh says. "All of us here together." Chris and I look at each other and smile, and it's all I can do not to burst into tears when I think about how lucky I really am.

■ ■ ■ ■

On Christmas morning, the kids wake us up at five fifteen. We were up way past midnight, assembling and wrapping toys. My eyes feel like they're cemented shut.

"Go back to bed," Chris mumbles. "Please, I'm begging you."

"But, Daddy, I want to see if Santa came," Jordan says. "I was actually naughty several times. I'm very worried."

Expecting them to go back to bed is highly unrealistic, so I sit up and yawn, rubbing my eyes.

"Yay, Mom's up," they shout. I nudge Chris.

"Come on. I'll dump some Baileys in your coffee."

He groans but finally sits up and swings his legs over the side of the bed. After he pulls on some pajama bottoms and a T-shirt we follow the kids' excited cheers and head downstairs. The wrapping paper flies, and we spend the morning eating eggs and bacon and cinnamon rolls, and putting batteries in all the new toys. Chris joins me on the couch where I'm drinking coffee and trying to figure out Jordan's new Barbie camcorder. He has a gift-wrapped box in his hand.

"Want to open your present?"

Just like last year, we'd both claimed that we didn't want or need anything for Christmas, but Chris insisted that I have at least one gift under the tree. I take the box from his outstretched hand.

"Sure."

The box is ornately wrapped in red and green. I open it. Nestled in the tissue paper is a sterling silver picture frame. It's a picture of Chris and the kids and me, taken at my parents' house on Thanksgiving. "Did my mom send you this?"

"Yeah, I asked her to e-mail me the pictures from her camera."

I laugh. "Did she know how to do that?"

"No. I had to walk her through it. It was hysterical."

In the picture, Chris and I are sitting on the raised hearth of my parents' fireplace. Josh is on my lap and Jordan is on Chris's. Everyone is smiling. "It's my fault that we didn't have a family picture taken last Christmas. And I wasn't home long enough this year to get one taken professionally. This is the best I could do."

"It's perfect," I say.

I hand him a square box wrapped in blue with a big bow on top. He unwraps it and pulls out a DVD case. The disk is silver, but the case is blank. "What is it?" he asks.

"You'll see. Play it on your laptop when you go back out on the road," I say. "Not before. Just trust me."

He nods and snaps the disk back into the case. "Okay. I'll wait." He leans over and places a soft, gentle kiss on my lips. "Merry Christmas."

We spend the next week together, as a family. I keep my contact with Daniel to a minimum. Chris tries his best not to work too much. The kids have never been happier.

And just when I feel as though we've made some progress, he's gone again.

43

CHRIS

I snap the DVD into the CD-ROM player on my laptop. I'm in some hotel in Oklahoma, and I've had a shit day. Being home for a week made it twice as hard to get on the plane this morning, not to mention the fact that I've been putting out fires and appeasing people all day long. It's ten thirty and I'll be lucky if I get to bed before 1:00 A.M.

The disk whirs to life and the first image in the slide show pops up on the screen. It's a family photo, taken the first Christmas after we had Josh. Then, in order after that, each subsequent Christmas card photo except for the year I was unemployed. I didn't want to take a picture that year, wouldn't come out of the office in fact. Claire posed the kids in front of the tree and if anyone noticed that Claire and I were missing, they didn't say anything. Well, they didn't say anything to me, but maybe they did to her. After the holiday photos there are individual photos of the kids. I smile as they slowly pass by. There are pictures of me and Claire when we were in Hawaii. I pause the one where she's splashing in the ocean, wearing a pink bikini. I haven't seen a smile like the one she has on her face in that picture in a long time. I play the slide show twice, watching as photo after photo of my wife and kids passes by, not unlike the way they are in real life because I'm not there. The slide show comes to an end, and I think about calling Claire. It's late, though, and if I don't get started on all the work I have to do, I'll be up all night.

I miss my family profoundly.

44

DANIEL

I call Claire at eleven thirty. It's a Tuesday night, so I know her husband won't be home.

"Too late?" I ask when she answers.

"No. Not too late," she says.

I love her voice when we talk late at night. It changes. Gets softer. Like she reserves it just for these calls. She sounds sleepy but she also sounds happy to hear from me.

"Are you in bed?" I ask.

"Yes. I was reading. I just closed my book and turned off the light. What are you doing?" she asks.

"Same thing you are," I say. "Just lying here." I haven't been able to stop thinking about her. She was on my mind all day and now that I'm in bed I'm really having trouble getting her out of my head. I picture her under the covers, wondering once again what she's wearing even though I know I shouldn't be thinking about that, because it's torture and it's pointless. "How are you feeling?" I ask. She's had a bad cold and hasn't stopped by in more than a week because she said she didn't want to give it to me.

"Much better," she says. "The kids will probably bring home more germs soon. I better enjoy the respite while I can."

"I've missed having you around."

"You have?"

"Yes."

"I've missed you, too," she says.

"I've gotten used to seeing you sitting on my couch." I like stealing looks at Claire when she's got her head down, reading or typing, with my blanket wrapped around her shoulders. Like she belongs there.

"I like sitting on your couch. I like it when you make me lunch," she says.

"That's because I'm an excellent cook," I say.

"It's not usually a *hot* lunch," she teases.

I laugh. "Details."

"I can hear the wind outside my window. The meteorologist on the news said that we might break the record for a January low."

"I'm sure you're plenty warm. Something tells me you're all bundled up." What I wouldn't give to be able to put my arms around her. Heat her up so that she wouldn't want anything covering her.

"I'm in flannel pajama pants and a sweatshirt."

"I'd be sweating."

"You run warmer than I do."

"You aren't going to ask me what I'm wearing?"

"I'm pretty sure I know what you're wearing," she says.

Of course she does. She's got a husband who's sometimes home. One who probably also sleeps in his underwear, or naked when she's beside him. I'm wearing boxer briefs, but being specific with her will accomplish nothing. As much as I'd love to really let loose and tell her — explicitly and in full detail — what I'm thinking about when I call her late at night, I can't. Crossing any kind of line, even on the phone, is up to Claire, and not me. And there's no one here to help me with the hard-on I already have, so I should probably stop while I'm ahead. "I've got Monday off. Come over?"

"Sure. I'll come over after yoga."

"Okay. Go to sleep," I tell her. "Stay warm."

"I will. You, too," she says.

For the first time in months, I think about calling Melissa. But that would be a real dick move, so I disregard it immediately. Even if she agreed to come over, I still wouldn't be satisfied. I'd only be pretending that it was Claire's hands stroking me. Claire's lips on mine. It's easier if I just take care of this solo, because in my mind Claire can do everything I desperately want her to do, and I can imagine it in full Technicolor, without the distraction of another woman.

It isn't quite the same. But it's less complicated than calling Melissa, and it's almost enough.

45

CLAIRE

To: Claire Canton
From: Chris Canton
Subject: Awards banquet

The annual awards banquet is Saturday, February 12th. It's black tie. Buy yourself something new. Anything you want.

To: Chris Canton
From: Claire Canton
Subject: Re: Awards banquet

Okay. I'll go dress shopping. Would you like me to rent you a tuxedo?

To: Claire Canton
From: Chris Canton
Subject: Re: re: Awards banquet

That would be great, thanks. I'll get fitted while I'm on the road and e-mail you my measurements.

I miss you guys.

Chris's confidence is at an all-time high since his promotion and this event is important to him. He's still waiting to come in from the field, though. "Any day now," they tell him, but they haven't hired his replacement and Chris doesn't think they're working all that hard to find someone else. He tries not to let his disappointment show. I try not to ask him about it. We're both glad we didn't say anything to the kids.

I drop Josh and Jordan off at Chris's parents the day of the banquet. His mother greets me with a kiss on the cheek and a hug. She smells like Shalimar. Chris once told me that his mother is one of the hardest women to buy a gift for. "I have everything I need," she always claims. "Four healthy and happy kids and now all these beautiful grandchildren." Finally, under duress, she mentioned once that she loved the scent of Shalimar and she received so many bottles of it on her next birthday and for Christmas that she says she'll never run out. It's a smell I'll always associate with her.

"Be good for Grandma and Grandpa," I

tell the kids, kissing them and giving each of them a hug.

At the hair salon, I settle into the stylist's chair and ask for a sleek blowout. She uses a multitude of products and styling tools to coax my waves into a shiny waterfall of hair. My dress is off the shoulder and maybe I should wear my hair up, but Chris likes my hair down. "Do you want to have your makeup done?" the stylist asks.

"Why not?" I sit perfectly still as she cleanses my skin, removing what little makeup I'm wearing, and starts over. She applies foundation and blush and lines my eye in blue and silver. These are colors I would never have chosen on my own, but when she holds up a hand mirror in front of my face I'm taken aback at how good it looks. She's smudged it a bit so the line isn't too harsh and she's painted my lips in a pale pink to offset the dramatic eye makeup. My lashes have been lengthened with three coats of mascara and then curled; I hardly recognize myself. I thank her and pay, adding a nice tip.

Chris's car isn't in the garage when I return home and a silent house greets me when I walk in the door. I pin my hair loosely on top of my head and run a bath, careful not to let the water get too hot and steamy so it won't ruin my makeup, then sink into the warm water. I should have remembered to light a candle or bring a book, but I don't have much time, so I wash and then close my eyes and relax. When I get out of the bath I pat myself dry and soothe my skin, parched by the cold air of a lingering winter, with a thin layer of my favorite scented moisturizer.

In our bedroom, I walk to the dresser and pull out a strapless bra, thong, and thigh-high stockings. I'm just about to step into the thong when Chris bursts through the bedroom door, startling me. He's already dressed in his tux. The black looks striking against his blond hair and the cut of the suit flatters his build. He stops in his tracks, a surprised expression on his face.

"Where were you?" I ask.

He doesn't answer me. Although it's been a while, Chris has seen me naked thousands of times. His hands and mouth are more than familiar with my most intimate places, and he's had an up close and personal view of both children being born. But as I step into the thong and fasten the bra his eyes track my movements as if he's seeing my body for the first time. I stop what I'm doing and look over at him.

"Chris?"

He clears his throat. "I went to fill the car up with gas. Then I ran into the office for a minute."

Chris watches as I sit down on the bed and carefully pull the stockings on. I slip my pump inside one of them. I take my dress off its padded hanger and step into it. It's knee length, fitted, and black, with a bit of shimmer. It hangs open as I step into my shoes and locate my earrings. Chris walks across the room and stands behind me. He zips me up, slowly, and rests his hands on my shoulders. "You'll be cold," he says, his voice husky.

His touch stirs something inside of me, and suddenly I can't breathe. "I'll wear a wrap."

His hands slide down my shoulders, along the bare skin of my arms where they linger. He finally steps back. "I'll let you finish getting ready."

"It won't take long." Chris retreats and I grab my evening bag and spritz myself with perfume. I pull the wrap off the hanger and drape it around my shoulders. Downstairs, Chris and I shut off lights and lock the door. In the garage he holds the car door open for me and we go.

The evening begins with cocktails and hors

d'oeuvres outside the banquet room of the Westin Crown Center in Kansas City. Chris brings me a flute of champagne and then fills a small plate of food for us to share; in his other hand he swirls whiskey around in his glass, the ice clinking. I scan the crowd, admiring the fancy dresses. Soon, the doors to the banquet room open and we make our way inside, finding the place cards with our names at a table elegantly set for eight.

A tall, gray-haired man makes his way toward us and Chris leans down and whispers in my ear, "This is Jim, my boss."

Jim beams when he reaches us and we both stand. He shakes Chris's hand. Turning to me, he introduces himself and then says, "You must be Claire. I've heard so much about you."

Perhaps it's just banter, but Jim's heard my name enough to remember it, and his expression is sincere. It never occurred to me that Chris might talk about his family at work. There's no hiding the warmth that emanates from Jim as he shakes my hand. "Your husband has become an invaluable member of my team. We're lucky to have him."

Jim's sentiments are shared by others, and throughout the evening, after the meal is served and the plates have been cleared away, several of Chris's coworkers congratulate him on his latest accomplishments. His direct reports flatter him, and I marvel at the posturing going on around me. This necessary hierarchy, and the relentless pursuit of the next rung on the corporate ladder, never fails to both amaze and exhaust me. It has the opposite effect on Chris. He draws incredible energy from it, and I can see why its absence has had such a negative effect on him. The golden boy radiates with happiness; it's Chris's night.

There's a dais near the front of the room, complete with a microphone stand. Chris does not receive an individual acknowledgment, but he's asked to rise when his team is honored. I clap loudly and smile for my husband. When they're done handing out the awards, a DJ begins playing a variety of music suitable for this kind of occasion. There are plenty of slow songs: Frank Sinatra, Etta James. Michael Bublé for a more modern selection.

"Do you want another glass of champagne?" Chris asks.

"No thanks."

"Then let's dance," he says. He leads me by the hand and we join the swirling couples on the dance floor. Chris clasps my left hand with his right and rests his other hand on my waist. We move to the music; he seems happy, and it's been so long since I've seen him this way. He looks into my eyes and says, "You look stunning tonight. You always do." He puts both arms around my waist and pulls me closer, and I rest my head on his shoulder. When the music ends we walk back to the table. The evening is winding down and the crowd in the banquet room is starting to disperse. "Are you ready to go?" Chris asks.

"Yes."

He holds my hand as we walk outside and wait for the valet to bring the car. He used to hold it all the time, but he stopped holding it during the months he was out of work. Maybe because we didn't go many places together or maybe because we just didn't feel all that loving toward each other. But I've always loved the feel of his hand holding mine. I still do.

My wrap is worthless against the freezing temperature, and my feet are like blocks of ice. Chris notices my shivering and takes off his tuxedo jacket and places it gently over my shoulders. "Put your arms in." I do as he says. He stands with his arm around my shoulders, impervious to the chill in his white dress shirt. My eyes are drawn to his wrist, and the onyx cuff links I gave him for our tenth wedding anniversary.

On the way home I say, "Your boss seems really nice."

Chris turns up the heat another notch and the warm air blows, filling the interior. "He's a giant asshole. You saw the good side, but believe me, I've seen the bad. It's unsettling. I'm just waiting for him to turn on me the minute I make a single misstep, which is why I don't."

"Seriously?" I try to envision Jim without a smile on his face. His tone harsh instead of welcoming. He had me snowed, that's for sure.

"Oh, yeah. It's like watching an anger bomb detonate."

"Why haven't you said anything?"

Chris shrugs slightly, hands firmly on the wheel. "What difference would it have made? I can't do anything about it."

"Because I would have known what was going on. You would have had my sympathy, Chris. All this time, I've thought that the job was going so well, and that you loved it." That the sacrifices our family made were worth something.

"I should never have taken this job, but at the time I didn't know what else to do. I don't think they have any intention of bringing me in from the field. They know that in this economy there aren't many of us who can afford to make waves. I've been networking again, surfing job sites late at night in my hotel room. So far nothing has come up. There just isn't much out there."

Why, why couldn't he talk to me like this before?

"It's okay," I tell him. "We'll get by."

"You keep saying that, Claire, and I appreciate it. But it isn't okay." He takes his eyes off the road for a second to look over at me. "I miss my family. I miss you."

His words warm me like nothing else can. "Try and hold on a little longer. It'll all work out eventually." I have no idea if it will, but I don't know what else to say.

At home, Chris locks up and sets the alarm. I leave my phone tucked inside my evening bag and for the first time in a long time, Chris doesn't disappear into the office. Instead, he lets Tucker out and tells me he'll be up in a minute. In our bedroom, I put on my warmest pajamas in an attempt to offset the lingering chill, then remove the elaborate makeup and brush my teeth. I burrow into the bed feeling drowsy, the warmth and softness lulling me into a state of relaxation.

Chris makes his way upstairs. He doesn't turn on the lights but the water runs and the toilet flushes in the master bathroom. Silently, he pulls back the covers and slides between the sheets. Before I drift off completely I'm aware of a shifting of weight, of movement that encircles me. I teeter at the precipice between wakefulness and sleep, and then I fall, wrapped tightly in the arms of my husband.

46

Chris

I close my eyes and hold Claire in my arms, replaying the events of the evening in my mind. The first image I revisit is Claire standing naked in our bedroom. Even the antidepressants and their unwelcome side effects couldn't dampen the way I felt when I walked into the room. To see her standing there like that took my breath away.

I watched her turn heads tonight, and I realized that I've been so wrapped up in my own life I never once thought about what she'd do if another man hit on her. I'm thinking about it now, and I don't like it.

I'm worried about what will happen if I stop taking the antidepressants. I don't know if I can handle the pressure. Maybe they're just a crutch, and I don't really need them anymore. Then instead of holding my wife I could make love to her.

If I'm wrong, I might lose everything I've gained.

But if I'm right, I might be able to have it all.

47

Claire

I'm driving home after dropping off Josh and Jordan at their respective after-school activities when my cell phone rings. A quick glance at the screen brings a smile to my face. "Hey," I say when I answer. "I was just thinking about you."

"One of my fellow officers just pulled over a friend of yours," Daniel says. "The one who drinks a lot. Julia."

"What?" I'm confused about how Daniel knows this information. "Where?"

"A couple of miles from your neighborhood. A neighbor noticed her swerving and called the police. She failed the field sobriety test and the Breathalyzer. Her kids are in the car."

Oh, Jesus.

Daniel continues. "She tried to talk him out of arresting her by giving him my name. She said I was 'Claire's friend.' "

"Where is she now?" I ask.

"She's still there. The officer is waiting to take her in because he needs someone to come get the kids. How far away are you?"

I give him my location and he tells me where Julia is.

"How long will it take you to get there?"

"Less than ten minutes."

Daniel stays on the line until I reach the flashing lights and the two cars parked on the shoulder of the road. It's heavily traveled and the cars in front of me slow to see what's going on. I pull up behind the police car.

"What am I supposed to do?"

"Just take the kids home with you. Call her husband and tell him he'll need to post bail. Are you okay, Claire? Can you handle this? I can come meet you if you need help."

My stomach does an odd flip. I want no part of this drama I've been unwillingly pulled into, but I think of Julia's girls and how scared and confused they must be. "No. I'm fine. I'll take care of it. I'll call you later," I tell Daniel and disconnect the call. I get out of the car and the officer approaches me. Julia is in the back of the police car but her girls are still in the backseat of her minivan.

"Hi. Thanks for coming. I'm Officer Hill."

"Claire Canton." I shake his proffered hand. "Can I speak to the girls first?"

"Yes. That's a good idea."

I open the door to the minivan and stick my head inside, a comforting smile on my face. The girls' frightened expressions tug at my heartstrings, so I smile warmly and speak in a soothing voice.

"Everything's okay. The police are here to make sure everyone drives safely and they just want to talk to your mom for a minute, okay?"

They nod silently, unsure of how to respond. Of course they don't know what to say. They're children.

"Stay in your seats. I'll be right back."

Tears run down five-year-old Hillary's face as she nods solemnly. Three-year-old Beth remains blissfully clueless.

I approach the police car and the officer opens the door so I can slide in beside Julia. Her hair hangs in her eyes and mascara streaks her cheeks. The smell of alcohol fills the car. She won't even look at me. I pull my cell phone out of my pocket.

"Where would Justin be right now? Is he on his way home?"

Suddenly, I have her attention. Her head snaps up and she begs silently, eyes blazing, imploring me not to make the call. I wait patiently. This ends now. Her shoulders slump in defeat.

"He's probably with his girlfriend," she says, slurring a bit. But she mostly sounds sad.

Justin has a girlfriend? And Julia knows about this?

I don't even know what to say about that, but I have more pressing things to worry about. I scroll through my contacts and call Justin. When he answers I begin to speak.

"It's Claire. Julia got pulled over for drunk driving. I have a friend on the police force and he called me. I'm with her now."

Justin inhales sharply and there's a slight pause before he says, "Fuck." He exhales and asks, "What now?"

"The officer is going to arrest her." Beside me, Julia starts crying. "Listen to me, Justin. Your daughters were with her. They were sitting in the backseat while your wife swerved her way out of our neighborhood. Check Julia into rehab immediately and pray they don't slap her with child endangerment."

Julia cries harder and a figurative thud echoes through the car as she hits rock bottom.

Of course he agrees.

I tell him I'll drive the girls home and wait

for him there.

"I'll head down to the station," he says. "Tell Julia I'm on my way."

"Okay."

"Claire?"

"Yes?"

"Thanks."

"Sure."

The officer helps me install Beth and Hillary's car and booster seats in my SUV and we strap the girls in. I'm grateful that they don't really know what's going on and that the memory will fade by the time they're old enough to realize what happened. At least I hope it will. After I shut the door I turn to Officer Hill and say, "Thank you."

"You're welcome," he says.

I lean back in the open door of the squad car. "I'm going to take the girls to my house. I'll make them dinner and they can play with Josh and Jordan when they get home."

Julia wipes her eyes and nods.

"It'll be okay," I say, giving her hand a quick squeeze.

Silence fills the car on our way home, and my mood feels as gray as the sky on this blustery March day. Spring seems a lifetime away. I turn up the heat so the girls won't be cold. Maybe I should open a dialogue with them, comfort them somehow with words, but then I decide that the less talking I do, the better. The radio plays softly and the minutes pass like hours.

At home, I get out some coloring books and crayons and ask the girls if they want a snack.

"When is my mom coming back?" Hillary asks.

"Your dad's going to pick her up and they'll both come here to get you in a little while." I smile and try my best to add some normalcy to the situation.

Later, when Josh and Jordan are home and all four children have eaten dinner, I put in a DVD and they huddle on the couch in the family room, engrossed in the film. I step into the kitchen and call Daniel.

"Hi," I say when he answers.

"Hey. How are you?" I can picture him sitting on the couch, feet on the coffee table. Smiling.

"I'm tired. That was a bit draining."

"I knew it would be," he says. "How are the kids?"

"They're doing okay."

"I made a call. Julia's been processed and released. They'll probably be there soon."

"Thanks."

"Think she'll get the help she needs?"

"I hope so. I'm hoping her husband will step up a little. But guess what — she told me he has a girlfriend!"

"What?"

"Yeah. So not only is he unfaithful to her, she knows about it." I can't condone her coping method, but she has my sympathy for her marital situation.

"Wow," Daniel says. "That's too bad."

A car door slams outside. "Listen. I think they're here. I have to go."

"I'll call you later," Daniel says.

I open the front door and watch as Justin leads Julia up the sidewalk, his arm around her. After several hours, she seems more sober. They come inside and it brings tears to my eyes when Julia softly calls out, "Girls?" They go to her, and she pulls them close, one arm thrown over each of them. They don't understand their mother's need for comfort, but they give it anyway, unconditionally. Justin stands nearby, watching. He looks me in the eye and he doesn't have to utter a word for me to know he's grateful. Whatever he's planning to say to Julia, the things he needs to say, can wait until tomorrow. But he will say them. Of this I am fairly certain.

He loves his girls and deep down I hope that he still loves Julia.

48

CLAIRE

Jordan has been invited to a slumber party, to celebrate a classmate's birthday. We carefully pack her overnight bag making sure to include her stuffed kitty and her pajamas. Her excitement knows no bounds, and she talks a mile a minute about the pizza they're going to eat and the movie they're going to see.

"I'll have my phone with me at all times, so if you need me, just call," I say, mostly to reassure myself.

"I won't need you," she says. She won't either, this self-assured social butterfly who enjoys the company of her friends almost as much as her own family. Maybe more.

"Okay. But you know where to find me if you change your mind."

Josh and I are on our way home from dropping Jordan off when my phone rings.

"Does Josh want to go to the speedway

with Skip and Travis tonight? It's the opening event of the season."

I know the answer to that without asking, but I pull the phone away from my ear and say, "Skip and Travis are going to watch the car races. Want to go with them?"

"Yes!"

I put the phone back to my ear. "I'm assuming you heard that," I say, laughing.

"Loud and clear. Skip will pick him up in an hour. Travis wants Josh to sleep over. Okay with you?"

"Sure. Let me know if you need anything."

"We'll be fine," Elisa says.

Daniel's working tonight. After Josh leaves with Skip and Travis I putter around the house, straightening up and doing a couple of loads of laundry. Restless, I turn on some music and flip through a magazine. My phone rings and I smile because I was hoping that he'd call.

"Hi," I say. "Are you on your dinner break?"

"Yep," he says. "What are you doing?"

"Skip just picked up Josh. He's going to the races with him and Travis. Jordan is at a slumber party."

Daniel processes this information quickly, and mere seconds pass before he asks, "Is he still out of town?"

"Yes, he's not flying home this weekend at all."

"Can you come over later?" he asks, his voice hopeful. "I'll try to get off early. You might have to wait a little while."

"That's okay. I'll watch TV or read until you get home." I've known since I received Elisa's call that I would say yes when he asked.

I finish a few things around the house and by eight fifteen I'm pulling into Daniel's driveway. There's a light on, in the kitchen I think, but maybe he forgot to turn it off before he left for work. I punch the code into the garage keypad and wait for the door to go up.

I open the door leading into the house and walk down the hallway, freezing in place when a man saunters out of the kitchen. He looks like a slightly younger version of Daniel, but a bit scruffier, and if I wasn't so sure of who it was, I'd be turning on my heel to bolt. His hair is longer, his jeans are ripped, and the well-worn leather jacket he's wearing gives him the opposite appearance of his clean-cut sibling. He holds a bottle of beer in his hand and he raises it to his mouth and takes a drink.

We study each other. "You must be Dylan," I finally say.

"I am." He takes a step forward, scrutinizing me. "Who are you?"

"Claire. I'm a friend of Daniel's."

His face transforms, and I see firsthand what Daniel meant when he said Dylan was a charmer; his eyes all but twinkle. "Daniel never mentioned you," he says, coming closer. "I wonder why that is. Want a beer?"

"No thanks."

"You sure?"

"Yes." I leave the kitchen and sit down on the couch in the living room, thumbing through the magazine that I left on Daniel's coffee table a week ago. Dylan follows and makes himself at home, sitting in the leather chair that's angled toward the couch.

"I didn't see a car," I say.

"A friend dropped me off."

"Did Daniel know you were coming?" I'd love to whip out my phone and send Daniel a text, but I'm pretty sure the message and recipient would be painfully obvious to Dylan.

"Maybe," he says vaguely, placing his empty beer bottle on the coffee table. I glance discreetly at my watch. It's only eight thirty. Hopefully Daniel won't be much longer.

"So, tell me about yourself, Claire."

I shake my head. "Not much to tell."

I'm saved from any further questioning when headlights sweep into the driveway. The garage door goes up, and a minute later, Daniel walks into the house. He doesn't miss a beat when he sees his brother. From what Daniel has told me, Dylan's appearances are sporadic and rarely planned.

"When did you show up?" he asks.

"Right before your girl."

Daniel shakes his head and mutters, "I don't know why I ever thought giving you the garage code was a good idea."

"Thanks for the warm welcome," Dylan says sarcastically, but his self-satisfied expression tells me he enjoys getting under Daniel's skin.

"Are you staying here tonight?" Daniel asks.

"Nope. Just dropped by to say hey."

Daniel catches my eye and smiles. He cocks his head in the direction of the bedroom and motions for me to come with him. I follow him down the hall and he closes the door once we're both inside.

"I'm glad you came," he says.

We haven't had an evening together since the night we dined at Bella Cucina, when I fell asleep on Daniel's lap. I vow there will be no repeat of that tonight, but I'm happy to be here with him.

I sit down on the bed as Daniel takes his gun out of the holster and opens the closet door. Crouching down, he opens the door of a small safe and places the gun inside. He unclips his radio and flashlight and connects them to the chargers that sit on the dresser. He takes off his belt and hangs it up in the closet.

"I'm not really in the mood for Dylan tonight." Daniel unbuttons the shirt of his uniform and takes it off. His T-shirt and body armor follow, leaving him in just his pants. Daniel's physical attributes rarely capture my attention, but occasionally, like right now, they're hard to ignore. "I have no idea how long he'll be here," he says.

"That's okay," I say.

Daniel pauses with his hand on his zipper. "I don't mind at all if you stay, but I'm going to take off my pants."

I stand up immediately and he chuckles. "Thanks for the warning," I say, smiling. "I'll be in the living room."

Dylan has helped himself to another beer and he's slouched in the chair where we left him, looking bored. Daniel, now wearing jeans and a T-shirt, grabs his own beer from the kitchen and joins me on the couch.

"So," Dylan says. "You and Claire. Is it serious? Mom and Dad didn't mention her."

I can't believe he asked that right in front of me. It's as if he's ignoring the fact that I'm sitting right here. Ignoring it or he just doesn't care.

"You've seen them?" Daniel asks.

"I stopped by earlier."

"Wow, you really are making the rounds," Daniel says, taking a drink of his beer. He sets down the bottle. "Mom and Dad have never met Claire."

"Oh, sorry," Dylan says. He turns toward me. "Don't worry. I'm sure he'll introduce you at some point. He's very proper that way."

His patronizing tone irks me. "I'm not worried," I say.

"It's doubtful that I'll be introducing Claire," Daniel says.

"Oh come on, give it time. You'll get there eventually."

I can't be sure if Dylan's condescending attitude is genuine or just an affectation. It's like watching someone play the part of the wronged and bitter sibling in a live stage play. Like it's a game for Dylan. Look what a big asshole I can be.

"Well, I'm pretty sure we won't, because Claire is married," Daniel says.

"You're kidding," Dylan says. His eyes flick from Daniel and then back to me.

Though it probably shouldn't, it pleases me a bit that Dylan didn't see that coming.

He lets out a long, low whistle. "Wow, you've got some balls." Dylan starts laughing, like it's the funniest thing he's ever said. He leans forward, resting his elbows on his knees. "What a fascinating juxtaposition. My brother, whose sole mission in life is to catch the wrongdoers, is messing with another man's wife."

"Sorry to ruin all your fun, but we're just friends," Daniel says, clenching and unclenching his fists.

"Then those balls must be blue as hell because I can tell from all the way over here how much you want her."

He did not just say that.

In a commanding tone, the kind he must reserve for the most hardened and serious offenders, Daniel says, "Get out."

"Oh come on, Dan. Surely we can have this conversation. I mean, if there's really nothing going on between the two of you."

"Claire?" Daniel says. He doesn't want me present for the epic argument they're about to have, and I know by the tone of his voice what he's asking. Looking over at him, I nod and walk down the hallway to his bedroom. I barely get the door shut and sit down cross-legged on Daniel's bed before the fighting starts.

Their voices carry, but I can't make out every word. Either they're cognizant of the fact that I can still hear them or they're trying hard to keep it civil. It really doesn't matter because they abandon this censoring almost immediately, and it doesn't take long before Daniel really lets loose. I will not be surprised if one of them throws a punch.

"You waltz into town, show up uninvited, and make a statement like that in front of a woman you met less than an hour ago? I know you don't give a shit about anything or anyone, but what the fuck is wrong with you?"

"Touched a nerve, did I?"

"I don't need you to offer your commentary on a situation you know nothing about."

"Well, you sure seem to want to give me your opinion on how I should live my life. You judge me constantly," Dylan yells.

"That's because you make fucking horrible choices!"

"How sanctimonious of you, especially considering the circumstances of your current relationship," Dylan retaliates. "Call it whatever you want, but a married woman doesn't let herself in on a Saturday night to wait for you if you're just friends. And by the way, this shit never ends well."

"Yes, you're such an expert. You come and go whenever you feel like it and you're gone again before anyone can get too comfortable. Don't talk to me about my relationships, or how I spend my time. I've got this."

"Really? You gonna build a life with her like you had with Jessie? Is she going to leave her husband for you?"

"I didn't ask her to leave her husband," Daniel says.

"Well, if she doesn't, she's just playing you, man."

There's more than a bit of truth to this statement, and hearing it out loud stings a bit. I'm not playing Daniel, but the truth is I have no intention of ripping my family apart. I never have.

"You know what, Dylan? We're done here. I'm sure you've got someplace you need to be." Daniel sounds more resigned than angry, like the fight's been drained right out of him.

A door slams and the house goes silent. Moments later, Daniel walks into the bedroom. I swing my legs around so that I'm sitting on the edge of the bed with my feet on the floor. Before I can stand up, Daniel crosses the room and kneels down in front of me.

"I'm sorry."

"Don't be." I smile sympathetically, knowing he's probably worn out. "Are you okay?"

"Yeah." Daniel leans in a bit so that his upper body is between my legs. He places his hands flat on the bed, alongside my hips. Not quite touching them, but close. "I'm used to it. Dylan and I are never going to see eye to eye on anything. We just won't."

It's so quiet and he's so near. I fight the urge to run my fingers through his hair. "He's right," I say. "I don't think anyone would understand if they knew how much time we spent together. Our phone calls. The texts . . ." It's our thing, mine and Daniel's. I don't know any other way to explain it.

"Do you want me to stop calling you? Stop texting?" Daniel places his hands on my hips, pressing firmly, pulling me a few inches closer. The feel of his hands on me sends delicate shivers over my skin. My heart pounds and I feel the pressure, the ache, start to build between my legs. My body ignores the panicked signals my conscience is sending in favor of the more pleasurable sensations. Even more alarming, I think Daniel can sense how turned on I am. It's the way he's staring at me, observing my breathing and the flush I can feel heating my skin. I'm in way over my head, but I'm momentarily paralyzed and can't seem to make myself swim to safer waters.

I answer his question with one of my own. "What he said? Is it true?" I already know the answer; I have for months. Just because we've never acted on it doesn't mean I don't hear the desire in his voice. See it in his eyes. But I want him to say it out loud.

"Of course it's true," he says. "But it's so much more than that."

When Daniel changed my flat tire he told me that friendship was all he was interested in, but I'm not entirely certain that he was telling the truth that night. Or maybe he was, because he thought he could handle it. Just like me.

My suspicions are confirmed a moment later when he stands and pulls me to my feet. Holding me close, his arms wrapped around me, he looks me in the eye and says, "I have no right to say this, and I'd never ask you to leave him." Daniel's voice is barely a whisper, but in the dead-silent room I have no trouble hearing what he says next. "But I wish you were mine."

49

DANIEL

I watch Claire drive away after I walk her to her car. I shouldn't have said that to her. I could blame it on Dylan, but I won't. Telling Claire the truth about how I feel was the one thing I told myself I could never do if I wanted her to keep coming back. And I do want her to come back.

Once I'm back inside the house I gather up the empty beer bottles and throw them in the bin in the garage, then sit down on the couch and turn on the TV. I click aimlessly through the channels and finally shut it off.

I wanted Claire so much. I wanted to kiss her and take her clothes off and lay her down on my bed. I know she wanted me, too. I could see it in her eyes, hear it in her breathing. Not capitalizing on it was the right thing to do, but unfortunately I don't feel noble at all and I sure as hell don't feel satisfied.

I don't know what I was thinking taking things so far with Claire.

And maybe it's better that I don't keep dragging things out with a woman who belongs to someone else.

50

CLAIRE

The doorbell rings in the afternoon two days later. I open the door and find Bridget standing on my porch, tears running down her face. "What is it?" I ask.

"We're going to lose our home."

I pull her inside, confused. "What do you mean?"

"Sam lost it all. Our savings, the boys' college funds, our retirement account. Everything. He got fired six months ago."

I think back to the day when I saw the man who looked like Sam walking into the credit union.

"He thought he could hide it from me, make gambling his full-time job." She drags the sleeve of her sweatshirt across her red-rimmed eyes. "The bank will take possession of the house on Friday."

Bridget loves her home. Her style is more ornate than any of ours, even with all those boys running around. She won't spend a cent more than she needs to on her wardrobe, and jewelry isn't her thing, but she'll hunt down a bargain on cashmere throws and plush rugs. The perfect crystal sculpture or one-of-a-kind painting. Her state-of-the-art kitchen, complete with a fireplace and a small nook where she can drink a cup of coffee and read the newspaper, is her favorite room in the whole house, and she spends hours there making Sam and the boys their favorite meals.

"Oh, Bridget," I say, pulling her into my arms. She sobs and I rub her back until she calms down. When she pulls away she sighs and tucks her short hair behind her ears. "I told him the gambling stops right now. He gets help and changes his ways, or we're done."

"Did he agree?"

"Yes. He's at a Gamblers Anonymous meeting right now."

I take her by the hand and lead her into the kitchen. "Sit down. Do you want some tea?"

She shakes her head. "No thanks. I just wanted to talk to somebody."

"Do the other girls know?"

"Not yet. Can you tell them? I'm just so ashamed and embarrassed. My poor boys,

Claire. They're old enough to understand. I can't hide this from them."

"They'll be okay. Not right this second, maybe, but eventually." I hand Bridget a box of Kleenex and she wipes her eyes. "You'll get through it as a family."

"I should have paid attention. I should have taken more of an interest in our finances instead of letting Sam take care of everything. It might not have gotten so bad and I wouldn't have been blindsided. I feel so foolish."

"Where will you go?" I ask. At that moment I'm furious with Sam. How dare he take his whole family down with him?

"We'll stay with my parents for a while, but I think it's safe to say that their condo is not remotely large enough to hold all of us. If I can get back on at the hospital, I'll rent something."

I put my arm around Bridget's shoulders as the sound of her sobbing fills my kitchen, and we stay like that until she's all cried out. "I'll do anything I can to help," I say.

"Thanks, Claire."

I walk her to the door and watch as she disappears into the house that's no longer going to be hers.

Daniel is on duty, but he calls shortly before I have to go meet the school bus.

What happened the night of Dylan's visit was a big wake-up call and we're both trying hard to pretend that what he said didn't change anything.

"How's your day been?" he asks.

"Good. How about you?"

"Great. I'm just taking a quick break."

We're overly cautious on the phone. Gone is the flirting tone I hadn't even realized I'd been using until I stopped using it and noticed how different I sounded. Daniel pauses before he speaks, as if he's weighing each word, choosing the ones that won't send me fleeing. The ones that aren't so brutally honest. So heavy.

"Are you off on Thursday?" I ask.

"Yeah."

"I'll come by."

"That would be great," he says.

I can hear the relief in his voice. "I need to go meet the kids. I'll call you later."

"Okay. Have a good night."

"You, too."

When he walked me to my car last Saturday night he asked me point-blank if I'd be back. "I'll understand if you say no."

I wasn't sure if I could. Realizing how close I'd come to crossing a line that would cause serious repercussions in my marriage had shaken me. Brought to light just how naïve I'd been. Because if Daniel hadn't remained a gentleman, hadn't been the one to end the embrace and take a literal step backward like he did, I'm not sure what would have happened.

"I need a few days," I said.

"Of course. Take as long as you need."

Everything feels different and there are so many things to think about. Most overwhelming is the guilt I feel about what I almost did, what I very much *wanted* to do in the heat of the moment. Then there's my sadness over losing a friend, because what I had with Daniel now feels awkward, broken. If we can get back on track, put what happened behind us, then we might be okay.

I'm not sure if we can. And I'm not sure if we should.

51

CLAIRE

That night, the door creaks slightly as someone creeps into the bedroom. In the pitch-black darkness I sense movement beside the bed and I climb toward wakefulness.

"Who's there?" I ask groggily.

"Mommy, I don't feel good," Jordan says.

I sit up and swing my legs over the side of the bed, gathering her in my arms. Pushing her hair back, I lay my cheek on her forehead. She feels feverish. I pull her into the bed and lay her head gently down on the pillow. "I'll be right back. Mommy's going to get some medicine, okay?"

She moans softly. "Okay."

I keep our drugs in the kitchen, on a cupboard shelf up high and out of reach. I'm relieved when I spot a half-full bottle of Children's Motrin and I hurry upstairs. Jordan squeezes her eyes shut when I turn on the lamp that sits on my nightstand.

"I'll turn it off as soon as you take this," I say, measuring out a dose and holding the medicine cup to her lips.

"Is it bubble gum?" she asks, as I help her sit up. "I don't like the purple kind."

"Yes," I answer.

She swallows the pink liquid and lies back down, flopping listlessly onto the pillow.

"Does your head hurt? Or your throat?" I ask.

"My head," she says. "And my tummy."

Uh-oh. I grab the garbage can from the bathroom and put it beside the bed. I turn off the light and stretch out next to her, pulling the covers over both of us. "It'll take a little while for the medicine to kick in," I say, stroking her hair. "You can stay with me, okay?"

"Okay."

I hold her until her breathing deepens and I think she's almost asleep, but then she sits bolt upright and I have just enough time to get the garbage can underneath her before she vomits. Jordan hates to puke more than anything, and she starts to cry.

"It's okay, baby," I say, as I lead her into the bathroom and fill a cup with water so she can rinse out her mouth. "Feel better?"

"Yeah," she says.

"Maybe now you can rest."

We crawl back into bed, and I hold her until we both drift off to sleep.

In the morning, I let her sleep while I make Josh's breakfast. I tell him his sister will be staying home and at eight I walk him to the bus stop.

"Where's Jordan?" Elisa asks.

"Stomach flu. I think she might be running a low-grade temp, too. Her forehead was pretty warm this morning." I glance over my shoulder at my house, nervous at leaving her inside. If she wakes up, she'll wonder where I am.

"Poor thing," Elisa says. "Go home. Julia and I will make sure Josh gets on the bus."

"Thanks."

Jordan is still sleeping, sprawled out in the middle of the king-size bed. I let her be and check my phone. There's a text from Daniel.

Good morning. What do you have planned for today?

I text him back. *Jordan isn't feeling well. I might not get much of anything done, other than keeping her comfortable.*

He responds a few minutes later. *That's too bad. Hope she feels better soon.*

I also text Chris. *Jordan has the stomach flu. I kept her home today.* I don't get a response because he's undoubtedly in the middle of a presentation or a meeting. He'll respond when he can. He always does eventually, especially if it's in regard to the kids.

Jordan wakes around 10:00 A.M. and doesn't want anything to eat. Her forehead feels hot and she says she's achy, so I give her another dose of Motrin and convince her to try some cold apple juice. She drinks half the juice and settles back down on the pillow, her eyes glassy. I turn on the TV, find a station playing cartoons, and take a quick shower, leaving the bathroom door open in case she calls out to me. The Motrin must have kicked in because when I come out of the bathroom wrapped in a towel, she's sleeping soundly again.

Daniel calls at noon. "How's Jordan doing?" he asks.

"She kept down her apple juice and she's sleeping now."

"Do you need anything?"

I'm running a little low on Motrin, but I don't want Daniel stopping by in the middle of the day. Elisa probably has an extra bottle, and if she doesn't, she'll gladly pick some up for me. "No. Thanks for asking, though." I lean over and brush Jordan's hair off her forehead, still blissfully cool. "I'll keep her home again tomorrow if she's still running a fever."

"I hope she feels better."

"She'll be fine. It's probably just a virus."

"I'll text you later," he says.

"Okay."

I bring my laptop upstairs and plug it into the outlet behind my nightstand. I tap away while Jordan sleeps. She stirs around three thirty, sits straight up, and vomits all over the bed. I scoop her into my arms and run toward the bathroom, holding her hair back as she dry-heaves into the toilet. Her forehead sizzles. I can tell when my children have a fever just by touching their skin, but I wipe her mouth, lay her down on the dry side of the bed, and rush downstairs to grab the ear thermometer. I gently insert the tip into Jordan's ear and when it beeps I'm relieved to see that it's only 102. I can handle that.

The vomiting and the fever have worn her out and she remains listless while I strip the sheets and comforter out from under her, balling them up so I can transport everything to the laundry room without making a huge mess. I retrieve her purple fleece blanket from her room and lay it gently over her, tucking it around her shoulders. Grabbing my phone from the nightstand, I thumb through my contacts and call Elisa.

"Can you get Josh from the bus stop?" I ask. "And do you by chance have any Children's Motrin?"

"I'm guessing Jordan still isn't feeling well," she says. "How's the fever?"

"It's still high and she just puked again. Spectacularly. She's miserable."

"I'll let Josh know what's up, and I'll send the Motrin home with him."

"Thanks."

I text Chris to give him an update on Jordan. He responds five minutes later with a phone call.

"Is she okay?" he asks when I answer, and I hear the concern in his voice.

"She's better now. I'm going to try and keep her hydrated and comfortable until this runs its course."

"I need to get back into my meeting. Let me know how she's doing, okay?"

"Okay."

A door slams downstairs and moments later Josh barrels into the room. "Is Jordan still sick, Mom?" he asks, thrusting a bottle of Motrin into my hands and flopping down on the bed.

"Yes, and she has some sort of stomach bug, so keep your distance," I warn.

He scoots away from Jordan and then puts

even more space between them by climbing off of the bed and heading toward the bedroom door. "I'm gonna go play with Travis, okay?"

"Backyard only. I don't want you in front since I can't be out there with you. Be home by six."

"Okay," he says.

I pick up Jordan and carefully navigate the stairs. The couch in the family room will have to do so I can make dinner and still keep an eye on her.

I urge Jordan to try some 7Up and saltines. She makes a valiant attempt but stops after two small sips and a tiny nibble of the cracker. I don't blame her; better safe than sorry where the stomach is concerned.

I pop in a Disney DVD and run upstairs to put clean sheets and an old comforter on the bed. I return with the soiled bedding and start a load in the washing machine. Dinner will consist of grilled cheese sandwiches and tomato soup, I decide. Though it's more of a winter meal, both kids enjoy it and it's easy to prepare.

Josh comes in as I'm setting the table. He pulls out a chair and drops into it. "I'm starving," he says.

"Go wash your hands first."

He protests but scrapes his chair back and

washes up at the kitchen sink. I set a grilled cheese sandwich on his plate and sprinkle goldfish crackers into his soup. He smiles. He notices the can of 7Up on the counter. "Can I have some pop, too?"

"Yes, since it's open. I don't think your sister is up for it." I pour the remainder of the can into his glass.

I give Jordan more Motrin. She declines my offer of dinner, but a half hour later, when the medicine has kicked in, she manages a few more crackers and drinks some 7Up. I start to relax and pray we're over the hump.

Daniel calls when the kids and I are in the middle of a movie so I let it go to voice mail. I call him back later, when both kids are in bed and I've texted Chris with an update and climbed between my clean sheets. "How's it going? Is Jordan feeling any better?"

"A little." I bring him up to speed on her symptoms.

"Let me know if you need me to bring you anything, okay?"

"I will."

We say goodnight and I watch TV for a while. At 10:00 P.M. I check on the kids one more time. Josh's legs are tangled in his sheets and his head hangs halfway off the bed. I rearrange him and pull the covers up. Jordan's forehead feels cool and her breathing is deep and steady.

I turn out the hallway lights, go to the bathroom one last time, and climb into bed, happy to put this day behind me.

All hell breaks loose in the middle of the night. Jordan's cries wake me, and I rush to her bedroom. She's heaving into the garbage can I put next to her bed, just in case. Her stomach doesn't have much in it, so it isn't long before the vomiting subsides. I should have known this wasn't over.

I help her into the bathroom and wipe her face. She rinses her mouth out when I hand her a Dixie cup of water, swishing and spitting. I'm just about to walk her back to bed when Josh runs through the doorway and barfs at our feet, spraying us both. The sight and smell of all that tomato soup in reverse triggers my gag reflex, and it's only sheer will that keeps me from spontaneously emptying the contents of my own stomach.

I move Jordan out of the way and position Josh's head over the toilet. Reaching over, I turn on the shower and strip off Jordan's nightgown. Once I settle her under the spray I rub Josh's back and wait until he's finished. I flush the toilet and close the lid. "Sit here," I say. I pull back the shower curtain and make sure Jordan is clean, then wrap her in a fluffy towel. "Get in the shower, Josh. I'm going to take Jordan to her room." He nods his head and strips off his pajama shirt. Jordan is almost asleep by the time I tuck her in. I quickly clean the bathroom floor, pull the puke-filled plastic liner out of her garbage can, and walk it down to the garage.

Josh is out of the shower and standing in the hallway, wrapped in a towel.

"Let's get some clean pajamas," I say.

He follows me into his room. I place the back of my hand against his forehead, but he's only a little warm. I decide to hold off on the Motrin in case he's not done vomiting. "Do you think you can go back to sleep?" I ask.

He nods and I give him a quick hug. He'll want privacy to change, so I tell him to come get me if he feels sick again.

I strip off my own clothes in the master bathroom and take a quick shower. My laundry pile will be astronomical tomorrow, but I'll worry about that in the morning. Clean and dry, I burrow under the covers and fall asleep. I awaken a while later and glance at the clock: 4:00 A.M.

My stomach churns and I have just enough time to sprint toward the bathroom before everything comes up.

In the morning, the kids are lethargic and feverish but I'm temporarily spared more vomiting because neither of them will eat. I don't blame them. I force down what I have to in order to keep my blood sugar steady and wait to see if it was a bad idea. I throw it right back up. I text Chris to give him an update on the kids and he writes back expressing his concern and asking me to keep him posted.

Daniel texts me a short time later. *How is everything going?*

We're all sick now. I'm placing our house under quarantine.

He texts back immediately. *Is there anything I can do?*

No thanks. We'll be fine. It just has to run its course.

The kids and I spend the day cuddled together on the large sectional in the family room. The washing machine runs around the clock because the vomiting has resumed and Josh and Jordan do not always grab the garbage can or make it to the bathroom in time. Around 8:00 P.M., I tuck the kids into bed and hope they both sleep through the night.

I feel awful. I can't keep anything down,

so I have to keep adjusting my insulin. I'm so incredibly thirsty but the water comes right back up when I try to drink it. I haven't eaten anything in almost twenty-four hours. It's been years since I had the stomach flu, and I've forgotten how miserable it can be.

When I walk downstairs Tucker is standing by the front door, waiting for me to let him out. I open it and notice the bag sitting on the front steps. Curious, I open it up and spot a six-pack of Diet 7Up, saltines, and a bottle of Children's Motrin. I smile because I know who left it.

I send Daniel a text. *Thank you.*

He responds five minutes later. *You're welcome.*

I won't be able to come tomorrow. I'm sorry.

That's okay. Just take care of yourself. I'll see you when you're feeling better.

By the time Chris walks in the door the following evening, the kids are over the worst of it. He finds them sprawled on the couch, eating crackers and sipping juice, Disney Channel blaring.

He gives them a hug, smoothing back Jordan's hair and squeezing Josh's shoulder. "You guys feeling better?" he asks.

They answer in unison, "Yes."

Chris looks over at me. I'm barely holding

my eyes open because I haven't slept more than a few hours at a time in the last twenty-four.

"You look really tired, Claire."

I nod. It takes all the energy I have.

He peers at me closely, realization dawning on his face. "Did you have it, too?"

"Yes." I still have it. I haven't been able to eat anything today and my raging thirst drives me to drink even though I know it will only come right back up.

"Why didn't you tell me?" he asks.

I answer honestly. "I don't know. I guess I didn't think there was any way you could come home." Now that I know the kind of scrutiny Chris is under, I'm more sympathetic to the amount of work he's responsible for. "I would have called my mom if I couldn't handle it." I can tell by his expression that the words hurt a little.

He sighs, blowing out a breath as he looks around the living room. "There are more important things than work," he says softly. He loosens his tie and sits down on the couch next to Jordan, stroking her hair. He looks at me. "Go lie down."

He doesn't have to tell me twice. I go upstairs and slip under the covers, but thirty seconds later I hurry to the bathroom because I have to throw up again. After I rinse my mouth I fill a cup at the bathroom sink and drink it down, trying desperately to quench my thirst. My lips are cracked and the inside of my mouth is so dry I can barely swallow. I just want to drink, drink, drink until I can't hold any more. My digestive system rejects the water almost immediately and I throw up in the sink. After I wipe my mouth with a towel I sink to the floor, resting my head against the bathroom wall, breathing rapidly. I pull out my pump and check my blood glucose. I blink because there's no way that number is right. It's way too high.

I tell myself that I have to stand up, to find the strength to walk downstairs and let Chris know that something is really wrong.

52

Claire

I open my eyes and squint because the lights above my head are blinding. My throat feels scratchy and sore and at first when I try to speak no words will come out. Lifting my head from the pillow takes a herculean effort and halfway through it my mom says, "Claire!"

I hear her, but I can't see her. She's somewhere off to the right, just out of reach of my peripheral vision, and my movement has apparently startled her. I let my head drop back down onto the pillow as she takes my hand in hers.

"Claire." Chris's voice sounds just as worried and frantic as my mom's. He leans over the bed and tries to draw me into his embrace, which is difficult because I'm still flat on my back.

I've never been so confused in my life.

There are IV needles taped to the back of

both hands and the strong antiseptic smell alone is enough to confirm that I'm in the hospital. But that's really all I know for sure.

"Do you want some water?" Chris asks.

I nod and he helps me sit up. He holds the glass and puts the bendy straw in my mouth. It's heavenly. He lays me back down when I'm done.

"DKA?" I ask.

Chris nods, his expression grim. "Yes. You're in the ICU."

Diabetic ketoacidosis is a potentially life-threatening condition that can develop in people who have type 1 diabetes. I didn't realize that the vomiting — one of the main symptoms of DKA — was no longer due to my stomach flu but rather because my blood sugar had reached a critically high level. It had happened to me once before, when I was twelve years old and first diagnosed. If Chris hadn't found me in time, I could have fallen into a coma, or worse.

"What happened?" I ask.

"I went upstairs to check on you. You were lying on your side, not moving. You'd thrown up on the floor and Tucker was barking, like he knew something was wrong. I tried to rouse you but you were so out of it I called 911."

"How long have I been here?" I ask.

"Two days," Chris says. He's still standing over my bed, looking down at me. Finally he sits, scooting his chair close to me.

"What's the last thing you remember, honey?" my mom asks.

The question frustrates me because no matter how hard I try, I can't answer it. "I don't know, Mom." I look around the room. "Where are the kids?"

"They're with your dad," my mom says. "He took them to the cafeteria."

This five-minute conversation has exhausted me. "I'm so tired," I say.

"Just get some rest," Chris says. "Don't worry about anything else."

My eyes are heavy and I fight the sleep, but the voices sound farther and farther away and I drift off.

I don't know what time it is when I wake up again, but the inky black darkness I see outside the small window on the other side of the room tells me that it's nighttime.

Chris is asleep, slumped in a chair that's pushed as close to my bed as the railing will allow. He stirs when I say his name and then leans over me, brushing the hair back from my face. "I'm here," he says.

I reach for his hand and squeeze, my grip so weak he probably can't feel it. But he must because he squeezes back and doesn't let go of my hand.

"I'm so wiped out," I say.

"The doctor said you will be, for a while."

"What day is it?" Maybe he told me already, but I can't remember.

"Saturday." He glances at his watch. "Well, technically it's now Sunday."

I have no memory of anything that happened after Chris got home on Thursday. It doesn't help that no matter how hard I try, I can't seem to hold back the tears. They spill from my eyes and run down my cheeks. I'm so tired of being out of control emotionally. Physically now, too.

"What is it?" he asks.

"My sugars were high. I should have known what was happening. I just thought it was taking me longer to shake the flu. I should have called my mom or said something to you when you came home. I should have been more aware. It's my responsibility to manage my disease."

"You walk a tightrope, Claire. You told me that a long time ago. You just need someone there to catch you when you fall."

A nurse comes in to take my vital signs. "Your condition is definitely improving. Are you feeling a little better?" she asks.

"Yes," I say. "Just tired."

"Everything looks good. The doctor will

probably talk to you about being discharged when he does his rounds in the morning."

"Okay."

After she leaves Chris tucks the covers around me. "Are you warm enough? Do you need anything?"

I try to answer him, but I fall back asleep before the words can come out.

In the morning, the doctor says I can go home tomorrow. He wants to keep me one more day, to make sure that my blood sugar remains stable. "We'll transition you back to your pump today," he says. "You can try some solid food and we'll see how you do."

Later that day, they let my parents bring the kids in for a short visit. "Go get something to eat," I tell Chris. He's been by my side since I was admitted, and he definitely needs a break.

I'm grateful that the IVs have been removed and that there is nothing particularly frightening for Josh and Jordan to see. They rush toward my bed and I embrace them. I can't hold back the tears when I think about how scared they must have been when the ambulance took me away.

"Why are you crying, Mommy?" Jordan asks.

"Because I've missed you guys. I can't

wait to come home."

"When are you getting out of here?"

I wipe my eyes and smile at her. "Daddy's going to bring me home tomorrow."

"Yay," she says. She tucks her gray kitty in next to me, then glances at it longingly, as if she might change her mind. Deciding I can keep it, she takes a few steps back so Josh can move in closer.

"Hey, buddy."

"Hi, Mom." He leans down and gives me a kiss. "There was a policeman at the house. When the ambulance came. It wasn't Officer Rush, though. I don't know who it was. He stayed until Elisa came to get us."

Daniel. Oh, God. He must be absolutely frantic. I calm myself with the knowledge that he would do whatever it took to figure out what happened to me. I know he would.

"Good. I'm glad he was there to help. Everyone did exactly what they were supposed to do to make sure I got the care I needed. Be good for Grandma and Grandpa, okay? I'll be home before you know it."

"We will," they say.

"I brought you some things from home," my mom says. She sets down a large tote bag near the bed. "There are clean clothes and your toiletries. I put your slippers and a few other things in there, too."

"Thanks, Mom."

My parents leave with the kids and Chris comes back from the cafeteria. "You just missed everyone," I say.

"I saw them in the hallway."

"Did you eat?" I ask.

"Yeah. I had a sandwich. It was actually pretty good."

"You were probably just really hungry."

The nurse comes in and I ask her if I can take a shower, now that I'm not attached to the various drips.

"Sure, honey," she says. "That will feel good."

Chris helps me out of bed and catches me around the waist when my knees buckle. I lean on him and take deep breaths until I'm steady. In the bathroom, I brush my teeth while Chris shuts the door and turns on the shower, waiting for the water to run warm. When I'm done brushing he strips off my hospital gown as if I'm a child. I shiver but the steam that has filled the room warms my bare skin. The walk to the bathroom and the exhausting prospect of standing long enough to wash my hair and body overwhelms me before I've even begun, and when I step into the shower I stand motionless under the spray, my limbs as useless as spaghetti. There's a built-in bench, so I sit down. Just for a minute.

"Claire?" Chris pulls back the curtain to check on me. "Are you okay?"

I'm pathetically incapable of attending to this most basic task. No matter how hard I try, I can't seem to stand back up. "Yes. I'm just resting for a minute."

I watch as Chris takes off his clothes and steps into the shower. He squirts the shampoo into his hand and when he massages my scalp I almost fall asleep. The hospital-issue washcloth is rough but the soap and water on my skin feel wonderful. He washes and rinses me and then washes himself while I remain on the bench, my head tilted to the side and resting on the shower wall.

"Stay here," he says. When he's dressed again he pulls back the curtain and shuts off the water. He pats my hair and skin gently with a towel and wraps my pink bathrobe around me. "I have your slippers. Step into them."

Chris tucks me back into bed and pulls the covers up. I've done my best to take care of everything at home while he's been on the road all these months, but I can't even shower without assistance and I'm going to need his help. For the last month, he's been flying out on Sunday evenings. I don't want him to go.

"You're not leaving tonight, are you?"

"No." I hear so many things in his voice: surprise, pain, sorrow. "I already told them I'd be out all week."

"You did?"

"Yes." He clenches the sheets in his fists. "You asked me once, 'what is the worst thing that could happen?' And it isn't being unemployed. Or having to sell the house. Or the cars. Or any of those things. I thought it was, but it's not. The worst thing that could happen to me is if something happened to you. Nothing matters but you and the kids."

"Do you still love me?" I ask suddenly.

"Of course I do." He looks confused and hurt, as if my words have cut him to the bone. "Why would you ask such a thing?"

"Because you haven't said it in a long time. And sometimes I still need to hear it to know that it's true."

"I love you, Claire. I always will."

"I love you, too."

He brings my hand to his lips, kisses the back of it, and holds it close to his cheek. He lowers the railing on the bed, and I pull him closer.

I stroke his damp hair, knowing that Chris is the one who needs reassuring now.

53

CHRIS

Claire has fallen asleep again and she doesn't wake up when the doctor walks into the room fifteen minutes later. He shakes my hand and keeps his voice low.

"Your wife is doing great," he says, flipping through her chart. "Blood glucose looks good, there's been no recurrence of ketosis, and she's done fine with the switch back to her pump. She can go home tomorrow."

"Great," I say. "That's wonderful to hear."

"I'll be back in the morning to go over some discharge instructions," he says before he leaves the room.

"Okay."

This report is a vast improvement compared to what they told me shortly after Claire and I arrived at the emergency room. She was barely conscious and they said if I hadn't found her when I did, the outcome could have been tragic.

She asked me if I was going to leave. I could see it on her face, the fear that I might actually get on a plane tonight like I have for the last month. Despite the fact that we were having this conversation while she was lying in a hospital bed.

What the hell kind of husband would leave his wife alone after something like this?

She thought you might, Chris.

And if that didn't drive home just how badly I need to make some changes, then I don't know what would. The image of her lying on the bathroom floor and thinking about what might have happened if I hadn't been home sends me over the edge.

I walk into the bathroom, shut the door, lean my head back against it, and cry.

54

DANIEL

Claire didn't respond to any of my texts, and all my calls went straight to voice mail. Fearing the worst, I made myself wait twenty-four hours and then I started calling the hospitals. I got lucky on the first try when the woman who answered the phone at Shawnee Mission Medical Center confirmed that there was a person admitted the day before by the name of Claire Canton. They couldn't tell me anything other than she was a patient, but I still felt relieved. The obvious reason for her dropping off the radar like that was her diabetes, but if she's under medical care, then at least I'm no longer thinking the worst.

That was two days ago. Now I'm waiting for her to call me. I know she will as soon as she's able. Part of me wanted to go down there, find out her room number, and see for myself that she was okay. But I couldn't do that to her because as far as I know, her husband still doesn't know about me.

And I sure as hell don't think he'd understand why I was there.

55

CLAIRE

I wake up the next morning when a nurse comes in to take my vital signs. Chris is still asleep, slumped over in the chair. My mom walks in a few minutes later and my spirits lift instantly.

"Hi," I say. I keep my voice low so I don't wake Chris. "What time is it?" For some inexplicable reason, my room does not have a clock. I've lost all sense of time, especially since I can't remember parts of my stay here, and I sleep in frequent, random intervals.

"A little after eight," she says, bending down to give me a kiss. "Your dad will be here with the kids in about an hour. He's taking them to breakfast at McDonald's. Did the doctor say what time he'd be discharging you today?"

"Chris talked to him last night, while I was taking one of my many naps. I should be able to go home around noon."

Chris wakes up when he hears us talking, stretching his legs out in front of him. He rises from the chair and approaches the bed. Resting one hand on the rail, he bends down and gives me a quick peck on the mouth. I like the kissing. It reminds me of before: before Chris lost his job, before I lost Chris. He used to kiss me all the time.

"How are you feeling?" he asks.

"Good. I'm ready to get out of here."

"I'm going to run home and take a quick shower. I'll be back to get you."

"Okay."

Chris returns an hour later, in time to listen as the doctor goes over my discharge instructions. When he tells me I'm free to go we start to gather my things.

"I brought your phone," Chris says, handing it to me. "The battery was dead, so I plugged it in while I was in the shower. Looks like you've got enough of a charge to check your messages. I'm sure you have some."

My stomach drops and my heart starts pounding as I pocket the phone, wondering whether Chris looked at the text history or the call log. He wouldn't normally, but maybe he did this time because of the circumstances. He doesn't seem angry or upset, though; he's acting quite calm. Because he was gone so often I never really worried about Chris seeing a message from Daniel, and therefore, I never really had to face just how duplicitous it was. I realize I wouldn't feel the way I'm feeling right now, wouldn't feel the guilt and shame, if Chris knew about my friendship with Daniel. If I'd told Chris about him instead of hiding everything. "Thanks," I say.

He smiles at me and we ride the elevator down to the lobby.

"Stay here," he says, pointing to a bench near the door. "I'm going to bring the car around."

"Okay." I watch him walk away and then I pull my phone out of my pocket. After I punch in the code I listen. The first five voice mails are from Daniel. His voice sounds progressively more panicked as I listen to, and delete, each one. The last one says he's called the hospitals and knows I'm alive. "I'm really scared, Claire."

There are also seven missed calls and six texts from him. I tap out a quick reply. *I'm okay. I'm so sorry you were worried.*

He responds immediately. *Are you home?*

Not yet. I'm about to leave the hospital. I'll call when I can.

I'll be waiting. Take care of yourself.

I won't be able to see Daniel anymore, and I've known this since he told me he wished I was his. You can't go back to simply being friends after a declaration like that. And if my precarious mortality was the wake-up call Chris needed, the things he told me in response were mine. It will take both of us working together to repair this relationship.

Maybe I should come clean about my friendship with Daniel. Get it out in the open. Accept whatever ramifications come my way. But I know Chris will not understand my friendship with Daniel. Neither would I if he told me there was a woman he kept in nearly constant contact with. A woman he laughed with. A woman whose words brightened his day. A woman he told his secrets to. A woman who knew of his heartache. Would he believe me if I tell him that Daniel was just a friend?

I may have never physically cheated on Chris with Daniel, but I wanted to and that's almost as bad. What's worse is that I gave Daniel the things I should be giving only to my husband, whether he was giving them back to me at the time or not: my emotions, my attention, my adoration, my desire. I have to be one hundred percent present in this marriage, and I can't be if

I'm sharing my time with Daniel. If I'm sharing anything with him at all.

Chris pulls up in front of the hospital and walks in to get me. He picks up my tote bag and puts his arm around my shoulders. Smiling down at me, he says, "Ready?"

I smile back. "Ready."

56

Claire

Chris spends the next week by my side. He works but he does it while he's sitting next to me on the couch, my feet in his lap. He closes the laptop while we watch a movie. He talks to me, hugs me, kisses me. He sleeps with me in his arms.

Daniel hasn't texted. He must know that the reason I'm not calling is because I'm not alone. The space he gives me, the demands he doesn't make, make me feel even worse for what I'm going to do.

I wish everything could remain status quo, but it can't.

It isn't fair to Daniel.

It isn't fair to Chris.

And I should have never let it go on so long.

Finally, when Chris has gone back out on the road and the house is empty, I pick up my phone and call him. "Hi," I say when he answers.

"Hi." Even over the phone, I know he is smiling. I can hear it in his voice. "How are you?"

"I'm much better," I say.

"I'm so glad."

"I'm sorry it's taken me so long to call."

"Don't be."

"What days are you off this week?"

"Thursday and Friday."

"Can I come on Thursday?"

"Of course."

"Okay."

"I feel like you're coming to tell me goodbye," he says.

It's hard for me to get the word out. "Yes."

"Then let's make this last day count. Can you do that?"

The tears start falling. "Of course. I can do that."

On Thursday I slide behind the wheel of my car and back out of the garage. The sun is shining brightly but the air still feels brisk. When I first met Daniel it was summertime. We haven't come full circle yet, but warmer weather is on the horizon.

Every other time I've driven to Daniel's it seemed as if it took forever, but today's drive is over in no time at all, and soon I'm pulling into his driveway. My heart feels as heavy as my footsteps when I park the car and walk up the steps. He waits in the open doorway, watching as I approach. He's smiling, but it's a subdued smile.

I smile, too. "Hi."

"Hi," he says. I put my arms around him and hug him tight. His arms encircle me and we stand like that for a minute, not speaking. Finally, we let go. He closes the door behind me and I follow him to the couch. My favorite blanket is folded neatly and draped over the arm. I'm not surprised; I'm the only one who ever used it.

"I've been so worried about you," he says.

"I know," I say. I tell him what happened, explain about the DKA.

"Is he taking care of you?" Daniel asks. "Making sure you're okay?"

"Yes. He stayed home for a week. He's back at work now."

Daniel nods and looks away. I know what he's thinking: If you were my wife, I would never leave you home alone, especially after something like this. But he would. He just doesn't know it. Chris didn't want to leave either, but I told him he had to. The world doesn't stop spinning because I got sick.

I take a look around the room I've spent so much time in. It's a room where there are no lost jobs or marital discord. No one discusses paying the bills or argues about whose turn it is to take out the trash. We brought the best, the most uncomplicated, aspects of our world into this room. Who wouldn't want that? But we fooled ourselves into thinking that our relationship was uncomplicated because of it.

"Do you want to go for a ride?" he asks. "It might be a little cold."

I smile. "Going for a ride is exactly what I want to do."

So we go. It's not a long ride, but I hold him tight and try to remember every detail: The way the sun shines down on us. The air that smells like fresh soil as the hard ground softens and readies itself for the grass and flowers. The way his shoulders feel when I lay my head on them. When I look back on this day I want to remember it all, no matter how much it hurts.

When we get back Daniel parks the bike in the driveway. I climb off and wait for him to do the same. We both know it's time for me to go. He stands in front of me and I look into his eyes.

"If things had been different, I would have given my whole heart to you."

He nods and gives me a smile. "I know."

My eyes fill with tears. "Good-bye, Daniel."

"Good-bye, Claire." He doesn't walk me to the car the way he always has before.

I'm almost at my door when I stop and turn back around. To hell with this reserve, this formality. I want a messy, emotional good-bye, to let everything that's been pent up inside of me out.

I could have loved this man. Maybe I already do.

It's as if he knows what I'm going to do because he opens his arms at the exact moment I start to run. He catches me when I jump, and I wrap my legs around him and hug him tightly. The tears start to fall. When he finally sets me down and both of my feet are back on the ground, he holds my gaze and I know what he's going to do, but I don't stop him. He takes my face in his hands, leans down, and slowly presses his lips to mine. The kiss is brief, gentle. Filled with love and longing and what will never be.

"I don't regret a single minute that we spent together," he says.

"Neither do I."

He wipes my tears and this time I make it all the way to my car. When I pull out of the driveway I head toward home, and I don't look back.

57

DANIEL

I watch Claire drive away. I've always been fairly certain that this day would come, but that doesn't make it hurt any less. I tell myself it doesn't matter that I laid my cards on the table; she was never available in the first place and she never tried to make me think she was.

It will be hard not knowing how she's doing. If she's okay. That was the hardest thing about losing Jessie. The way she felt about me didn't change the way I felt about her, and it didn't mean that I stopped caring. I let her go only because I thought it was what she wanted.

Claire's the second woman in a row that I've lost and I don't know how much more of this I can take.

58

Claire

I'm quiet the next morning when Elisa and I drive to yoga. I wait until we're seated on our mats before I tell her about Daniel. "I'm not going to spend time with Daniel anymore."

"You're not?"

"No. It turns out that men and women can't be friends. Not really," I say.

Elisa takes a drink from her water bottle. "How do you feel about that?"

"Sad. There's this space that he used to occupy and now it's empty." I stretch my arms over my head and exhale. "It was the right thing to do, though."

"Are you going to tell Chris about Daniel?"

"I don't know. I don't want to hurt him, and I'm not sure what would hurt him more: telling him about it now that it's over, or not telling him about it at all." The instructor is moments away from starting the class when I say, “Elisa?”

She looks over at me. “Yes?”

“Do you think it’s possible to love more than one person? At the same time?”

“I think just about anything is possible when it comes to love,” she says.

59

CHRIS

It's late when I get back to my hotel room. I'm so goddamned tired of key cards, plastic-wrapped glasses, and ice buckets that I'd be happy to never see another hotel room again. They even have a smell I can't stand. I don't know what it is, only that it doesn't smell remotely like home.

Being back out on the road these last three weeks, after staying home with Claire and the kids, has been hard. Jim made a big deal of welcoming me back and asking about Claire during our last conference call, but that was for the benefit of the twenty other people who were also on the line. I know this because when I called him from the hospital to tell him I was taking a week off he acted like a complete dick.

"It isn't a good time, Chris," he said.

"This is my wife, Jim. I'm staying home." Fuck him. It makes me nervous to leave

Claire alone now. It's been so long since there was a problem that I got way too comfortable. If I hadn't found her in time . . . well. I still can't get it out of my head.

Claire assured me that she would be fine. "Mom and Dad will be checking on me," she said. "Elisa is close by."

I haven't said anything to Claire yet, but I've been spending a lot of time with Seth, one of the senior software engineers who's been traveling with us and assisting the implementation team. He joined me for drinks one night and we started talking. He doesn't say much, but when he does open his mouth, what comes out is brilliant. What he told me the other day, what we stayed up until 4:00 A.M. discussing, blew me away. The possibility of what it could mean for Seth, for me, for my family, is the only thing that's keeping me motivated right now.

I loosen my tie and sit down on the bed to call Claire. "Hey. How are you?" I ask when she answers.

"I'm fine," she says. "Feeling good. Are you at the hotel?"

"Just got back. We took the clients out. Some sports bar they wanted to go to. Same old shit," I say. "How are the kids?"

"They're good. Josh is building a volcano

for science class."

"The kind with the vinegar and baking soda?"

"Oh, yeah. It's a regular rite of passage."

"How about my daughter?"

"She's okay. A little quiet tonight. She spent a long time in her room rearranging her stuffed animals. I think it soothes her."

Jordan struggles the most with my absence. I sigh and walk over to the fridge. Use the opener to pry the cap off a bottle.

"Minibar?" Claire asks.

"Amstel," I say.

"Everything will be fine," she says.

"Yeah." I'm no longer satisfied with fine. I used to be, but I'm not anymore. "You should get some sleep. It's getting late."

"Okay," she says. "I'll see you when you get home."

"Sleep tight," I say.

"You, too."

Later, when I've shut my laptop and I'm lying in my hotel bed alone I think about Claire and how much I've missed her. I think about how Jim says, "Jump," and until now, I've always said, "How high?" All this for a man who couldn't understand why I wanted to stay home with my wife after she almost died. If I hadn't pulled my head out of my own ass and figured out what was really important, how long would it have taken before I turned into someone just like him?

60

CLAIRE

I lift the lid on the pot and inhale the smell of basil and tomatoes. The water in the other pot is just coming to a bubble and I grab the box of pasta out of the cupboard. After giving the marinara a final stir, I turn the heat down to low and replace the lid. The door that leads from the garage into the kitchen opens. "Wipe your feet," I say, without turning around. It rained earlier and the kids have been tracking in mud ever since they got home from school.

"It's me," Chris says. I didn't hear his car pull in, and I whip around, surprised that he's home so early on a Friday.

"I thought you weren't supposed to land until eight?"

"I wanted to get home sooner," he says, setting down his suitcase and his laptop. "I had to fly standby, but I got lucky." Yawning and rubbing his eyes, he joins me at the stove and lifts the lid on the marinara, inhaling just like I did moments earlier. "That smells good."

"I used your mom's recipe," I say. "It's the best." I dump the pasta into the water that's finally come to a rolling boil and set the timer. "I thought I'd be heating it up for you hours from now."

Chris loosens his tie and says, "Nope. I can eat with you and the kids tonight." He removes the tie completely, throws it on the island, and unbuttons the top two buttons on his shirt. "Are they outside?" he asks.

"They're at Elisa's, playing with Travis."

I cross the kitchen to the cupboard where I keep my colander and after I locate it I set it near the edge of the sink. I need a bowl for the pasta and I finally spot the one I want on a high shelf, but I can't quite reach it even when I'm standing on my tiptoes.

Chris walks up behind me and reaches over my shoulder to grab the bowl. His front is pressed up against my back and he doesn't move after he sets the bowl on the counter. We don't speak and suddenly the only sound in the kitchen is the sound of our breathing. He uses one hand to brush my hair to the side and then nuzzles my neck.

"I came home early because I missed you,

and I couldn't stop thinking about you. The other night, when we talked on the phone — after we hung up I laid in that hotel room bed all alone and I couldn't remember what you smelled like. How you taste. I couldn't remember, Claire."

His words make me feel cherished and I want to stand there in the kitchen with his arms wrapped around me and just bask in them. But then something shifts and I feel him. I *feel* what he's saying, and the physical side takes over. The side that wants him the way I always have. My desire pushes his affection away and replaces it with something more primal.

Chris flutters a series of soft kisses along my neck and pulls the collar of my shirt to the side so he can reach my shoulder. And he is hard. Very hard. I can tell how much he wants me and a wave of desire reaches the innermost parts of my body. Turning me around, he cups my face in his hands and kisses me as if his life depended on it. I kiss him with just as much intensity, my tongue meeting his and our mouths moving instinctively into the right position, the right angle, the way they have been since he kissed me for the first time over a decade ago.

The edge of the countertop digs into my

back, but I don't care. Chris is sucking on my neck, biting softly, and I run my hands through his hair and press my body as firmly against him as I can. He lifts me up on the counter and starts unbuttoning my shirt. I help him with the buttons and it takes only seconds with us working together for the job to be done. He doesn't bother taking my shirt off, but once my bra is exposed he reaches around to unhook it and then shoves it up toward my neck so he can get to my breasts. I nearly scream when his tongue makes contact with my nipple. He licks it a few times and then takes the whole thing into his mouth. He's pulling gently on my other nipple with his thumb and forefinger, and I grab the back of his head and wrap my legs around his waist. The edge of the hard granite countertop prevents him from grinding our lower bodies together and he finally gives up and pulls on the button of my jeans instead. He plunges his hand inside them before he gets the zipper even halfway down. "Oh, Jesus," he says, when he touches me and discovers how wet I am. He strokes me and the sound of my whimpering fills the kitchen. This only seems to fuel his desire because his breathing is out of control and he starts making a few noises of his own.

I'm reaching for the button on his pants when Josh bangs on the locked sliding glass door off of the kitchen; I can see him out of the corner of my eye. At the same exact time the doorbell rings. It's Jordan. I know this by the *ding-dong-ding-dong-ding-dong-ding-dong* that reaches the kitchen and will continue until someone goes to the front door. Why don't they ever use the same entrance? Thankfully, Chris shut the garage when he got home, otherwise they would have burst into the kitchen and caught us in flagrante delicto. The timer for the pasta goes off and the telephone rings, because apparently there's not enough going on.

Chris groans in frustration and I want time to stand still, because Chris and I desperately need to finish what we've started. But instead I remove Chris's hand, jump off the counter, and quickly zip my jeans and button my shirt, leaving my bra unhooked, focusing only on covering up my nakedness so my children won't be traumatized. Chris opens the back door for Josh and I go to the front. *Ding-dong-ding-dong-ding-dong.*

"Stop ringing the doorbell," I say when I unlock the door and fling it open.

"Hi, Mommy," Jordan says. "Whatcha doin'?"

I step aside so she can come in. "Nothing," I say. "Just making dinner. Go wash up."

I turn off the stove, drain the pasta, and combine it with the marinara, then dash into the bathroom to fasten my bra and button my jeans. When I come out, Chris is standing there with rumpled hair and a smile on his face.

"Hungry?" I ask.

"You don't even know how much," he says.

I set the salad and pasta on the table and Chris and I transition into parenting mode. Jordan wants butter on her pasta, and a sprinkling of parmesan. "I don't like Grandma Canton's sauce. It's too spicy," she says.

"It's not spicy at all," I say. But Jordan thinks everything is spicy, and I knew this was coming, which is why I scooped some of the pasta into a separate bowl before I added the sauce. I decide this battle is not worth fighting and grab the butter and cheese.

Josh informs us he's not eating any salad. "I only like ranch," he says. He points to the bottle of Italian dressing. "I don't like that kind."

I get up and grab a new bottle of ranch

from the cupboard and hand it to him.

"Thanks, Mom," he says. Harmony restored. "How come you're home so early, Dad?" Josh asks.

"I took an earlier flight. I missed you guys," Chris says, reaching over to ruffle Josh's hair. "Tell me about what's going on at school."

They take turns regaling Chris with their accomplishments and he splits his attention equally between them. At the end of the meal, when he asks them to help clear the table, they do his bidding eagerly, fighting over who gets to carry more dishes to the sink.

I send them off to play while I clean up the kitchen. A thought occurs to me when I'm loading the dishwasher, and I wipe my hands on a towel and open the cupboard. No matter how much I move things around, no matter how hard I search, I can't find Chris's bottle of antidepressants. I'd bet money that I will not be able to find the other bottle, the one he keeps in his suitcase, either.

At eight we give the kids a five-minute warning. We can perform this bedtime routine in our sleep: pajamas, brushing teeth, reading, and tucking in. Tonight, Chris takes Jordan and I take Josh. We field requests for one more kiss, a drink of water. Finally, we turn off their bedroom lights and reconvene downstairs.

"Goddamn it," Chris yells. He's gone into our home office to check his e-mail one last time.

I pop my head in. "What's wrong?"

"Jim needs my reports. The ones I didn't finish because I caught the earlier flight." Chris exhales in frustration and pinches the bridge of his nose. "He said he didn't need them until Monday, so I didn't work on them on the plane. For once, I didn't want to work on the plane."

"It's okay," I say. "I'll wait for you."

Chris gets out of his chair and walks around to the front of the desk, where I'm standing. "I'll be up as soon as I can. I promise. Give me one hour, two at the most." He pulls me toward him and puts his arms around me. The kiss he places on my lips is tender and my joy knows no bounds because I feel as if my husband is finally trying to make his way back to me.

61

Chris

My hatred of Jim grows every day. I have no doubt that asking for the reports is some kind of power play designed to make him feel as though he has the upper hand. He's been extra difficult since I took that time off after Claire got out of the hospital.

I power up my laptop and open my spreadsheet, working as fast as I can. But then it hits me. If Claire is upstairs waiting for me, why the hell am I down here? Shouldn't Jim be the one who has to wait? Hasn't Claire waited long enough? I slam the lid of my laptop shut and take the stairs two at a time.

She's lying in bed reading a book and she looks up when I open the door. "That was fast," she says, smiling. "Are you done already?"

"No. I'll work later." I lock the door to ensure there are no interruptions. She's wearing lingerie — I don't know what it's called, but it's the kind I like: short, black, and low-cut, with thin straps. I strip off my shirt and unbutton my jeans as I walk toward the bed.

When I reach her I take the book out of her hands and lay it on the nightstand. I kick off my jeans and ease in next to her, leaning over to move one of the thin straps aside. I kiss her collarbone and work my way up her neck, inhaling the scent of her perfume.

"You smell so good," I say.

She places her hands on my chest and runs her fingers lightly over my skin, leaving sparks trailing in their wake. Claire has always been able to turn me on with a touch of her hand and tonight is no exception. The first kiss I place on her lips is gentle, but when she opens her mouth to me I deepen it, taking my time. Gone is the frantic feeling of earlier today, because this time I'm not stopping until we're done.

I grab the hem of her nightgown and pull the whole thing over her head. The site of Claire stripped down to her lacy black underwear almost sends me over the edge. I have no intention of turning off the lamp because I want to see every bit of this. She sighs when I rub her nipples. They harden instantly and I groan, loving the way they feel under my fingertips. I replace my fingers with my mouth and circle each nipple with my tongue. When I start to suck, Claire runs her hands through my hair and tells me how good it feels.

I kiss my way down, past her stomach. Kneeling between her legs, I hook my thumbs in the waistband of her underwear, dragging them down and throwing them on the floor. I look at her — laid out before me — and wonder how I was able to stand not being with her for so long.

I put my hand between her legs and stroke her. Her eyes are half lidded and her lips are parted as she draws in increasingly ragged breaths. I love watching Claire when she's turned on, and all of her inhibitions are gone. I push her legs farther apart and use my mouth and my tongue. When I told her I'd forgotten what she tastes like, this is what I really meant.

Claire moans softly and repeatedly, and that's a sound I love hearing her make. Always have. I can tell she's close, very close, so I keep stroking and licking and I don't stop until she comes.

When the aftershocks have subsided she pulls me up toward her and removes my boxer shorts. I'm dying for Claire to touch me, but I'd rather be inside of her, so I roll onto my back and pull her on top of me. She straddles me and guides me inside. We rock together and it feels incredible, and when I come I say her name over and over. I'm still inside her when she stretches out on top of me. I wrap my arms around her and we lay still, catching our breath.

"I never stopped wanting you, Claire," I whisper. "Never."

I hold her in my arms and as soon as I'm able, I make love to her again, just because I can. Afterward, when I'm certain that she's fallen asleep, I slip out of bed and finish my reports. Jim has sent three increasingly angry e-mails, asking where they are. I'll get an earful on Monday, but I really don't care.

Fuck you, Jim. I still win.

62

CLAIRE

Chris and I tuck the kids into bed one night a few weeks later, and reconvene on the couch to watch TV. It's Sunday and he worked most of the day, but he took a break to go to Josh's soccer game and he stopped early enough so we could take the kids out for dinner. He seems happier, even with his stressful workload and the large amount of time he has to spend away from home. Even without the antidepressants. Instead of shutting me out he answers my questions when I ask about work. He shares with me how frustrated he is.

We're watching the end of a *CSI* rerun when the local news interrupts programming with a special report. I watch the BREAKING NEWS banner flashing at the top of the screen and feel a prickle of unease because whatever we're about to learn is significant enough to disrupt prime-time programming.

The news anchor begins speaking and I lean forward a bit, listening as he reports that two police officers have been shot during a routine traffic stop. The station cuts to live footage, which shows flashing lights, police cars, fire trucks, and barricades. "Can you tell where that is?" Chris asks. I don't answer him because I'm searching the faces of the police officers who are trying to maintain order and hold back the onlookers. The anxiety increases a bit when I realize that Daniel isn't one of the officers I can identify in the crowd.

It can't be him. There's no way it's him.

But it might be him. I don't know if he's on duty tonight, but this is the shift he works. I fight the urge to slip out of the room, send him a text. I might not be able to see him anymore, but that doesn't mean I stopped caring about his well-being. The news report ends with a promise from the anchor to keep viewers updated as more information becomes available.

"That doesn't sound good," Chris says.

"No," I say. My worry increases. You're being foolish, I tell myself. Daniel wouldn't have anyone in his police car. He patrols alone. But Daniel told me once that a routine traffic stop is one of the most dangerous things a police officer faces. "You never know what the person behind the wheel is thinking," he said. "What they're going to do. If they're armed."

CSI comes back on, but I'm no longer paying attention. The nightly news will start in a few minutes and then I'll know more. I'll know that Daniel is safe.

The shooting is the first story the nightly news covers. For five minutes they repeat the same information they've already given viewers, but then Daniel's name suddenly flashes on the screen and I stand up so fast that my knee hits the coffee table and sends my glass of water flying.

"Claire!" Chris says. "What is it?"

I scramble for the remote control and turn up the volume. The anchor reports that Daniel Rush and Justin Chambers, the reserve officer riding along with him, have been transported to the hospital. Their conditions are unknown.

I sit down on the very edge of the couch, feeling panicked. I can't answer Chris. It's as if the wind has been knocked right out of me, and I can't speak.

"Tell me what's wrong," he says.

My heart is pounding and I have that awful feeling, the kind where the adrenaline makes your whole body vibrate with anxiety.

"I know one of those officers. He's a friend of mine."

His forehead creases in confusion. "Which one?"

Hysteria bubbles up inside me. I feel it building and want to shout, "The ridiculously good-looking one!" but I take a deep breath and say, "Daniel Rush."

Chris ponders this for a moment. "I don't understand. How do you know him?"

"I did a freelance assignment for the police department."

"But you said you were friends with him. What do you mean?"

I thought breaking things off with Daniel would mean that I'd never have this conversation with Chris. But suddenly I want to have this conversation. Need to have it. Daniel's life could be hanging in the balance, and I'm not going to downplay our friendship, even if I have to pay for it. "We got to know each other pretty well," I say.

"How well?"

I can almost see the lightbulb flickering above Chris's head.

He stands up and takes a step back, exhaling in one fast breath. "Jesus, Claire. Are you trying to tell me you were having an affair with this guy? Because if you are, just say it."

I shake my head. "I never slept with him. I never did anything like that with him."

"Well, what did you do?" Chris asks, appearing only slightly relieved.

"We talked," I say. "We texted. We went to lunch, to dinner. We spent time together."

"How much time?" Chris's face is flushed and he's getting louder by the second. "And why didn't you ever tell me about him?"

"When would you have had time to listen?" I ask, my voice also getting louder. "Do you know how many times I stood outside your office door waiting for you to come out and talk to me? Or laid there in bed wondering if you were going to join me? Put your arms around me and let me know in some small way that you still cared? There was always something more important to you than me." I take a deep breath and lower my voice. "He was there when you weren't."

"I thought you would wait for me. You're my wife. I thought you of all people would understand." Chris's shoulders slump and he runs a hand through his hair. "I feel like I don't know you at all. How am I supposed to trust you now, Claire?"

If Chris only knew how many times I longed for Daniel to hold me in his arms, and how many times I resisted the physical pull of him. But that won't help anything now. He won't want to hear any of it.

"I'm sorry if I hurt you, Chris. That was never my intent. But Daniel could be dying right now, and I will not be okay if that happens. He was important to me. I need to know that he's all right."

Chris walks away and moments later I hear the office door slam.

I relocate to the bedroom and watch news coverage continually, flipping between all the stations, desperate for an update on Daniel's condition. I feel powerless. There's no one I can call, and I have a better understanding of how Daniel must have felt when I was in the hospital. I keep the bedroom door closed because I don't want to be bothered, but it doesn't matter because Chris never comes upstairs. Additional details trickle in and I gasp in horror when I learn that Daniel — and the reserve officer who rushed to his aid — both sustained gunshot wounds to the head.

My thoughts race and images of Daniel flash before my eyes like a slide show that's moving too fast toward an outcome I can't even contemplate.

63

Chris

I walk into the kitchen to grab a bottle of whiskey and a glass from the cupboard. Claire has gone upstairs, which is a good thing because I really don't feel like talking right now. I take the bottle into the office and pour myself a drink, hoping it will numb me but knowing the only thing I'm likely to achieve is a hangover.

I feel like I've been blindsided. To find out that some guy spent time with my wife, had some kind of relationship with her — no matter how platonic she says it was — hurts more than I ever imagined it would.

I can't stop picturing them together. Talking and doing whatever it was that they did.

I want to know, but I don't.

I should be grateful she didn't sleep with him, but I'm not. I feel as if we've taken one giant step backward.

And I'm too pissed off to listen to the

voice inside my head that's saying it's mostly my fault.

After spending a restless night on the couch I finally walk upstairs to our bedroom. Claire has fallen asleep with the TV on, but I don't bother shutting it off. Once I'm out of the shower and dressed I look in on the kids and then I get in my car and drive to the airport.

64

CLAIRE

I don't remember what time I finally fell asleep, and when I wake up at 6:00 A.M. the TV is still on. Chris's side of the bed is empty and hasn't been slept in. When I go to the bathroom I see his damp towel on the floor and smell the faint traces of his cologne, and when I check the garage I discover that he's already left for the airport.

I watch the morning news as I make breakfast for the kids. The newscasters recycle the same information that I already learned last night before I dozed off: that Daniel and the reserve officer were flown by Life Flight helicopter to the University of Kansas Hospital and taken directly to surgery. They're both in critical condition. The shooter — whom Daniel pulled over for running a red light — was strung out on drugs and wanted for a parole violation. He took his own life at the scene.

Elisa follows me home after we put the kids on the bus. "I've been watching the news coverage. You must be so worried," she says.

"I am. I called the hospital, but they won't give me any information. He's in the ICU, so I can't go there. I'll have to wait until he's transferred to a regular room. If he's transferred." I blink away tears.

Elisa nods and hands me a Kleenex from the box on the counter, and I dab at my eyes.

"I had it out with Chris last night, too. I told him about Daniel. He didn't take it very well, shattered trust and all that."

"I'm sorry," she says.

I shake my head. "I deserved it. We were just finding our way back to each other, Elisa. It's my fault. All of it."

"Not all of it, Claire. Don't be so hard on yourself."

"I still care for Daniel. I can't just shut that off."

"Of course not. There are lots of people pulling for him right now. For both officers. People that don't even know them. It's tragic when something like this happens. Give Chris some time. He'll come around."

I know she's right, and that Chris needs time to process everything. I send him a text. *Are you okay?*

He answers an hour later. *I'm fine.*

Fine. A word that means the opposite if there ever was one.

I spend most of the day on mundane chores, leaving the TV on and refreshing the browser on my laptop every fifteen minutes. A little before 3:00 P.M. the BREAKING NEWS banner flashes at the top of the TV, and I hold my breath. I start crying when they announce that the reserve officer has died.

And I feel horribly guilty for being relieved that it wasn't Daniel.

65

Claire

"Mom?"

I struggle to open my eyes.

Josh is standing beside my bed, dressed in his pajamas. "Aren't we supposed to be up by now?" he asks.

The clock on the nightstand reads 7:34. I was still awake at 3:00 this morning, despite my repeated attempts to fall asleep. I tried everything: reading, watching a boring TV show, lying in the dark trying to empty my mind. Nothing worked. I hate not knowing how Daniel is doing, and Chris is responding to my texts with short, terse replies. The tension, the anxiety of it all, keeps building and I feel constantly on edge, mind whirring with possibilities, none of them positive. Finally, at a little before 4:00 A.M., when I couldn't take it anymore, I took a dose of Benadryl, which worked very well. Too well, it seems.

My heart races when I realize how late we're running, and I fling back the covers. "Go get dressed, Josh. I'm going to wake up your sister."

"Okay," he says, hurrying off to do what I asked.

I rouse a sleepy Jordan from her bed and tell her to get ready, then hurry to the kitchen to make breakfast. Cereal bars, bananas, and juice are all we have time for this morning.

Josh sits down at the table and starts eating while Jordan wanders in, sharing none of her brother's sense of urgency.

"Come on, Jordan," I say. "Pick up the pace a little, okay?"

My eyes burn, my head pounds, and my feet feel like cement blocks as we walk to the corner, reaching it a scant fifteen seconds before the big yellow bus pulls up. Elisa and Travis are the only ones there and I'm grateful that Julia and Bridget are absent this morning. In the vague recesses of my mind I remember that Julia is still in rehab and that Bridget's house is now empty.

"How are you doing today?" Elisa asks.

I take comfort in her soothing tone and sympathetic expression. "I'm okay," I say. "Just really tired. Chris still isn't really talking to me. We're communicating mostly through texts."

"Do you want some company? I can skip yoga."

"No," I say. "Thanks. I think I'll go back to bed."

She squeezes my hand. "Okay."

When I return home I drop a slice of bread in the toaster and when it pops up I spread a thin layer of peanut butter on it. I don't want to eat it, don't know if I can eat it, but I have no choice so I do. I gag on the third bite and hold it down by sheer will, then finish the rest. There are dirty dishes in the sink and fingerprints cover every inch of the granite countertops, but I leave everything the way it is. I'll pull myself — and the house — together later. Chris will be flying home tonight, which means we'll have to give Oscar-worthy performances if we hope to get through dinner without the kids picking up on the tension. It's something we know all too well how to do, but I'm exhausted just thinking about it.

Tucker waits patiently next to his empty food and water bowls and I fill the metal containers with fresh, cold water and his kibble.

"Sorry, boy," I say, reaching down to scoop him up. I hug him, burying my face in his soft fur.

Upstairs, I strip down to my tank top and underwear and crawl back into bed, pulling the covers over my head. Anything to temper the sunlight that filters in through the bedroom curtains. I suddenly understand why people like blackout shades. I need a break from the TV, from my life. I toss and turn, but I'm so tired that my mind eventually stops spinning.

I close my eyes and soon the sleep returns.

"Claire, wake up." Chris opens the curtains, and the simultaneous assault of his voice and the blinding sunlight has me squinting and wishing I could put my hands over my ears like a child. His voice is so loud, or maybe it just seems that way because the room was so blissfully quiet. I have no idea why he's here and one glance at the clock doesn't make it any clearer. It's noon on Friday. Chris should be getting ready to fly home, not standing in our bedroom looking down at me.

"Why are you here?" I ask.

"I wanted to talk to you. I caught the first flight out this morning."

"Give me a minute." Slowly, I sit up and swing my legs over the side of the bed because I really need to pee. After I pull on my yoga pants I walk into the bathroom to relieve my close-to-bursting bladder. When I'm washing my hands I look in the mirror.

I do not look good.

My skin is ashen and there are dark circles under my eyes. I brush my teeth and then pull my hair back into a sloppy bun. When I come out of the bathroom Chris is waiting for me.

"Let's go downstairs."

"Okay," I say.

"Okay," he echoes, and follows me out of the room.

"Why were you sleeping?" he asks when we sit down on the couch. "You hardly ever nap during the day."

"I was sleeping because I'm tired. I'm tired of you shutting me out whenever we hit a rough patch. I'm tired of worrying about whether Daniel is okay."

Chris flinches, as though the very mention of Daniel's name has caused him a fresh wave of pain.

"I'm tired of everything, Chris." I can't look at him. I'm afraid I'll start crying again, and I'm tired of doing that, too. Swallowing the lump in my throat and looking at the clock on the wall over his shoulder, I wait for him to say whatever it is he flew home early to say so we can clear the air, once and for all.

"I know I didn't handle things very well the other night, Claire. I just never expected you to tell me something like that."

"I didn't have to tell you at all," I say.

"Yeah, well. I almost wish you hadn't."

Neither of us says anything for a minute, but then we both try to talk at once.

"Go ahead," he says.

"When I got out of the hospital I told Daniel I couldn't see him anymore. Even though nothing physical ever happened between us, we came close."

Chris's jaw clenches and he looks as if he'd rather hear anything other than the words that are coming out of my mouth.

"But I felt like you were finally going to fight for me instead of letting me slip away. And I *was* slipping away, Chris. A little more every day."

"Why did you spend so much time with him?"

He looks as though he might not really want to hear the answer, but he asked, so I tell him the truth. "I was lonely, Chris. Lonely and sad and frustrated. I spent time with him because he gave it to me." I angle my body toward his. "I wanted you to be the one I turned to, but you weren't there."

"I know. I'm sorry," Chris says. "For everything."

"You were doing what you thought you had to do," I say. "What you thought was best for this family."

He shrugs and shakes his head, runs his fingers through his hair. "At what cost?" he asks.

I think I've already given him the answer to that question. "I'm sorry, too," I say.

Chris stares out the window at the backyard and doesn't say anything for a minute. He turns back around and looks me in the eye. "How close did I come?" he asks. "To losing you."

"Not as close as you think," I say, because there are some things that a man never needs to hear.

Chris reaches over and pulls me into his arms. He doesn't speak, but he strokes my hair and holds me tight, like he'll never let me go. We stay like that for a long time. And I think to myself that maybe Chris talks to me the loudest when he says nothing at all.

66

Claire

We join together at Skip and Elisa's once again, to celebrate the last day of school. I smile, listening to the kids' excited voices as they chase each other across the freshly cut grass, reveling in the noise of happy children.

Chris stands beside me, a smile on his face. The golden boy shimmers in the sunshine, the way he once did, and I swear that man's happiness can light a room.

He turned in his resignation at work this morning. He told me what he wanted to do a few nights ago while we were lying in bed. "I want to form a new company. There's this guy at work named Seth — he's a software engineer from the implementation team — and we've been talking about it for a while, discussing every possible scenario. We've mapped out timelines and gone over the budget a thousand times. I feel like we have a pretty solid business plan."

"So it would be a partnership?" I asked.

"Yes. Seth's not very expressive — he's really more of a head-down programmer — so he would design and create the software and it would be my job to sell it."

"What about the start-up costs?"

"They'd be fairly low. And we wouldn't have any overhead, at least at first. We'd work out of our homes. I don't know if you've noticed anything about our bank accounts."

"I've noticed that they seem to have a nice balance in them." I never stopped economizing. I never changed the money-saving habits I formed when Chris was unemployed. I still shop at discount retailers. I clean the house myself. And I maintain a fairly high volume of freelance assignments. Chris spent next to nothing after he went back to work because his expense account paid for everything when he was on the road. Our financial situation has never been better.

"Enough for us to get by for at least a year, maybe longer," he said.

"No insurance company is going to cover me individually."

"We would apply for group health insurance. As long as we have at least two employees, we can do this. In the meantime, we could extend my health insurance benefits like we did when I got laid off. We'd all be covered for eighteen months. It will be expensive, but we've included the premiums in the estimation of our operating costs."

I could hear the excitement in Chris's voice, but I proceeded cautiously. "A start-up requires a lot of time. Hours upon hours. How do I know we won't be trading one problem for another? Even if you're home, you could be too busy." I thought about the office door being closed all the time. The late nights and weekends spent working.

"I know that. A start-up isn't easy. And I'm not going to lie. There's a ton of competition in this market. I'd still have to travel, but not nearly as much. Eventually, we'd hire people to do that. We wouldn't have to answer to anyone but each other. But I can't promise you this will work, Claire. It's a huge gamble. There's a good chance we'll fail."

I gave him my blessing anyway. If Chris didn't take his career into his own hands, he'd never be free of the possibility of a layoff, or a less than desirable work situation, or a temperamental boss. If we had to economize even further, we would. At least

Chris would be working toward something he believed in.

So now we wait and see. Sink or swim. Fingers crossed.

Chris and I find drinks and settle into a couple of empty chairs on the patio. Julia and Justin arrive with their girls. Two months out of rehab, Julia's sobriety is still tenuous, the thread connecting her to this new, sober life as delicate as gossamer. She relapsed, but just once. She's thirty-three days sober now, and she fought for every single one of them. I'm praying for thirty-four.

I thought Justin might cut and run, abandon her in her desperate time of need, but he didn't. After Julia joined AA she told him he was free to go. That if the other woman was who he really wanted, there was no reason for him to stick around. But he did, and I hope that he stays. Her daily affirmations, Justin's support, and her daughters will help her stay the course, but the decision not to drink will always rest on Julia's shoulders. I believe she has what it takes.

Bridget can't be with us tonight because she's working at the hospital. She does three twelve-hour shifts a week, from 7:00 P.M. to 7:00 A.M., relying on Sebastian to keep his brothers out of harm's way. Her child care arrangement isn't ideal, but her boys don't seem to mind. They moved into a three-bedroom apartment, and Bridget pays the rent, and all other expenses, by herself. She hasn't heard from Sam in more than a month. It turned out that gambling was more important to him than Bridget and the boys. He didn't show up for his initial court date after Bridget initiated divorce proceedings, and she hasn't been able to reach him since. It's as if he disappeared.

"Claire," Elisa says. She sounds a bit frantic. "Can you help me for a second?"

I look up and see that Elisa does indeed have her hands full. She holds eleven-month-old Lauren with one arm and balances a plate of burgers for the grill in the other. Four-year-old Layla, who is so frightened of being alone that she is never far from Elisa, clings to her leg, making it almost impossible for her to walk.

According to a social worker, a neighbor reported Layla and Lauren sitting in their front yard unattended, Lauren dressed in only a dirty diaper despite the fifty-degree temperature. The police found their mother inside the garbage-strewn home smoking a crack pipe. The kitchen cupboards held only a box of stale crackers and a container of formula with enough left in it for a few more feedings. Elisa broke down sobbing when she told me that. She and Skip hope to make the transition from foster parents to adoptive parents, and I'm keeping my fingers crossed that it works out. Someday, those little girls will realize just how lucky they really are.

I jump out of my chair and walk toward her. "Do you want me to take the burgers or the baby?" I ask.

"The baby, for now," she says, handing a sleeping Lauren to me. She stirs a bit, but I hold her close and she closes her eyes again.

Elisa grabs Layla's hand. "Let's go drop off these burgers, okay?"

Layla nods eagerly, appearing happy to be asked. Happy to be taken care of at all.

Julia sits down beside me and strokes the baby's head. "She's precious," she says.

I look at Julia and smile. "She is. Do you want to hold her?"

She nods, so I hand over the baby. She looks down at Lauren and then out into the yard, to where her own girls are playing. "Children. They're so helpless," Julia says. "It's our responsibility to take care of them."

I know at this moment that her remorse runs as deep as an ocean. "Yes," I agree. "But they're resilient, too." I reach out and grab Julia's hand and she squeezes it. I squeeze back.

After dinner, we put on some music. The sun goes down and the candles Elisa lights and places in the lanterns that hang from the trees, and the full moon, create a magical glow. Justin stands and extends his hand to Julia. I swallow the lump in my throat, and it's all I can do not to burst into tears when he holds her close and sways to the music. Watching them restores my faith in a lot of things. I feel hopeful, not just for Justin and Julia but for Chris and me. Daniel, too. I read in the newspaper that he's been moved to a rehab center and though he'll have a long road ahead of him, he's expected to make a full recovery.

Chris pulls me to my feet. "Dance with me," he says. He holds me close and I lay my head on his shoulder.

Chris knows me better than anyone ever has or ever will. This is the man I'll grow old with.

Skips dances with Layla in his arms while Elisa holds Lauren and smiles, and now I do tear up, just a little. The remaining kids join hands and do something that looks a little like ring-around-the-rosy except they laugh, and instead of falling down, they run faster and faster.

Chris and I got lost somewhere, and I

don't think we've completely found our way back yet, but we're close.

Losing him would have been one of the worst things to ever happen to me. And the best thing I can do is put my whole heart back in his hands.

So I do.

At the end of the evening we gather our children and Chris laces his fingers together with mine.

"Let's go home," he says, and the word means something different than it did a year ago. It isn't just the place we live. It's the life we built together. The one we came very close to tearing down.

I hold his hand tight and say, "Home."

Epilogue

Claire

I poke my head into the office. Chris is whistling as he types.

"The kids are over at Elisa's," I say. "The boys are playing and Jordan is helping with the girls."

Jordan loves following Elisa around, assisting in any way she can; Layla worships the ground she walks on. Jordan can't wait until she's old enough to babysit them and this is her way of practicing. Elisa graciously indulges her.

"I'm heading out for a bit."

He looks up from the computer and smiles. "Sounds good. Seth will be here in about fifteen minutes."

I slide behind the wheel of my car and program the address for the rehabilitation center into my GPS. When I arrive I park and walk through the double front doors to a reception desk.

The woman sitting behind it says, "Can I help you?"

"I'm here to see Daniel Rush."

She types his name into the computer. "He's in room 104. Go down the hall and take a left."

"Thank you," I say. He doesn't know I'm coming, and I debated about calling first. In the end I decided I'd visit and if it was a bad time, I'd come back another day. As I near his room a woman with blonde hair exits and heads down the hallway. There's something familiar about her, but I can't figure out what it is.

I'm suddenly nervous. I have no doubt that Daniel's still in pain and maybe he doesn't want company. I take a deep breath and knock softly. His door is ajar, but he doesn't answer, so I push it open a little more and peer around it.

His eyes are closed, but they flutter open when the door creaks. He smiles at me and the smile that lights up my face in return rivals any that he has ever given me. My chest feels tight and tears fill my eyes.

"I'm okay. Don't cry," he says when I reach his side. His voice sounds raspy.

"I'm not," I say, although I am clearly in danger of breaking down and bawling any second. Trying hard to get my emotions under control, I sit down in the chair next to the bed and reach for Daniel's hand. "I'm so happy to see you," I say. His head has been shaved and there's a light dressing over his wound. He's wearing a T-shirt and looks thinner.

He gives my hand a squeeze. "I'm happy to see you, too."

"I was going to text you, but it seemed so impersonal. I didn't know if you were taking phone calls. I've been so worried."

"I know. But I was very lucky," he says.

"How long will you be here?"

"About three more weeks. Then I'll have outpatient therapy every day. I need help relearning some of my motor skills, and I have quite a bit of weakness on my left side. Recovery is going to be slow."

"Are you in pain?"

"A little. Some days hurt more than others."

"I'm so sorry about the reserve officer."

Daniel nods. "I am, too."

"Who's taking care of you?" I can't bear the thought of him being alone.

"My parents are here every day. Dylan has even stopped by."

"Oh, that's good."

"Jessie's here, too," he says, and I think back to the woman I passed in the hall. The one with blonde hair who looked a little like me. "I still had her listed as my emergency contact and they called her when I was brought in. She was the first person I saw when I finally woke up."

"That's wonderful," I say. I squeeze Daniel's hand hard, and I don't even try to stem the tears as they spill out of my eyes. It makes me wonder if Jessie never found someone else after Daniel let her go. Maybe she really didn't want someone else. Maybe time really does heal all wounds.

"She'll be back soon," he says.

Please let her stay by his side.

"It means a lot that you came, Claire."

"I had to. I had to see for myself that you were okay." I lean over and kiss Daniel's forehead. He looks tired. "I'm going to leave so you can get some rest."

He gives my hand a final squeeze and says good-bye.

"Take care, Daniel," I say, and then I head home, confident that all is right in the world.

Chris is standing in the kitchen when I get home. "Hey," he says. "You're back. I never did ask you where you were going."

"I went to visit Daniel at the rehab center."

Chris stands very still, his face expressionless.

"I don't know if you can understand this,

but I needed to know that he was okay. To let him know that I was concerned, that I'd been thinking about him. I won't be going back, but I needed the closure."

"Is he going to be okay?"

"Yes," I say, holding back the tears. "He's going to be just fine."

Chris doesn't smile, but he nods. "I'm glad to hear it."

I walk over to him and bury my face in his shirt. He puts his arms around me, squeezes me tight, and kisses my cheek.

"Thank you," I say.

Something wakes me up in the middle of the night. I open my eyes and listen, but my senses register nothing but darkness and the absolute stillness of the room. I'll always love this time of night, before dawn crests on the horizon and brings light and a new day.

Chris sleeps beside me, one arm thrown over my waist, breathing softly. The weight of his arm anchors me to the bed, to him, to this life.

I roll from my back onto my side, toward him, this man that I could not leave. He murmurs in his sleep as I bury my face in his neck, pressing the length of my body against him, the smell of his skin as familiar and comforting as anything I've ever known.

I do think we have the capacity to love more than one person at a time, and that the love we feel for someone can be displaced, transferred, shifted. Even shared with another. But not lost. At least not forever.

The kisses I flutter along Chris's jaw rouse him from sleep, slowly, but I know the exact moment he awakens fully because he tangles his fingers in my hair and pulls me closer, lips pressing firmly onto mine, the desire rolling off him in waves.

Maybe love is like a pendulum. It swings back and forth, slowly, steadily, and sometimes you don't know where it will come to rest.

We made it through the first real test of our marriage, of our life together. Neither of us came out of it unscathed. Neither of us will ever forget what happened.

But both of us can forgive.

ACKNOWLEDGMENTS

First and foremost, I want to thank my husband, David, and my children, Matthew and Lauren: You've waited patiently while I spent hour upon hour in my writing chair, with fictional people. To be clear, these people will never mean more to me than the three of you.

To my US editor, Jill Schwartzman: Thank you for your excellent guidance and your friendship. Thank you also for reading about me in *Variety* and taking the ball and running with it. I truly believe that all things happen for a reason. To Brian Tart, Ben Sevier, Christine Ball, Carrie Swetonic, Phil Budnick, Stephanie Hitchcock, Erica Ferguson, and the rest of the team at Penguin: Thank you for being just as excited as Jill and for making me feel so welcome.

To my UK editor, Sam Humphreys: Thank you for your wonderful insights and your unwavering support.

To Jane Dystel, Miriam Goderich, and Lauren Abramo: I couldn't ask for better literary representation. Thank you for all that you've done for me.

To Amanda Walker and Elizabeth Keenan: Thank you for being the most awesome publicists an author could ever hope for.

I owe a debt of gratitude to the people who so graciously gave me their time in the name of research. Officer Jeff Casey of the Urbandale, Iowa, police department shared his knowledge of all things police-related, and never once complained about my barrage of text messages when I thought of "just one more thing."

To Tracie Banister and Kristy Slining: Thank you for sharing your knowledge and your personal anecdotes about type 1 diabetes. I so appreciate your willingness to share your stories with me.

To Julie Gieseman: Thank you for demonstrating the intricacies of an insulin pump.

To Elisa Abner-Taschwer: Thank you for your cheerleading and for being all-around amazing.

To Colleen Hoover: Thank you for reading the early draft of *Covet* and for giving me that great idea when I ran the alternate ending by you. Beta feedback is truly a magical thing.

To my copyeditor, Mikayla Butchart: Thank you for your extraordinary attention to detail. Because of you, I will spell the word *barbecue* correctly from now on.

And last, but certainly not least, thank you to the readers who have made all of this possible.

ABOUT THE AUTHOR

Tracey Garvis Graves is the author of the *USA Today, Wall Street Journal,* and *New York Times* bestseller *On the Island.* She lives in Des Moines, Iowa.

The employees of Thorndike Press hope you have enjoyed this Large Print book. All our Thorndike, Wheeler, and Kennebec Large Print titles are designed for easy reading, and all our books are made to last. Other Thorndike Press Large Print books are available at your library, through selected bookstores, or directly from us.

For information about titles, please call:

(800) 223-1244

or visit our Web site at:

http://gale.cengage.com/thorndike

To share your comments, please write:

Publisher
Thorndike Press
10 Water St., Suite 310
Waterville, ME 04901